FORGET ME NOT

A REGENCY GOTHIC ROMANCE

MICHELLE M. PILLOW

MICHELLE M. PILLOW® - MICHELLEPILLOW.COM

17TH ANNIVERSARY EDITION

This edition has been re-edited and revised from its original version.

Revised 17th Anniversary Edition

Forget Me Not © copyright 2004 – 2020 by Michelle M. Pillow

17th Anniversary Printing November 2020, The Raven Books LLC

This edition has been re-edited and revised from its original version.

Previously Titled: The Mists of Midnight

Fifth Edition Printing July 2018

Fourth Edition Printing April 2018

Third Edition Printing November 2016

Second Edition Printing February 2011

First Edition Printing April 2004

Published by The Raven Books LLC

ALL RIGHTS RESERVED.

ISBN 978-1-62501-260-9

Published by The Raven Books LLC

This book or any portion thereof may not be reproduced or used in any manner whatsoever without the express written permission of the publisher except for the use of brief quotations in a book review.

This novel is a work of fiction. Any and all characters, events, and places are of the author's imagination and should not be confused with fact. Any resemblance to persons, living or dead, or events or places is merely coincidence.

Michelle M. Pillow® is a registered trademark of The Raven Books LLC

FORGET ME NOT

John, your encouragement and support mean the world to me.

Mandy, thank you for all the wonderful years in this crazy business. I couldn't have done it without you.

B, you are amazing.

To my parents, thank you.

ABOUT FORGET ME NOT
GHOST PARANORMAL REGENCY HISTORICAL ROMANCE

From NYT Bestselling Author Michelle M. Pillow comes a tragically beautiful love story that defies perception.

When the scandalously independent Isabel Drake refuses to marry the man her parents choose for her, they force her to take lessons on how to become a respectable lady. However, her new tutor makes her feel anything but proper. Although her attraction to Mr. Weston is instantaneous, he resolves to keep her in her place—even as his desires for her become unmistakable.

Things are not what they seem at Rothfield Park. With Mr. Weston's arrival, there comes an abundance of restless spirits who insinuate themselves into her life. Quickly, Isabel loses her grasp on reality, not knowing who's alive or dead. Time is running out, and Isabel must solve the ghostly mystery of the eerie night mist that surrounds the manor before it comes to claim everyone she holds dear—including her Mr. Weston.

This edition has been re-edited and revised from its original version.

Original Title: *The Mists of Midnight*

NOTE FROM THE AUTHOR

This book holds a very dear place in my heart. It was originally titled *The Mists of Midnight*. It is with this story that my career was launched back in April 2004 and I've been a full-time author ever since. Though it was the 9th novel that I had written at the time, it was the very first of my published novels. Now, even as my book list is closer to 100 than to 1, I still remember this book fondly as where it all started. Some of those first books have never seen the top of a publisher's desk (though I'm sure that will soon change).

So much has happened to me since the book first released, and I wouldn't change any of it for the world. Forget Me Not (aka The Mists of Midnight) represents several of my loves—historicals, paranormals, and romances. This book has been modified and updated from its original version.

I am grateful to all of the readers and publishers who have given me a chance over the years, and to the authors with whom I've become friends. You all are such a big part of my life.

Thank You and Happy Reading!
Michelle M. Pillow
www.michellepillow.com

AUTHOR UPDATES

To stay informed about when a new book is released sign up for updates:

michellepillow.com/author-updates

THE LEGEND OF A FLOWER

Forget Me Not

"There is a legend about this flower. Long ago a knight was picking blue flowers for his lady near a stream. He loved her greatly with all his heart and planned to make her his wife. But fate was not kind to the lovers, and he fell in. Though he fought to return to shore, the weight of his armor, combined by the recent floodwaters overtook him. Before he drowned, he threw the flowers at the lady and yelled, 'Forget me not!'" – *Mr. Dougal Weston*

For this reason, the Forget Me Not flower is the symbol of true love.

1

ROTHFIELD PARK, ENGLAND, 1812

"My heart pounded in a violent fit, and the child wouldn't quit screaming." Jane Drake's words rushed at her oldest sister. Her round eyes shone through her spectacles, echoing the strength of her conviction. "I swear to you, Isabel. It was real. There are unrested spirits at the manor."

"It was a dream," Isabel assured her, remaining calm. Jane was a sweet girl, and Isabel loved her dearly. However, her bookish sister had somewhat of a wild imagination when it came to Rothfield Park.

"I'm not explaining it well." Jane's usually meek expression had stiffened with fright. Absently, she pushed the sliding spectacles up her nose. Her pink linen gown flowed as she paced about the floor. The color matched the flush of her cheeks.

The high empire waist was belted with a dark pink sash, and complementing ribbons bound her dark brown hair. Despite her gown's richness, Jane had an indifferent air to her manners, an untidiness that was rather endearing.

Isabel sighed. Her concerned blue eyes met her sister's brown ones. She had half a mind to reprimand the servants for telling the girl such fanciful tales upon the family's arrival to the home. Patting her sister's cheek with a soft kidskin glove, she whispered, "Oh, Jane, we have let Rothfield Park for nigh six whole months. If spirits were lurking about the manor, they would have made themselves known before now."

"But I think they *are* making themselves known. I have heard them moving about this past week," Jane insisted. "I know there are more than one. There is a terrified child. And a man—"

"Jane, I'll hear no more of this. Quit trying to frighten me." Isabel shivered, disliking talk of the supernatural. She had no idea why Jane had been so apprehensive lately, but it needed to stop. Then an idea struck her. "Did you just read that new *shilling shocker* that Harriet sent to you from London?"

"Yes. But, I—" Jane began.

"Shh," Isabel hushed her. "Therein lies your problem. You've been staying up late reading in bed, haven't you? Oh, Jane, and to waste such a gifted mind on such rubbish."

Jane merely nodded at the loving correction.

Satisfied that her sister's fears were for naught, Isabel relaxed. She smiled at the girl and gave her an impish wink to cheer her. Jane was only sixteen and still very impressionable. Harriet loved to exploit the youngest Drake's fantasies by giving her useless gifts.

"You had best be careful when speaking of such things, especially to Mother. She will have Reverend Campbell here in an instant to exorcise this house from demons." Isabel paused mischievously. "Can you imagine such a thing? The Scotsman would—"

"Issie, please," Jane broke in before her sister could say anything that would insult the poor vicar. "He's a man of God."

"He's a self-righteous prig who I believe has taken to drink."

Jane frowned and turned her attention to the floor.

The fine muslin of her blue and cream gown swished as Isabel moved past her sister to the sideboard. Seeing the customary tray of pastries the servants had set out for breakfast, she ignored the stacked plates, chose a scone, and took a bite, leaning over the tray and using her gloved hand to catch any crumbs that fell. She noticed her distorted reflection in the polished silver, and she liked the way her prettily coiffured hair bounced around her head in gentle, dark curls.

"Allow me, Miss Drake." A maid hurried forward, shaking her head. The servant grabbed a plate and held it under the crumbling breakfast.

Isabel sighed. With a heavenward roll of her eyes, she relinquished the pastry to the fine china. The maid rushed the plate to the table, pulling back a chair for her mistress. Isabel dusted her gloves and waved the woman away with an annoyed toss of her hand.

"Miss Jane?" The maid gestured to the food.

Jane shook her head. "No, thank you."

The maid backed from the room with a polite curtsey.

"Issie," Jane said when they were once again alone. "Please, you must believe me. There was a child in my chamber last night. I could hardly sleep from the fright of it."

"Oh, my most prudent sister, I would believe you if the idea were not so fantastic of a notion. But I think I would be more apt to believe you if you told me my horse grew another set of legs overnight. This house is *not* haunted. And, hating the isolation of Rothfield Park as I do, I can't give credence to such a conjecture."

"You think me a silly girl, don't you?"

"No, sweet Jane." Isabel smiled tenderly; a look saved only for her sister. Jane was her truest friend. "I do not."

Viscount Sutherfeld, their father, had moved his three daughters far from London and the influence of its high society, believing it had bred insensible ideas into the girls' heads. The middle sister, Harriet Drake, was the first to protest to their Aunt Mildred so that the older woman took pity and invited her to stay in her home in London. Once a month, they would receive a dutiful letter from Harriet, gloating about the fine society she enjoyed and filled with her hopes of snagging a suitably rich husband of consequence. The thought brought a frown to Isabel's features.

Jane looked at her in worry.

"I don't think you're silly," Isabel asserted. "I think you're bored, as you must be in such a place as this. Too bad a regiment of soldiers won't come to stay in Haventon so that we might for once give a ball."

"I don't mind it so much," Jane allowed. She'd been out for only one season. That one season was enough to convince the youngest Drake that she preferred to stay in the country. Scratching thoughtfully at her mousy brown hair, she pushed her spectacles up on her nose. "I shouldn't like it with Aunt Mildred. I do hate having to make conversation with men at balls. I never know what to say to them, and they never seem to listen to me unless I speak of you or Harriet."

"You do say the strangest things," Isabel mused.

Clearly deciding it best to change the subject, Jane forgot her ghosts for a moment. "You look very pretty, Issie. Is Mr. Tanner coming to call on you?"

"Yes." Isabel smiled, disregarding her oncoming melancholy with the name of her gallant suitor. Sighing wistfully, she thought of his dark blond hair and laughing brown eyes. Her Edward was always in fine spirits, and he made it impossible to think of anything contrary to happiness. "He is. I'm sure he will seek permission from Father soon. And, though he does not have much money, I think with my dowry and his smart investing, we will be reasonably well off. Already I have expressed my desire to go to London and Bath. I have it on good authority that he might have expectations of his own though he wouldn't tell me the exact details."

Jane tried to smile but couldn't seem to muster it. She often said she didn't want to think of Isabel leaving her. "And what of the colonel? He seems very smitten."

"Colonel Wallace?" Isabel shot in surprise. Her hand fluttered to her chest. "Please, Jane. Whatever made you think of the colonel?"

"When you were sleeping this morning, he came to visit Father. I don't flatter myself that he came for me," Jane said.

Isabel didn't pay attention to the jealous tinge in her sister's tone. She turned toward the side window overlooking the front drive. The long, straight gravel road disappeared into the distance, barring all of their neighbors' homes from sight. Along each side of the driveway were numerous shrubs, sculpted to perfection.

"Is he still here?" Isabel asked, hating that she might be forced to entertain the quiet man. He was as sparing with his smiles as he was with his praise. She would abhor having such a man for company, let alone as a husband. The only thing recommending Colonel Wallace besides his uncle's ownership of Rothfield Park, which in essence made him their future landlord, was that he had wealth in his own right. Once the colonel's uncle died, he would come into an even greater fortune.

Isabel shivered. What was wealth if it brought with it no happiness?

"No, I believe he must have gone away by now. Even so, Father wishes me to send you to the library when you're of a mind to come from your room. I suppose I should have told you right off, but I wanted you to myself before he puts you in a mood."

"It's not Father who I find to be disagreeable. It's Mother." Isabel naughtily grimaced as she walked past her sister toward the large paneled doors. Resting her gloved hand on the mahogany, she grumbled, "Too bad she couldn't have gone to London with Harriet. Maybe, you should speak to her and convince her to go. I would like country life better if she were not in it."

Isabel turned around to face her sister.

Jane didn't bother to scold her. Instead, she smiled. Isabel and her mother were rarely on speaking terms. It wasn't unusual for weeks to pass with hardly a word uttered between the two of them.

"If it would please you, we can exchange rooms. I swear I have never heard so much as a single moan in my chamber," Isabel said.

Jane's eyes lit up. "But that's because my room is in the area of the house rebuilt after the fire. I'm sure something tragic happened that night, though I can't prove it. I would very much like to help that poor child's spirit."

"Nonsense." Isabel refused to pay heed to such thing as ghosts. "But we will trade if it helps you to sleep easier."

"Yes, thank you."

Isabel nodded, forgetting the bothersome business as soon as she left the dining room.

Rothfield Park was an old estate, having been renamed for the Marquis of Rothfield, who had restored and expanded the place to one of grandeur and good taste some sixty years past. Soon after having finished the very last detail of the very last room, however, a fire had mysteriously started and burned down a sizeable section of the house. The flames were said to have killed a few servants and a child. It was also rumored that the meticulous Marquis went mad from the destruction and, soon after, died himself, leaving the estate and title to a cousin—Colonel Wallace's uncle.

No wonder Jane believes this house is haunted, thought Isabel in hard-pressed amusement. She barely gave credence to the story. She assumed it was exaggerated for the sake of entertaining bored country folk. *How else are the good people of Haventon going to get London's high society to visit them way up north in the middle of nowhere?*

Still, even Isabel had to admit that it was a wondrous home for the generously lenient price of the lease. She couldn't understand why the marquis would have built it in such an area. Still, nevertheless, she appreciated his eye for details, from the tall white walls of the main hall, trimmed and outlined with mahogany, to the expansive archways and shutters of the same wood, to the pristine marble floors of the adequately sized ballroom. Only a few pieces of furniture had arrived with the Drake family, the weathered pieces oddly out of place with the understated elegance of the furnishings that belonged to the house. The gentle curves of the Rothfield collection were of an older style, not the Palladian style of the modern-day, but still gracious and befitting of a great estate.

Rich tapestry lined the chairs and settees. Candleholders and fireplaces, sweeping draperies and paned windows, all graced their proper places. Along the carved stone mantles and wooden tabletops strewed an immense variety of vases, sculptures, and clocks. Large portraits of people and dogs lined the vast walls, hanging on damask and Genoa velvet. Their clothing was antiquated, and their faces were so unrecognizable that Isabel found they were hardly worth looking at except out of boredom.

Bedrooms flanked the east wing, each large and exceptional. Isabel imagined they were not so fine as they should have been, belonging to a Marquis, but they met the Drake family's needs. The bedrooms had fireplaces and colossal four-poster beds, potted plants, and sturdy furniture. Drawing rooms and dressing rooms adjoined each one.

The house was built in the shape of a 'U' with a paved courtyard and a working fountain in the center. Beyond the house fanned the dense woods in one direction—great for hunting deer her father claimed, though he never hunted—and a stream cut through the woods.

Between the house and woods sprawled beautifully landscaped gardens, not so well manicured as one would desire, but adequate. There was a beauty to the untamed rose vines in the spring and summer and to the broken cobblestone pathways that led around the grounds, transforming to earthen byways as they twisted through part of the woods. There, various plants and flowers grew— some of them wild. Their bright colors dotted the land and added a sweet fragrance to the air.

Regularly in the morning hours, the land fogged with a mist that gathered in the night. It wasn't so unusual an occurrence since they were close to Scotland. However, the mist only added to the servants' superstitious fears, and often they would warn the Drakes about venturing out in it too late or too early. Isabel laughed at such warnings, shaking her head in tolerating bemusement.

Turning her steps toward the library where her father could usually be found, Isabel took a deep breath and patted her hair. As she reached for the door, it opened. To her dismay, she came face to chest with Colonel Wallace. Realizing there was no escaping the social necessity, she curtsied. Her gaze barely moved over his stern face and, what Isabel believed to be, a persistently disapproving expression.

"Colonel Wallace," she acknowledged with a polite nod. She refused to smile at him, discouraging any misplaced affection he might have for her.

"Miss Drake," he returned in his usual curt fashion. "I was hoping to meet with you this morning."

"Oh." Isabel looked away. With forced airiness, she claimed, "I can't imagine what for."

"It's my wish to call on you this evening—before supper, of course," said the colonel. His tone was matter of fact, leaving no room for doubts of his intentions.

He speaks to me as if I were one of his men to be ordered about, Isabel thought in disgust.

Flippantly, she responded, "Well, alas, good sir. It can't be my wish. My afternoon is already promised to another. I believe you have been introduced to Mr. Tanner?" She waited for his reluctant nod. "I thought as much."

Before she could continue, the colonel said, "Most unfortunate for me. Your parents, however, have invited me to dine tonight, and I should be happy to speak with you at that time. Good day, Miss Drake."

"Good day, Colonel," she answered with a curtsey to match his bow, unable to do otherwise after such an abrupt dismissal. She waited until he was out the front door before moving to join her father.

"Isabel!" the Viscountess, Lady Sutherfeld, exclaimed. Her mother graciously smiled as she stood from her place in a low chair.

Isabel eyed her mother with a sense of foreboding, not trusting the woman's good humor. Nodding, she acknowledged, "Mother. Father."

"Come in, Issie. Come in." Lord Sutherfeld gave a merry wave, favoring his eldest daughter with a smile as he motioned for her to take a seat.

Isabel dutifully obeyed. Her father cleared his throat and then turned to some of the papers on his desk. Gathering them up, he organized and stacked them neatly into a pile.

Isabel waited as her father went through the ritual of looking busy as he collected his thoughts. Seeing a frown develop the more he collected, she began to fidget. Her mother's happy blue eyes gave away nothing beyond the fact she was pleased with herself, as was always the case where her mother was concerned.

The viscountess was a pretty woman for her

advanced years. And though she was prone to a hearty dislike of her eldest child—whom she blamed for the slight roundness of her figure—she often hid it behind a smiling mask, knowing that many men had admired her for her dainty contrivances of pleasure.

When her father didn't readily speak, she said, "The colonel told me you asked him to dine this evening. I wish it were not so, for I have already allowed Mr. Tanner to come this afternoon. I hoped that you would also allow him to dine."

"Well, of course, we wouldn't want to appear inhospitable to your guest," said the viscountess. She looked helplessly at her husband, clearly desiring him to deny his daughter's request. When he didn't answer, her mother muttered, "But perhaps the invitation would be better if postponed to another night."

"I don't see why, Mother," Isabel protested as meekly as she could manage. "Colonel Wallace shouldn't mind. Already, I've told him of Mr. Tanner's visit—"

"Oh, Isabel," the viscountess gasped. "You did no such thing!"

"Why, yes, Mother. I saw no reason not to. Besides, the colonel is rather tiresome company, and I think the evening's conversation will be lightened by what Mr. Tanner has to impart." Her smile might have appeared sweet, but inside she wanted to scream.

"I'm sorry to hear you say that," the viscount stated before his wife could speak—attempting to stop the fight brewing between the two women. Isabel watched her father expectantly. The viscountess looked demurely at her lap. He continued, "We shall get to the colonel in a moment. First, I have to discuss something of great discontent to us all. Miss Martens."

Isabel cringed, having forgotten her latest disagreement with the governess. "Oh, Father, you can't believe anything that dreadful woman says."

"That dreadful woman is the finest governess we could get to come—" her mother started.

The viscount cleared his throat, interrupting his wife. "Miss Martens is a highly competent woman, and you vexed her quite grievously. She has left her position here as of this morning."

Good! Isabel thought. She hid her triumphant smile. It had taken her only two short months to get rid of the insufferable woman. "I wish I could say I was sorry for it, but the woman was a bore. And I daresay her French was that of...*lower society*."

The viscountess paled at such a thought and was for once at a loss for words.

"Be that as it may, you need someone to guide you," her father said.

"I'm above the age of needing a governess," Isabel complained, unable to hide her pout. "I have just turned twenty-one. I'm not a child to be led about by the hand."

"That has yet to be proven," the viscount muttered under his breath. Seeing his daughter's stricken face, he added, "I have decided not to get you another governess."

"That *is* wonderful news," Isabel exclaimed happily.

"What?" the viscountess demanded in horror. "My dear, dear husband, you can't mean for me to chaperone our daughters everywhere? Whenever would I have the time?"

"No, my lady." The viscount's expression held only a passing fondness for his wife. She was an amiable companion to him, one who had still been blessed with charm and looks even after children. For that, he gave small thanks. "I have decided that our daughters need someone more commanding: to educate Jane properly and to prevail over Isabel's outspokenness."

"Father?" Isabel grew apprehensive.

"I will hire you a tutor." Her father was clearly proud of his own cleverness. "I think an educated man is just the thing for our Issie."

"But, propriety." The viscountess paled and fanned her face with the threat of a swoon.

"Take control of yourself, my lady," the viscount said, unaffected by his wife's theatrics. "Mr.—"

"Father?" Isabel whispered, not hearing him. "Tell me you're joking."

The viscount continued as if she hadn't spoken. "He's beyond reproach. I have the highest recommendation of his character and have spoken extensively about him with the colonel. Now, Colonel Wallace has allowed that such a fine character of sound mind and impeccable reputation won't be improper at all, considering Isabel is never alone with the man in private. And it's my hope that you, my dear Issie, will learn from him the proper discourse to be had with a gentleman. No more speaking of horseflesh and breeding, do you hear me?"

Isabel flinched. Miss Martens had caught her conversation with Mr. Tanner the week before and had harped on her endlessly. She should have known the woman would tattle to her father about it.

"And why would the colonel be involved in such a decision as to my tutor?" Isabel frowned. Seeing her mother's teary smile, she felt her stomach tighten.

"Colonel Wallace is rather taken with your charms, my dear," her father answered.

"Yes, quite taken," echoed her mother with a nod.

"What are you saying, Father? By all means, speak plainly." Isabel gripped the sides of the chair, her gloved hands working hard against the rough material. Her cheeks burned with the first simmer of anger.

"He wishes to marry you, Daughter, and I have given him my consent. We agree that, after some intensive training of your mind and actions, he will claim you as his wife and formally introduce you to his uncle." The viscount appeared a bit puzzled by her reaction. "Surely, you know of his feelings?"

"No, I do not," Isabel answered.

"Isabel, your tone," her mother scolded.

"I will not mind my tone." She stood, desiring nothing more than to run away. "You must send him notice at once that you have changed your mind."

"I will do no such thing." Her father remained calm. "A gentleman does not rescind on his word without good cause. And you can forget Mr. Tanner. I will never consent to such a disagreeable man as he."

"But the *colonel*? He wishes to change me," Isabel whispered in a mix of anger and mortification. "Am I not suited as I am? He would turn me into a meek and mild plaything?"

"You overreact." The viscount scowled in displeasure, and his tone became hard. "We merely wish to see your more desirable traits polished before you are to be a wife."

"Our family remaining in this home may very well be dependent on the impression you make upon his uncle," her mother inserted.

"And you won't be entertaining Mr. Tanner tonight or ever again unless it's with the colonel's consent," her father said. "Mr. Tanner has been a most unwelcome influence over you, Issie."

"You *will* receive the colonel's attentions tonight, Daughter," her mother insisted.

"I will not," Isabel managed through clenched teeth. "If he wishes to speak to me, he will hear my thoughts. I won't have him. He'll be wasting his time for the very character of my person, which he finds so objectionable, cannot and will not be changed. So I beg you, spare the colonel the embarrassment of asking."

"Won't have him? He's worth nearly seven thousand a year." Her mother fluttered her hands nervously before her face, hovering between the desire to scold her daughter and the need to faint to prove how upset she was. "You couldn't hope to do much better. And as to change, a wife's place is nothing if not sacrifice."

"And, after his uncle passes, he will own Rothfield Park," her father added logically. "He will be the new Marquis of Rothfield."

Isabel took several deep breaths. Her parents were serious. They wanted her to give up her chance at happiness for a man with seven thousand a year and a house whose location she abhorred.

"If you don't marry him," her mother threatened, "I shall never speak to you again. And neither shall your father."

"Then I look forward to a long and happy silence," Isabel shouted. She rushed through the library door. Seeing Jane as she passed through the front hall, Isabel met her sister's stricken expression and experienced a moment's regret.

Ignoring Jane's gentle entreaties, Isabel ran from the house as fast as she could. She refused to cry as she made her way to the stables. The heat of anger stung her features.

Without a groom to help her, she collected her mare. Isabel grabbed a set of reins from the stall and fashioned them around the horse's neck. Then, leading the palfrey out into the diffuse sunlight, she brought the horse to the stairs so that she could maneuver onto its back with as much incensed grace as possible.

Seated without the benefit of a sidesaddle, she nudged the mare. The spirited animal bolted forward with a jerk and tore off toward the north field where the grass was the most open.

Isabel, having ridden since the age of four, didn't think twice about her wild ride. Her skirts flew behind her, pressing against her legs and fanning over the backside of the horse. When she was well into the field, she discovered she had two choices. Either she could ride out into the clearing within view of the library window, or she could ride into the gathering mist, far from her father's watchful gaze.

Isabel chose the mist.

Once out of sight, she swung her leg over the mare's back and adjusted her skirts, so she was better seated astride the horse. The mist grew heavier, but she ignored it. She raced past shrubs and then trees, and the mare found an easy path. Its hooves pounded down a gentle incline through a limb-covered alcove.

The fog thickened. Isabel reined the horse to a rough stop. She heard the gentle babble of the nearby stream, but she couldn't see the water. The horse's hooves pattered nervously. The mist continued to expand and thicken until she could barely see the trees in front of her.

She looked around in mounting fright. Her

attention snapped to one side and then the other. The trees faded entirely, leaving behind an all-consuming whiteness. The water grew louder until she couldn't tell from which direction it came. Maneuvering the horse around, she urged the palfrey to move. At first, the animal resisted but finally obeyed as she yelled at it to go.

Isabel leaned close to the horse's neck, willing it to find its way home. The fog continued to thicken. The horse's movements became slow and cautious. The animal's ears twitched, and its head bobbed in agitation.

Isabel forced a nervous laugh, even as she trembled. The flesh on the back of her neck prickled in warning. She hugged closer to the skittish mare. She could feel its hot, sweaty flesh pressing into her gown. As they moved, she watched the white fog. She willed her eyes to detect anything familiar. A tree limb passed close to her face. She jolted back in alarm.

And then she heard singing, the sweet chime of a child's voice in play. The hollow melody was haunted, despite the girl's joyful laughter. It echoed in the trees. At first, the sound was behind her, as if the child ran through the mist. However, Isabel urged the horse faster. The voice was beside her; its bearer keeping pace with the mare.

"Play," she heard the childlike whisper near her ear.

Isabel jolted in fright. No one was there. Tears slid over her cheeks. She bit her lip to keep from crying out. The singing resumed in the forest and grew louder than before. The fog became so dense she could hardly make out the horse's alert ears.

"Hello?" she called, her voice cracking. "Who's there?"

"Play," demanded the pouting voice.

"Who are you?" Isabel insisted. She couldn't see her hands. Her limbs shook. She was too afraid to move from the familiarity of the horse's back. She felt the mare shake and jolt with each ring of laughter, each note of an eerie ballad. "What do you want?"

Suddenly, the laughing turned into crying. The mist felt as if it pressed into Isabel's skin. She breathed it into her lungs like the smoke from a fire. Coughing, she tried to catch her breath. Almost instantly, perspiration dotted her flesh. The horse neighed and bucked in protest. Her fingers found her throat, tearing at her gown as she fought for air.

"I want to play with you," the child answered with a sulk in her voice. The words sounded hollow, garbled by a roaring Isabel couldn't make out. She coughed louder, desperate to get out of the fog. Sweetly, the girl asked, "Are you my mother? Are you the girl from my bedchamber?"

She would much rather take her chances against the forest.

"No!" Isabel kicked her horse in the ribs, urging it forward, not caring if she were still in the woods.

As the startled mare began to run, movement shot out from the fog. Isabel saw the ruffling of a shirt. It was the hand of a man—pale, strained, and strong. He tried to grab hold of the reins.

Isabel screamed louder. The horse jolted violently, and she lost her grip. The hand disappeared behind her. She sat up, looking over her shoulder to see if the man was chasing her. There was nothing but mist all around.

With a relieved sigh, she turned to look forward. Her eyes didn't have time to focus as a branch materialized out of the fog. It struck her across the forehead, knocking her back with a sharp crack. Blood filled her mouth. Her head hit the jolting movements of the animal's galloping rump. Her feet loosened their hold, and she flipped over the back of the horse to the ground. And, as her head struck the earth, the white mist turned into an enveloping darkness.

2

THE EARLY DAWN came and went, dragging into the lateness of morning. The sun moved high and warm over the fields and valleys of Rothfield Park, dispersing the night's misty fog with the warmth of the day. Trees danced gently in the graceful wind, and flowers colored the land in the full bloom of spring. The perfumed air crept into every crack and crevice of the manor until all was fresh and clean.

To this wondrous delight, Isabel opened her heavy eyes. She moaned, stroking her hands over the comfortable linen of her bed, and then sweeping dreamily beneath her pillow. Sighing to test her voice, she reached to feel her forehead. It ached lightly but was nothing to be concerned over, and she quickly forgot the dull pain.

Isabel's bedchamber was a large square filled with woven rugs and quaint furniture. The raised four-poster bed had been carved from dark wood, contrasting nicely with the white-painted walls. An embroidered cloth covered her dressing table. Someone had placed a low chair by the fireplace, which was raised on a circular platform.

A long window with paned glass that opened inward was on the side of the fireplace, letting in enough light to see. There was no fire burning on such a brilliant day as this, so the room's far corner was darker than usual. She sat up, crawling from the fluffy bed to stand on the floor. Her bare feet crushed the mauve floral rug beneath them.

Seeing that she was alone, she decided not to call a maid to attend her and hurriedly dressed herself for the day. The lateness of the morning hour was alarming since she never slept so long. She wondered why no one had been sent to wake her. Then, with a rueful smile, she remembered her mother was angry with her for refusing to wed the colonel and had undoubtedly extended her displeasure to depriving her of servants.

Isabel donned a lightweight gown of green floral design on white linen and gauze. She smoothed the skirts and managed to tie the little bow in the back of the high waist herself. The draping sleeves were short, so she decided it would be best to wear her long gloves, pulling the material up her arms to rest above her elbows. From the look of the delicate sunlight, it would be a perfect day to walk alone in the gardens, maybe with a book.

Next came her white stockings and low-cut slippers. She brushed her hair into a quick coiffure, hiding the dark locks under a floral green bonnet. Ribbons adorned the shallow crown and deep brim.

Tying the hat under her chin, she looked into the mirror with satisfaction. Her complexion shone like fine porcelain, and her eyes were bright with life. Even her mother wouldn't be able to find fault with her appearance this morning.

She patted her hair and, without a backward glance, picked up a stole from her chair as she went to join the family downstairs. She hoped her parents had gotten over their disappointment of her rejection of the colonel. Propriety and good breeding could only get a man so far. He was such a dreadful bore.

Threading the stole through her gloved fingers, she pulled absently at the fringe. Then, draping the material around her arms as she came to the main hall, she frowned. Outside she could hear a carriage pulling away from the house. Curious, she went to the window, pulling back the drapes. It was their family carriage leaving the estate.

Before she could investigate, a manservant opened the front door. He bowed slightly as her mother walked in. The viscountess glanced around the hall. Then, nodding to the servant in dismissal, she came to look out the window beside Isabel.

The viscountess lifted her hand to pull aside the curtain. She didn't look at her daughter, choosing instead to sigh out toward the lawn. Isabel studied her mother's face carefully. It was strained, more so than usual. Her eyes were sad and wet from crying.

"Mother?" Isabel questioned softly. She lifted a hand to her mother's shoulder. "Is anything amiss? Who is in the carriage? Where are they going?"

The viscountess glanced at her shoulder, shivering as she shook her daughter's hand from her. For a moment, Lady Sutherfeld looked toward Isabel, not meeting her daughter's eye. Then, turning back to the window, the viscountess whispered, "There goes the last of my daughters from Rothfield Park. Godspeed, my dear Jane. May your visit with Harriet bring you a comfort I cannot feel."

Isabel gasped at the deliberate slight. She stiffened in understanding. Desperately, she whispered, "Mother? What do you mean? You can't be so angry with me as to ignore me forever. The colonel—"

"The colonel?" the viscountess echoed in a dramatic whisper. She furrowed her brows, lifted her chin proudly into the air, and sniffed. More tears wet the woman's blue eyes. She dabbed at them lightly with an embroidered handkerchief. Then, without one look at her waiting daughter, she turned away. The handkerchief dropped from her hand as she walked, the light fabric skimming across the floor as it fell, forgotten by its owner.

Isabel started to call out to the viscountess. However, seeing the little square still stained with tears, she picked up the fabric and rubbed her gloved fingers over the damp material. Clutching it, she felt like weeping.

Her mother had callously dismissed her. Isabel knew the woman was given to theatrics, but surely such an extreme punishment was unwarranted. Although being treated with silence was nothing new to her, the pointed refusal to acknowledge her was.

Just as she knew the bend of the viscountess' nature, she knew too that her mother was stubborn in her convictions, and it might be ages until she deemed her eldest daughter worthy of conversation. Isabel had no idea the colonel's fortune meant that much to the viscountess. It's not like they were poor, and the daughters needed to marry to save the family fortune.

"Fine, don't speak to me," Isabel whispered angrily. She refused to cry as she went back to the window. The carriage was gone. Remembering what her mother had told her, if not directly, she frowned. She sent Jane to London.

"Oh, Jane." Isabel already missed her sister. Jane wouldn't have chosen to go to London on her own. Undoubtedly this was another of her mother's punishments—to take away her confidant. Her unhappiness was overridden by anger toward her mother, and she found herself storming into the dining room.

She grabbed a pastry off of a tray. Hearing a gasp behind her, she turned to see an offended maid's pale face. It was the same girl who had given her the plate the day before.

The maid's mouth opened as if she might speak. Isabel cut her off with a grimace. "Not you, too. I will not suffer your accusing glances on top of my mother's. Begone from my sight at once!"

The maid gave a pitiful whimper and scampered off. Throwing the pastry down on the tray, Isabel strode from the room without eating anything.

"If no one wants me here, I shall go out." In part, she felt sorry for her animosity toward the maid, but she didn't go back to apologize. Without waiting for a servant to attend her, she went out of the front door, slamming it shut behind her.

Outside, the day was as fresh and clean as the morning sunlight in her bedroom window had promised. Isabel strolled over the graveled drive, through the grass, and then into the garden. She ignored the paved courtyard close to the house, choosing instead to follow the earthen walkways leading through the rows of flowers and benches.

The farther she wandered from the house, the easier her steps became until she could feel no anger, only joy in a beautiful day. Making her way to a bench, she sat on the stone seat. She realized then that she'd forgotten to bring a book with her. Not that she felt like reading, she assured herself, refusing to go back.

Time passed with the rolling of grasses in the gentle breeze. Isabel closed her eyes, letting the sun warm her as she turned her face toward it. She unfastened her bonnet, letting it fall from her fingers. Her stole clung loosely to her arms.

Suddenly, a chill swept over her, and she shivered violently. Crunching footfall drew near, coming from the house. She turned her head to confront the noise.

The heavy footsteps came steadily closer. Had her parents sent the colonel to join her?

A figure appeared from behind a shrub, his tall frame outlined by sunlight. Isabel relaxed some as she realized she wasn't acquainted with the man. He was much too slender to be Edward, and his gait too relaxed to be the colonel. Lifting her chin, she waited for him to approach her. His attention turned away from her to admire a bird taking flight in the distance. The sun bounced off the shiny dark hair bound at the nape of his neck. He leaned on a slender walking stick.

Isabel coughed delicately, watching him in expectation. At the noise, the man's head whipped toward her. He took a step forward into the shade. At first, he didn't make a move to acknowledge her with words as he watched with veiled curiosity. Grayish green eyes stared out from beneath a worried brow. They struck her with their unmistaken depth.

If ever in her wild youth she'd been stunned to dry-mouthed silence, this moment was it. Her heartbeat sped up from its usually steady rhythm. Another chill worked its way over her, and she was forced to blink and look away as she assessed his effect on her composure.

The man appeared to relax when her attention turned from him. Without comment, he took another step as if to pass her completely. Isabel propelled into action and stood to block his way.

Confusion passed over his features as he studied her. Slowly, he bowed. Isabel curtsied in return.

"Good day, sir," she said politely. Her voice was as weak as her legs, but she did her best to control it. She wouldn't let this man move on without discovering who he was. She waited to hear his voice, hoping it was high or off-pitch to counteract the disturbing effect of his handsome face.

Her gaze traveled over his attire. His clothes were of sufficient quality but by no means of the latest style. A stiff cravat fitted around his throat, the tall points of his high collar nearly touching his ears. His dark gray waistcoat looked solemn next to the black of his knee-length jacket. She realized his attire was more suited to the styles when she was a young girl.

"Good day," the man answered carefully. His tone was stern and disapproving, though it wasn't at all unpleasant, much to Isabel's delight and dismay.

"Are you lost, sir?" she asked.

"No, Miss, I am not." His words were stunted as if he were afraid to use them. He swallowed a bit nervously, making no attempt to go around her or to leave her, as he waited for her to speak.

Isabel studied his eyes and imagined they swam with thoughts, or perhaps dark emotions. Then an idea struck her. She expected a new tutor, and without a doubt, this had to be him. His old clothes were probably gifts from a previous lord he had served. His uneasiness could only mean her parents were still not talking to her and had sent him to introduce himself. It was clear by his stiff demeanor that he was displeased by the arrangement.

Isabel sighed. "You must be the new tutor my father has arranged for my sister and me. However, Jane has left for London this morning, and I do not require your services."

This seemed to surprise him. The man tilted his head thoughtfully and furrowed his brow. The look could only be interpreted as distaste for her bluntness.

"Oh, don't tell me you're at a loss for words," she laughed. "You're a tutor and must know of a great many things to say. Surely you know that it's up to me to introduce myself since my parents won't do it. And I expect you're the man they have hired to change my very disagreeable nature."

"I—" he began, cut off by the expectant lift of her brow. Then, with a worried frown, he questioned, "You don't know—?"

"Oh, I know that you're here to be my tutor. My father thinks I'm still in need of an education though I quite disagree. Already I have had nigh thirteen governesses." Isabel gave an airy laugh, purposefully trying to put him off. "I alarm you with my straightforward nature, do I not? I must warn you it only gets worse. If I were you, I would leave your post immediately."

The man didn't move. Instead, he studied her, his eyes roaming over her unruly hair to the bonnet lying on the ground.

Isabel patted her windswept locks. She hated his disapproval and wondered why his ill opinion upset her, especially when she'd gone out of her way to annoy him.

"I can see by your look that you will consider no such thing. Well, you can't say I didn't warn you. Whatever happens from here is entirely your fault. Now, you must be called something, what is it again?" She tried to make her tone more amicable.

"Dougal Weston."

"Mr. Weston, it's a pleasure to make your acquaintance. I'm Miss Drake, but please, if we are to be forced into each other's company, do call me Isabel, or even Issie. I much prefer it."

"Miss Drake."

"I do hope your journey to Rothfield Park was pleasant? We are a long way from…well, *everything*. I must apologize in advance for any disagreeableness you'll encounter here. I'm not on speaking terms with my parents, or should I more accurately state they're not speaking to me. You see, they're greatly disappointed in me at the moment."

At that bit of personal information, his frown deepened into one of grave distaste, "Surely you don't wish to discuss such matters with me."

"Oh? Whatever do you mean?"

"I have no wish to clarify at risk of insulting you, Miss Drake." Mr. Weston watched her carefully.

The crease between his eyes only deepened. She noticed he had the most distracting birthmark beneath his eye, near his cheek. The small mark was both disarming and handsome. She had the strangest urge to touch it, and from that urge grew the desire to feel his skin against her hand.

"Please speak candidly, Mr. Weston. For how else am I to learn?" she said before she could stop the words. Her attention moved from the mark on his cheek back to his eyes. She couldn't help but meet the challenge in his gaze. Any admiration she'd felt just moments before left her, replaced by the prospect of a stimulating rivalry. If this man were trying to disarm her with his superior attitude, she wouldn't allow it.

"I think your words thus far indicate you're very much in need of a tutor. You lack propriety. I can only hope that by expanding your mind, you will grow more assured and less...*frivolous*." Mr.

Weston gave her a curt nod of dismissal. He moved to walk around her, but she stepped to the side and blocked his retreat. His lips pressed in a straight line.

"Indeed." Isabel felt like a scolded child. She tried to keep the hurt from filtering through her expression. Her lips trembled, but she held her own. "And do you propose to be the man who will teach me this propriety I appear to lack?"

Mr. Weston instantly looked sorry for his harsh words.

"I daresay we will be spending a great deal of time together," he answered, the severity of his brow lightening.

"So that's my mother's game, is it?" Isabel forced a laugh. Turning from him so he wouldn't see her insecurity, she leaned over to pick up her bonnet. Dusting it, she studied the ribbons. She formed them into curls by winding the straps over her fingers. She couldn't meet his gaze as she said, "They wish to bore me with your teachings until I relent and marry the colonel. I suppose she is refusing to talk to me and has sent away my only confidant in an effort to make me want to take your lessons out of nothing better to do."

After a long moment passed and he didn't answer, she glanced up at him.

"They intend for you to start right away, don't they?" Isabel asked quietly.

Mr. Weston nodded. He appeared as if he wasn't sure what to say.

Isabel refused to acknowledge anything likable in him. As far as she was concerned, he was a hard man with an overly disapproving nature and an overbearing sense of himself. And the arrogance of him! It was inconceivable that he could have anything to teach her about how to be a proper lady.

"Well, I'm not ready to begin my lessons. I wish to flounder a bit more in my insufferable impropriety. Why don't you sit with my mother? I'm sure both of you can find enough faults with me to while away the entire afternoon. Please inform her I shall be dining alone in my room tonight and for possibly every meal until the end of time. I want nothing to do with either of you."

Isabel skirted around the stunned tutor without giving him time to answer. She felt his gaze on her back as she stalked off. Stomping as hard as she dared in her slippers, she did her best to appear as uncivilized as possible. If she were lucky, he would declare her so far gone and beyond hope and would therefore leave Rothfield Park at once.

Reaching the front of the house in a breathless flutter, she thrust open the door. The heavy wood crashed behind her as she stormed inside. In the front hall, her pale mother gaped in surprise, turning in fright at the sound. Isabel ignored her, hurrying past the viscountess to go to her room. Her mother rushed to close the door behind her. Isabel was gone before the viscountess could scold her.

3

Curse that Mr. Weston, Isabel fumed inwardly. *And his arrogant, insufferable disposition. I shouldn't be forced to endure his presence.*

She stopped near the window, tapping her fingers impatiently against the wood frame. It was nearly five hours since she'd introduced herself to the man, and still, his coldness stung just as fresh as the first bite of his haughty disparagements of her character. Resuming her pacing, she grumbled, "Who does he think he is, speaking to me as if I needed manners? Was it I who stared blankly as if the other didn't exist? Was it I who left all the awkwardness of the introductions to a gentlewoman? No, it wasn't."

Isabel refused to leave her bedroom. She wouldn't find a sympathetic ear with her parents.

They were the ones who'd hired the man. Besides, she hated to admit that she was too much of a coward to see her father. After the way her mother had acted, she was sure her father was just as displeased, if not because of her stubborn disobedience, then for her mother's ill humor, of which he would undoubtedly suffer.

Frustration seeped from every pore. She shook with indignation.

There was no one left to distract her attention or ease the displeasure of her bad mood. Jane was off to London without even a word. Her father had undoubtedly informed Mr. Tanner he wasn't to visit, as was the viscount's intention. And the colonel? Well, he was the last man Isabel wished to see. In her opinion, all of this was his fault.

Isabel was trapped at Rothfield Park, and it would seem her only company in her imprisonment was to be Mr. Dougal Weston. She paused in her pacing to stare at the plastered wall of her bedchamber. She pictured the image of his handsome face. He'd been rightly disturbed by her actions. A man as proper as he was would have been offended by her outburst. It wasn't Mr. Weston whom she'd been mad at, but he had, nevertheless, endured the brunt of her wrath.

A knock on the door broke through her thoughts, and she called for the visitor to enter. A maid carried a tray laden with food. Isabel tried to smile.

"Miss." The maid curtsied and averted her gaze to stare at the floor. Isabel saw the young woman peek curiously from the corner of her eye when Isabel motioned to a table. The maid quickly set the tray down before turning to leave.

"Wait," Isabel ordered. Then softening her tone, she asked, "Do I know you?"

"No, Miss," the maid answered. Her impeccable red hair was pinned beneath a white servant's cap, which bobbed as she again nervously curtsied. Isabel detected a northern dialect to the maid's words. "I'm Charlotte."

"Pleased to make your acquaintance, Charlotte." Isabel tilted her head to see if the maid would look at her. "Have you recently arrived at Rothfield Park?"

The maid did glance up at that. She seemed to struggle with her answer before saying, "New to your household, Miss."

"And are you from the area?" Isabel was desperate for company, even that of a servant. Again the maid appeared pained as she answered, "From the North."

It was clear the maid would willingly say no more.

Sighing, Isabel waved her hand in dismissal. "That will be all. Thank you, Charlotte."

"Yes, Miss," the maid again curtsied and hurried from the room.

When she was alone, Isabel muttered, "Well, I guess I can strike the servants from my short list of allies. Undoubtedly my mother has already spoken to them. She even sent a timid stranger to wait on me."

It always bothered her when her mother laid bare familial difficulties in front of the servants.

Isabel walked over to the tray of cold mutton and bread. It was a simple fare, but no doubt all her mother thought she deserved.

"I suppose I should try to get along with Mr. Weston if such a thing is possible. Maybe if I please my parents, they will be more apt to see reason and abandon the foolish idea of me marrying a man I don't love."

Taking a bite of the bread, she didn't taste it. She ignored the meat, preferring to drink the one glass of wine she was allotted. The liquid was thicker than she was used to and had a stronger, unusually salty taste. She gulped it down.

Isabel tore pieces of bread and placed the morsels in her mouth as she continued to pace. Her decision was made. She would make amends with Mr. Weston.

4

"Mr. Weston." Isabel curtsied. She watched his gaze move to her in surprise from over the top of his newspaper. Upon seeing her, his eyes narrowed in mild disapproval. She stiffened and tempered her expression. Could she blame him for being defensive toward her? "Good morning, sir."

"Good morning." Mr. Weston appeared weary as if waiting for her next tirade. His head bowed as he turned back to his paper, hiding his eyes behind the shield of print.

Isabel pressed her lips together, waiting to see if he would finish reading and speak to her. Already her mother had refused to look at her, and the servants bustled past without saying a word. Once, she caught Charlotte looking at her. The maid quickly turned away with a stack of clean linens hugged to her chest.

Isabel stood, her hands entwined before her blue gown. She felt like a soldier waiting to be reprimanded. When he continued to read, she insisted, "Mr. Weston?"

He flipped the edge of the paper down to study her again. Isabel swore she heard him sigh.

"Are we to begin?" she asked with forced meekness.

"Begin?" His gaze roamed over her with no clue as to what she was referring.

"Yes," she said. Pleasing her parents might be more complicated than she thought—especially if Mr. Weston continued to stare at her.

His gaze again darted over her gown. Weakly, she looked down only to brush the back of her hand over her skirt to straighten it. Realizing what she was doing, she tried to hide her scowl. Already she wanted to yell at him, and they had yet to complete one of his lessons. Through tight lips, she managed, "Are we to begin my lessons this morning?"

"Quite right." Looking around the library, he didn't appear to give her question much thought. "Read one of those books, and we will discuss it later."

Mr. Weston flipped the paper before his face

once more. Isabel made a childish face toward the irritating man. His long forefinger tapped the back of the newspaper as if he'd seen the rude gesture but was above responding to it.

Isabel crossed the room to the extensive bookshelf and exhaled noisily. "Which?"

The paper snapped in the silent room.

"I'm sorry?" Mr. Weston asked, looking blankly at her again.

"Never mind," she muttered.

He nodded once, just as abruptly turning his attention away from her as the paper lifted.

❦

Dougal patiently waited while Isabel ran her fingers over the library shelves. He was familiar with many of the volumes lining the walls. Watching her from the corner of his eye, he saw her hand pause by a thick old tome of a book. Then, glancing over her shoulder at him, her fingers skimmed hurriedly past, as if afraid he'd detect her interest in it.

Dougal was sorry for scolding her but doubted she gave it a second thought. It had been a long time since he'd spoken to a beautiful woman. Today, he'd known she was near him the moment she came into the room and could tell that his ignoring her wounded her ego. He hid his smile, trying to concentrate on the words that had captured his attention before she walked in. They faded and blurred, and yet he pretended to study them.

"I can't find one that interests me," she admitted at length, giving a small pout. "What would you recommend?"

"Would you take pleasure from the paper? We could discuss current events if you like," he offered. He tilted the paper toward her. She eyed him thoughtfully. A small wave of hope washed over him as he waited for her to take the suggestion.

"I have no interest in the affairs of men," she said with an airy laugh, shading her eyes with her lashes. "What does it matter what current intrigue Napoleon Bonaparte is engaged in? Let the French tend to him. He's their man, is he not? I see no threat of him here at Rothfield Park. And who cares about the war with the New World? I daresay we English should never have discovered so troublesome of a land."

Dougal stared in surprise at her unashamed ignorance. Isabel tried to hide a small smile as she carefully turned back to the books.

At length, he said, "You cannot mean that."

"What?" She waved a hand in dismissal. "Oh, you mean about the French? Well, you may be right. Perhaps the general is Spanish? I can never keep the two races apart, being as their cultures are so very similar. Ugh, and the chattering nonsense they insist on speaking. Every civilized person speaks English and always has. I see no reason to learn gibberish, just as I see no reason to rub elbows with the lower classes. I daresay both activities would be pointless and would ruin a good day."

Dougal was caught between being appalled and fascinated. He didn't like his reaction to her. Her beauty diminished with each untaught slash of her tongue. And though she repulsed his mind, his senses reminded him just how long it had been since he'd held a woman in his arms.

Nothing would ever come of his attraction, and so he pushed the impropriety far from his thoughts. He was at Rothfield Park to do one thing and one thing only. He wouldn't deviate from his task, especially not for a mere slip of a woman who held no real thought in her head.

Dougal assured himself that he couldn't find loveliness in a thoughtless vessel, but then, he knew that wasn't entirely true as he looked at her face. If she didn't speak, he would be quite content to look at her as one would look at an exquisite painting. However, her naiveté was much worse than he could ever imagine. She was indeed a product of foolishness encouraged by societal audacity, and he dreaded the idea of being forced to spend too much time in her company.

※

Isabel carefully watched her tutor's expressions, delighted that her ruse worked so well. Her parents wanted her to be an insipid, silly woman with no real opinions of her own, hadn't they? She kept an expression of false innocence, and her smile never once faltered. Seeing a frown descend upon Mr. Weston's handsome face, she said, "I don't see any books here worth reading. They're all very dull. Whichever man chose to read them would be a bore of a companion."

"None of worth?" he repeated in disbelief. Dougal looked over the shelves. If he'd thought she could be no less feeble-witted than she'd already shown herself, he was sadly mistaken. "I assure you, I know almost every line and—"

"Oh," she exclaimed. She scrunched her nose to emphasize her excitement. "My sister Jane recently received a novel from my other sister Harriet before going away to London. I will see if she left it behind. I think it's about spirits."

At this comment, Mr. Weston froze. Folding the paper, he set it aside without looking at it. Carefully, he stood from the chair, refusing to turn to her until his emotionless mask was well in place.

Isabel took a small step back at his height. His slender build moved with elegance and grace. Every line of him was rigid with perfection—the neatly queued pull of his dark hair held by a black tie, the stiffness of his white cravat against his skin, the mark beneath his eye. Again he'd dressed in an older fashion, his jacket the same long black with a gray waistcoat, albeit a darker gray than the day before. His booted feet planted apart, holding his weight evenly as he waited for her to continue.

She turned away, trying to look busy while she faced the books. Her heart quickened with an unfamiliar emotion, and she became very nervous. The library was too small, and she could feel him watching her with steady eyes. Her throat constricted as if invisible hands were choking her. Her skin tingled warmly.

Isabel twirled a lock of hair behind her ear, unable to meet his probing gaze. His eyes were full of disappointment, and though she'd given an ill opinion of herself to him, she couldn't help being sorry for it now.

"Are you trying to tell me something?" His words were barely above a whisper.

The leather-bound pages blurred before her eyes. A shiver worked its way up her back. She glanced at the floor, hoping to see him from the corner of her eye. She could not. "What, pray tell, would I be trying to say?"

He cleared his throat. Her head didn't move, and she gave no indication of retreating from the books. The silence stretched. Finally, he said, "Nothing."

"Is it the rumors of the house to which you are referring?" When she heard his intake of air, she turned slowly to face him. "Rothfield Park is haunted. Haven't you heard?"

Mr. Weston refused to meet her gaze. Instead, he turned to look out the window to the northern yard. Pushing the blue velvet drapes aside, he stared over the curving paths leading to the long, open field.

"It's said all kinds of spirits reside in the house," Isabel continued. "There is a child—"

"Have you seen her?" he asked, his tone strangely desperate. "Have you seen any of the spirits, I mean."

Isabel studied his back. She wanted to laugh. Surely this educated man didn't believe in such things as ghosts? Unable to stop herself from teasing him, she said, "No, but I think my sister might have once. She mentioned hearing a child crying in her chamber one night."

His grip tightened on the curtain, and she

wondered if he might pull it down. Turning around, his voice strained, he asked, "Is that all she said? Where was the child?"

Isabel became nervous. The hopelessness almost poured from his expression. With a perplexed frown, she said, "It's a jest, Mr. Weston. Ghosts don't exist. Jane learned of the story from the servants and then had a bad dream. You're not seriously giving credence to this story, are you?"

"No. Certainly not." He turned away.

"There are no such things as ghosts," she asserted.

"Are you saying you don't believe?" The mask once more dropped over his face. He leaned back against the windowsill, crossing his arms over his chest. A smile tugged on the corner of his mouth. She was delighted—and disturbed—to discover a dimple threatening to peek out from his cheek.

"I have never seen nor experienced reason to," she answered. Pretending to be stupid was one thing, insane quite another.

"Then," he began carefully.

Isabel waited for him to continue.

"Forgive my forthrightness, but what about your accident, Miss Drake?"

"Accident?" Isabel echoed. "I have no idea what you're referring to."

"I must be thinking of someone else." For a

moment, his eyes captured hers. His expression softened, and his lips curled up at the corner.

"Is this part of your lesson? I must say it's unconventional." She smiled, endeavoring to mask her blush at his direct attention. Her breath caught in her throat, and she had to look away.

"Read the paper," he ordered brusquely, pushing up from his perch on the windowsill. He grabbed his walking cane and swung it like a pendulum. "After you give me an account of what you've learned, we will discuss it. I hope you'll discover something of consequence."

Isabel glanced at her hands, not liking the harshness of his words. Pursing her lips to hide her displeasure, she turned around. Mr. Weston was gone.

She sighed heavily in disdain. On her father's chair rested the paper from London, a gift no doubt from Aunt Mildred to her father. She walked over to the chair, carefully removing her gloves so the print wouldn't stain them.

"All right, Mr. Weston. You wish to speak on current events," Isabel muttered, a mischievous idea forming as she picked up the news. Riffling through the paper, she found a page of public interest and grinned. "Then, by all means, let us find some current events."

As she sat down, her thoughts were not on

pleasing her parents or avoiding the most dreadful Colonel Wallace. Her aim was of a much more devious purpose. She was going to vex the rude Mr. Weston and drive him mad until he left Rothfield Park and took his high-handed manners with him. Only, she hoped he didn't go too soon. She had a feeling that vexing him would be one of the most pleasurable experiences of her life.

❦

Dougal watched the woman smile. He wondered what she was planning. She was unaware he studied her from the cracked library door.

Frowning, he scratched his head. He sensed she was contriving something, but he couldn't determine what.

Then, scowling, he remembered her remarks about the world's current events. Could the girl really be so empty-headed? A simpleton wouldn't make his task easier. Muttering a curse under his breath, he strode away from the library and out of the house. He needed to get far away from Miss Isabel Drake.

5

THE SUN SPARKLED over the flower garden in brilliant summer splendor. Isabel lifted her face to the warmth, letting the rays kiss her skin. Sighing, she felt restless and abandoned. It had been hours since Mr. Weston left her to read the paper. She wondered if he figured it would take her a long time. The notion made her chuckle.

Then, as if materializing out of her thoughts, Mr. Weston was there. Isabel shivered at his abrupt appearance, peering at him from the stone bench. Self-consciously, she stood and brushed off her long skirt.

"Miss Drake." He nodded. "Have you finished reading?"

She smiled at him to disguise her uneasiness.

Well, right to the point, she thought, not liking his stark manners.

Isabel's simple smile remained intact. "Why yes, Mr. Weston, I have—a few moments ago, in fact."

He studied her carefully. She had the feeling he wanted more than regurgitated political facts. "And what did you learn?"

"Oh, Mr. Weston," Isabel gushed. "Please, do sit down first. My head is so full that it might take me a while to collect all my thoughts into the proper order."

She turned from him, unable to help her smug grin. He glowered in disgust. His sharp eyes cut through her, willing her to be silent, yet his lips bade her to speak. She coughed delicately into her hand to keep from laughing. When she turned back to him, her eyes were bright, but her smile was innocently unaltered.

"Shall we start simply then?" The crease between his tired eyes deepened, and the severe line of his mouth made Isabel worry his face might be in danger of cracking open.

"Oh, yes, please." She adjusted her hands in her lap. "Let me start from the beginning. Mr. Darnell of Baker's Street is to wed with Miss Katherine Prynne, daughter of Mr. Prynne of Cunningham's, this fall. And I believe that he will be receiving four hundred pounds for his trouble."

He paled but didn't move. Isabel pretended not to notice as she leaned in secretively to him.

"I have met Miss Katherine, and I can say that Mr. Darnell is getting far too little money to take her on," Isabel added. That confidence shared, she continued, "And let me see...oh yes. His Grace the Duke of Hollingsworth is to wed with the Lady Catherine, with a C not a K like Mr. Darnell's Katherine. The Duke is to wed with Lady Catherine, daughter of the Earl of Ravenshire, next spring. I think it a more sensible time to marry in the spring—the fall is bad luck, you know? And I do hope she wears a reasonable color—not brown. Brown should be reserved for old men and stoic gentlemen who never smile, much like you. However, you wear gray, and that is overly dignified, as well."

Isabel paused, ignoring her slight against his character. Mr. Weston watched her, speechless.

"Be that as it may, I believe that the Duke and Lady Catherine are an excellent match. Neither one of them is graced with fine features. The Duke has a large nose, very disproportionate to his slender face, and Lady Catherine—well, I'm not one to speak ill of nobility—but she has rather large cheeks."

She tapped her cheek and nodded thoughtfully. He looked as if he might become sick. She gazed up at him to hide her mischief.

"Yes, yes, it's a fine match they have made of it. Marriage is a terrible business, but necessary, I'm afraid. If I didn't desperately want a handsome man, I might be content with the title alone. Though Mother wishes me to marry more money and Father wishes my husband to be of little humor and of much common sense. I daresay that if you were rich, he might be courting you as one of my prospects. Luckily, you're only a tutor, and I will never have to meet with such an expectation. And I'm sure you're happy not to be engaged to me."

Isabel waited for his outrage. It didn't come. She searched him for repulsion. If it was there, he hid it well. Usually, talk of marriage sent men scurrying without so much as a *by your leave*. Or, with the ones who hunted fortune, it brought on amusing declarations of love that they didn't mean.

He cleared his throat uncomfortably. He wasn't immune to her performance.

Isabel smiled with a sweetness that had melted most men and began to open her mouth.

Before she could speak, Mr. Weston said evenly, "Did you happen to read anything beyond the social pages?"

"Why, yes!" Isabel nodded enthusiastically. She thought of her sister Harriet. How proud the girl would be of her conversation. Almost every nonsensical phrase she took from her sister's pattern of speaking. And for years she had thought Harriet was a useless sibling. She again tried not to laugh.

"By all means," he urged, lacing his fingers in his lap. He looked as if he didn't dare to hope as she continued her report. With each word, tiny muscles in his face twitched. She imagined his mind began to go numb from her insensible conversation.

"It appears that pink is quite the sensation in London. Which is funny since I have read it was blue. Regardless..." She sighed before continuing in her brightly exaggerated way. She waved her hand in distraction and proceeded to prattle on about ribbons and sashes and what exact shades were to be worn and not worn. With each of her words, he grew more exasperated. Isabel was hard-pressed not to let him in on the joke. Except if she wanted to get rid of the high-and-mighty man, she would have to continue to put him off.

Isabel took a breath in between explaining the exact way that a man was to knot his cravat. She lifted her hands to pull rudely at the lace at his throat to demonstrate how he'd utterly miscalculated his knot. Mr. Weston lifted his hand and politely, but firmly, brushed her fingers aside. "What have you read from the first pages?"

"The first pages?" she asked in surprise. "There is nothing of importance on the first pages. I told you that I have no concern for men's affairs—so many battles and names. I daresay it's difficult enough to remember one's own name, let alone all the cities and places that you men go off to. Besides, there is nothing of interest beyond English borders. Even you, Mr. Weston, should be able to agree to that—being as you're a learned man of vast knowledge, I'm sure."

"I will admit to no such thing, Miss Drake." His hand stiffened on his cane until she thought he might splinter it with his grip.

"I'm afraid you have caught me," she admitted. "I only read your dull paper for a short time before finding a delightful copy of a lady's journal. The viscountess left it in the library on my father's desk.

"Tell me, did you at least learn the date from the first page of my dull paper?"

"The date?" Isabel wondered at the odd question. Then, deciding he was being purposefully condescending, she giggled. Part of her wanted to slap him, but she had to remind herself that any unfavorable opinion he had of her was her own doing.

"Yes," he said gravely. His eyes narrowed as if the answer were of great importance. "Did you happen to see the date?"

Isabel's smile faltered. She turned away from his probing glare. "It is June 1812."

"Is it?" he asked in his droll manner, with his eyebrow slightly raised.

"Why, yes, I know what date it is." She had little time to wonder at his remarks for in the distance, she saw a rider on a black horse. The man sat within the shade of the trees, staring at them. A dull ache began in the back of her head, quickly spreading to her temples and behind her eyes. Turning to Mr. Weston, she realized that he'd been speaking to her. Absently, she said, "I'm sorry? I didn't hear you."

He sighed in exasperation. "Where did you put the paper? We shall go over it together."

Ignoring him, she touched her temple. The pain started to throb. "Do you know that man, Mr. Weston? He's staring as if he is acquainted with us. Yet, I don't recognize him."

"What man?" he asked, looking into the distance. "I see no one."

"That man there," Isabel insisted. She pointed toward the trees where the man on the black horse still watched them. She couldn't make out his exact features, yet she detected the nobleness of his bearing and the arrogant tilt in his head. Slowly, she stood. There was something very odd in the way he seated his horse. The horse pawed at the ground nervously. What should have been the animal's dark coat was paled with white powder, which hid the black depths. "Don't you see the very large stallion beneath that tree there?"

How could he not?

Mr. Weston stood next to her, undoubtedly wondering if she were having fun at his expense. However, seeing what could only be construed as panic in her countenance, he squinted toward the tree-line. "Are you sure you're not mistaken, Miss Drake? Could it be a shadow?"

"No," she whispered. Panicking, she took a step forward and pointed, jabbing her finger toward it. "Can't you see him, sir?"

Mr. Weston shook his head. His brow creased in what was becoming an all too familiar expression around her. She studied his eyes before spinning back around.

"Right th—" Isabel gasped when she saw the rider was gone. She hadn't heard the thud of hooves that would have taken him away. She swayed on her feet, her knees growing weak. In a hush, she reasoned, "But he was there."

Instantly, Mr. Weston was by her side. He slipped his hands onto her elbows. She looked up at him in confusion. His touch sent a chill over her. She jerked away from him.

"Are you well?" He reached for her again, but she backed away. "You're not going to swoon, are you?"

"No," she managed to say, trembling. Her heart raced at his nearness. She felt heat coming from his chest as he tried to hold her. He looked at the trees in confusion.

Isabel tried to shake off the feeling of his hands. His touch did something very unfamiliar to her. Her gaze flew over his handsome profile as if seeing the stark beauty of him for the first time in his open expression. The pain in her head grew, becoming unbearable.

Weakly, she protested, "I do not swoon."

❧

Dougal's gaze darted back to her just in time to see her blue lips quiver. Isabel fell forward into his arms. Catching her in surprise, he dropped his walking cane on the ground. Her soft body pressed into his jacket. He felt the warmth of her yielding curves against him. Her head lolled back on her shoulders, and her arms hung limp and lifeless at her sides. For an instant, he took in her lips, tempted to taste them. He denied himself, wondering why the urge would come at such a moment.

Dougal studied her face, lifting a finger to brush a piece of wayward hair from her forehead. With a gentle bounce, he lifted her and adjusted her in his arms. Her hair blew against his chest. Her lips parted in breath.

Dougal closed his eyes to regain control of himself. Ignoring his rampant desire, he quickly carried her toward the manor.

6

Isabel moaned as her eyelashes fluttered open to reveal a stormy sky. She couldn't help the dreamy smile that crossed her features. Her loosened hair tickled her cheek.

Mr. Weston tenderly brushed her hair back. The gentleness startled her, and she blinked rapidly, trying to clear her mind. Her headache was gone, but not her confusion.

Her lips parted. She looked up at Mr. Weston in surprise. His face was close to hers. She could see the texture of his skin, the shape of his tiny birthmark beneath the fields of his eyes. When his hand stroked over her cheek, an unfamiliar energy buzzed over her skin, almost painfully. She hid her troubled gaze beneath a long sweep of lashes.

Mr. Weston caught himself and abruptly pulled

away. Then, as if to cover his actions, he placed the backs of his fingers to her forehead before standing. "You appear to be recovered."

Isabel swallowed nervously, only able to nod. She wondered at his gruff voice. The sudden withdrawal of his nearness left her feeling exposed, which made her lightheaded. She felt the darkness creeping back over her mind. Isabel fought it.

"How…?" Pushing slowly up, she looked around her father's library. What happened to the stormy sky?

"You swooned," he said at length.

"I don't swoon." She pressed her hands together. Her entire body trembled with a peculiar sensation.

Mr. Weston tried to hide a small smile of amusement and failed. His eyes sparkled.

She stared at him, completely spellbound by the look.

"Are you recovered, then?" he asked.

She shook her head in denial while mumbling, "Yes, yes, of course."

"Yes?"

Isabel rubbed her temple.

"Should I leave you?" he asked. The movements of his mouth drew her attention.

Touching her hand to her lips, she whispered, "Tell me you saw him."

"No," he stated. "I saw no one."

"I'm not losing my mind," she insisted.

"I never said you were." Mr. Weston took pity on her and sat next to her on the small settee, careful to keep distance between them. "Perhaps you were mistaken?"

"No, there was a man on a black horse," Isabel said, barely registering Mr. Weston's deepening frown or the concern in his eyes. "He was strange. I think he is a spirit. The horse was too large to be missed, and when he moved, it was unusual. Almost like his legs floated but yet were intact. I can't explain it."

"Miss Drake, I don't think—"

"I did not imagine it," she broke in, "and I'm not delusional. I know what I said earlier about ghosts not being real. Nevertheless, I think I saw the late Marquis of Rothfield."

At that, he stiffened. He pulled away from her and stood. He paced to the window. "What makes you think it was the marquis?"

"It's said that the marquis is still around. Oh, I wish Jane were here. She knows all about the legends. I should have believed her when she tried to talk to me. I think I shall write to her in London and tell her about it. I'll ask her to come back as soon as she can."

Mr. Weston turned to her. "You mustn't do that."

"Why? She's my sister, and I trust her above all others." Isabel pushed to her feet. His serious expression worried her.

It was then she realized he wasn't trying to convince her that ghosts didn't exist. In fact, he appeared to believe her. His acceptance alarmed her, and she knew there was something Mr. Weston wasn't telling her. Doubt caused a shiver to trail up her spine.

"Who are you?" she asked.

"Your tutor," he stated, not meeting her gaze.

She backed away from him. "You don't act like a tutor."

His head tilted up with pride. Why hadn't she noticed the bearing before? She thought of his regal manners. This man was no tutor. There was more to him, a quality that bespoke of not only intelligence but of secrecy.

"How do you know what a tutor acts like? I'm your first one." He dared her to contradict him with his steadfast gaze.

"That is true, but I don't imagine a tutor would act as you have. You've not given me a single lesson."

"What about the paper?" he inquired, coming toward her. "Were we not discussing it?"

"No tutor would have let me prattle on about nonsense as you did without so much as a scolding," she said. "Who are you?"

Mr. Weston raised a brow. A smirk lined his mouth at her words.

Unmindful of what she revealed to him, she said, "No. A tutor would have corrected me when I said that wars and battles didn't matter. A tutor would have instructed me otherwise when I claimed the French and Spanish were the same. A tutor wouldn't have listened to my insane ideals of marriage and the endless chattering of social color. A tutor would have corrected all this. Who are you? What do you want? Why have you come to Rothfield?"

Mr. Weston frowned. Lifting his fingers to his mouth, he shook his head and hushed, "Shh."

Isabel saw him move. Her vision blurred in fear, and she moaned weakly, swaying on her feet.

❀

Dougal went to Isabel in three long strides, capturing her quickly in his arms as she fainted. Sighing over her head, he carried her back to the settee. He didn't trust himself to get too close. He couldn't afford to get involved with her.

Her skin was smooth beneath the back of his

hand as he checked her forehead to see if he could rouse her. A dark curl clung to his finger. He watched her closely, entranced by her peaceful expression. When she was resting quietly, not speaking of ignorant things, she was ravishing. There was no other word for it. He trembled. It had been a long time since he had caressed a woman.

It had become evident that she didn't remember falling from her horse or what had happened afterward. She didn't recall any of the things he needed her to remember. His scowl deepened as he whispered, "Let us try this again."

7

With a light groan, Isabel opened her eyes. Her body was fatigued, and her limbs heavy. Blinking hard, she looked around in confusion, detecting the pale morning sky outside her window. She was in her bedchamber.

A nearly spent candle caught her attention. It appeared to have been left burning all night, which was strange. Wax pooled in a drying puddle on her table.

When she sat up, she saw that she still wore her gown from the day before. How had she gotten into bed? She couldn't remember anything past the garden. No, that wasn't exactly true. She remembered teasing Mr. Weston, but then it all went blank.

A knock sounded on the door. Isabel jumped, inhaling sharply as it opened.

"Miss Drake." Charlotte curtseyed. "I thought you might desire breakfast."

"Ah, yes," Isabel mumbled, leaning back as Charlotte entered with a tray of tea and muffins. "How did you know I would be awake? It's early."

"You ordered a tray brought to your room at dawn, Miss, last night before you retired for bed. You said you wished to go for a ride this morning in the forest. I have instructed the groom to have your horse readied."

Isabel remembered no such order. Shaking her head, she said, "Tell him I have changed my mind. I won't ride this morning."

"Miss?" Charlotte probed.

"I don't feel like riding in the forest." Isabel waved her hand before lying, "I think it's too cold to go outside. I shall go to the library instead."

"Yes, Miss."

Isabel hummed weakly, trying to smile and failing miserably. She pushed her messy hair back from her face and waited until the maid left before rising to remove her gown. She washed quickly in the water basin, scenting her skin with rose-oil perfume. Then, after shrugging into a thin chemise and pulling on silk hose, she chose a pale blue gown of soft crêpe de chine.

Isabel hated being nervous. Her heart beat hard, and her head spun with unusual thoughts and all of them were of Mr. Weston. She couldn't imagine how all her feelings about him had changed so drastically. Now when she thought of his face, she felt like blushing, and her lips tingled with a peculiar sensation. She had the strangest urge to impress him, yet she knew the damage she'd done in pretending to be dimwitted.

Isabel finished her toilette, not bothering with the food on the tray. She left the room and slipped silently through the hallway. Portraits lined the walls. The painted eyes appeared to watch her progress. She caught movement out of the corner of her eye and gasped as she stumbled to a stop.

She thought one of the painted men dropped his arms from his chest to hang at his side. Swallowing nervously, she stared up at the opposing figure, waiting and watching. His dark eyes bore into her. After several minutes, when nothing happened, Isabel forced a laugh. She shook her head and rushed down the hall, refusing to look at another portrait.

The library's fireplace had been lit, and it cast the room in a fiery glow. The warmth offered comfort in the coolness of the early morning. The house was quiet, its inhabitants asleep except for Mr. Weston, whom she found sitting at her father's desk with a book. When she entered, he glanced at her. His eyes carried a gentle affection she wasn't used to seeing in him. The look took her by surprise, and she froze. Something wasn't right.

Mr. Weston watched her curiously as she took a step back. He placed his book on a nearby table and stood, waiting for her to speak.

"Mr. Weston." Isabel trembled and wished her voice was stronger. His handsome face agitated emotions deep within her.

An array of responses stirred inside her, fighting to be freed. But a lady couldn't give in to such bold propositions, no matter how hard her body tried to convince her mind to allow it pleasure. She couldn't run to her tutor and throw her arms around his neck. He'd probably recommend her parents place her in an asylum for emotionally disturbed women.

"I…" She couldn't form the words.

At the sound of her tortured voice, he took a step forward. He lifted his hand as if to touch her. Isabel jerked back in surprise.

When had his demeanor toward her changed? Where was the silent condemnation? What was this softness in his gaze?

She watched his lips fighting between a scowl and a smile. A memory tried to force its way from the back of her mind. His mouth drew her full attention as her own began to ache with sensitivity. She bit her lips to keep them from shivering.

What was her mind trying so desperately to tell her? And why was she so afraid to find out? She felt as if the answer was right there, begging to be discovered, but she couldn't see it.

"What is the matter?" Mr. Weston's gaze searched her. His hand again lifted as if to draw her forward by his very will, but she didn't move. "Has something happened?"

"Nothing, Mr. Weston," Isabel replied a bit harshly.

"Mr. Weston?" he echoed. His expression hardened. His hand fell to his side, balling into a frustrated fist.

"Yes. That is your name, isn't it?" She saw the filtering of early morning light glowing on his shoulders, haloing him. Her eyes were drawn to the strength of his neck, visible beneath his untied cravat. He didn't look so proper this morning. He'd discarded his jacket behind him. His waistcoat hung open, revealing the fine linen of his shirt. She saw the base of his throat beneath the revealing fall of the shirt's collar. His flat stomach darkened the white linen as it showed from behind the thin material.

Isabel's pulse began to race. She shook violently, wanting to test the firmness of his body for herself. Unable to divert her gaze, she continued to look him over.

"Yesterday, you called me something else." He was aware of her attention to his person. How could he not be?

"I'm sorry for whatever I said," she said. Isabel wondered what she could have called him but came up blank. "I must not have been myself. I can't remember a thing beyond speaking to you in the garden."

Mr. Weston's expression steeled itself to her, but there was a deep agony within his gaze. Breathing hard, he turned from her. Quickly, he buttoned his waistcoat and straightened his cravat. Then, taking his jacket, he slid it over his shoulders.

When he turned back to her, his manner was cold and impersonal like she remembered him. There should have been comfort in that normality, but all she felt was loss.

He stared blankly at her for a moment. A war waged behind his eyes, and she wondered why she thought him tortured and alone. Isabel was drawn to go to him, to comfort him, but she nervously held back.

Mr. Weston took a step toward her. He was rigid and proper. His gaze probed her, willing her to remember something. She could only stare back in confusion. Then, without speaking, he curtly bowed his head and moved past her to the library door as if he didn't trust himself to speak.

"Mr. Wes-Weston," she stuttered.

"Yes, Miss Drake?" He didn't look at her. His shoulders slumped forward as he waited for her words.

"What would you have me do today for my lesson? I should like to get started." She desperately wanted to go to him. Her entire being begged her to hold him. Her lips tingled, wanting something she couldn't describe. Her mind reached out, willing him to answer a question she didn't know how to ask.

"Read," he said, his voice a little hoarse. "Pick a book—anything."

He moved to go.

Isabel stopped him by insisting, "And we shall discuss it later in the garden?"

She waited to see if he would smile at her. He did not. Back was his cold demeanor.

"Yes, Miss Drake. We shall." He bowed his head in her direction, not turning to look fully at her before he left her alone in the library.

She dropped onto the settee, finding it difficult to breathe. What had happened? What couldn't she remember? Why did Mr. Weston think she should call him anything but his name? Had they fought? Isabel felt dizzy. Or was it much worse than that? Had she shamed herself with him?

She took a steadying breath and refused to think about it. The previous evening was a blank mystery. Taking her time, she went to the bookshelves, not seeing the binding for the nervous tears threatening to spill from her eyes. She couldn't determine why her lips shook or why her arms trembled with a strange need to hold her tutor. And why, when he looked at her, did it feel like her heart was being ripped apart?

Gaining control, she grabbed a book from the shelf—the first her fingers touched. Then, making her way back to the chair, she sat with a resolve she didn't know she possessed and read.

The long shadows cast from sunlight moved over the floor until they had journeyed from one end to the other. Isabel couldn't make it past the first page of the nameless treatise on animal husbandry and its relations to social economics. A duller book she couldn't have found. But, refusing to replace it, she read and reread the first page, not remembering a single word past the very first "The."

More often than not, her eyes would wander to the embroidered roses on the bodice of her gown. Her fingers would pluck at them absentmindedly. With a delicate yawn, she opened her eyes to gaze dreamily about the room. The light had softened into the golden hue of late afternoon.

Isabel blinked heavily and forced her eyes to focus on the orange patterns reflecting off the rows of books, not really seeing them. She recalled every detail of Mr. Weston's soft look when his clothes had been disheveled, lovely in their disarray before he once more became rigid and gruff and proper. The memory only brought with it a profound sense of loss. Her mind tried to recapture the look of him when she closed her eyes—a soft smile, a tender expression, the gentle reach of his hand as if he'd wanted to touch her.

Isabel groaned. Rising from her seat, she went to the window to gaze out over the garden. The book she'd left on the settee was easily forgotten. A gentle mist surrounded the garden, the sight of it tugging painfully at her memory. Her mind begged her to remember. She struggled to grasp a thought, but as she detected a hand—slender and pale—coming into focus in her mind's eye, she jolted in fear, and the image was gone.

Behind her, the door opened. She turned, hopeful to see Mr. Weston again. Instead, she found her father—his cravat loosened, his brown eyes brimmed red from drink. Shocked to find him thus so early in the day, Isabel stayed motionless by the window. The viscount didn't see her as he stumbled into the room. He glanced at the roaring fire in surprise before kicking off his wet boots.

Lumbering across the carpeted floor, he swayed only a little and stopped at his favorite chair. Wearily, he sank into the stiff folds. Isabel saw the balding top of his head and realized he still didn't notice her. The viscount stretched out his stocking feet with a sigh. She started to go to him when he cursed. Sitting up, he leaned forward, his gaze on the settee.

"Not again," he muttered, shaking his head.

The viscount pushed himself up with a groan and went to the settee to pick up the book. Looking at it despondently, he walked over to the shelf and put it back in its place. "Who the devil reads such in this house?"

Isabel cleared her throat delicately, thinking it high time she made herself known to her drunken father. The viscount spun on his heels. Grabbing his head in his hands at the quick motion, he paused, endeavoring not to weave.

"Father?" Isabel questioned.

"What?" he muttered. Looking up, he squinted. His gaze found her briefly before he rubbed his eyes to clear them of his self-induced discomfort. Under his breath, he cursed, "Bloody Hell! I must have drunk more than I figured."

His laugh was choked as he stumbled back to

his chair and fell more than sat into it. His eyes closed.

"Father, can I get you something?" Isabel asked.

"Ah," he muttered, his mind falling into a stupor. "Leave me, child."

"Father, what has happened?" She placed a hand on his head. His skin was warm. He moved his forehead away from her, but her fingers followed him.

"Blast it all, Issie," he slurred. "You were always a stubborn child. It's the reason I took you from London's influences. And you resent me for it. I should have taken a heavier hand with you. Possibly then things would be different."

"You mean because I won't marry the colonel?" She willed his eyes to open once more. It wasn't to be. A drunken snore escaped his lips.

Isabel dropped her hand from his forehead. Lovingly, she smoothed the tousled hair back from his flushed, round cheeks. She arranged his limbs into a more comfortable position. Her father mumbled but didn't open his eyes. Isabel left him to meet Mr. Weston in the garden.

Isabel walked along the curved paths, drawn back to the stone bench of their first meeting. She waited for the remainder of the day, but her tutor didn't keep their meeting. It was just as well. He preoccupied her thoughts.

The wind blew over her gown, pressing it to her body. Occasionally, a chill would work its way over her spine, and she felt like she wasn't alone. Then the moment would pass, and she would decide the chill was from the cool breeze, and the feeling was from her desire for Mr. Weston to join her.

With a wry smile, she realized she hadn't heard from Mr. Tanner. Not that Edward's absence surprised her. It had only been a few days since her father had ordered him not to call on her. With luck, one of the local families would throw a ball or a small garden party where she might happen upon him. Her father couldn't very well keep her from talking to him under those conditions.

Thinking about it, Isabel realized that she hadn't seen any mail or invitations. Beyond that, no one had been calling on Rothfield Park. Had her mother driven all guests away? Or worse, with the sweet Jane gone, did no one think to visit her?

Suddenly, Isabel wished she'd been a little more hospitable to the poor country folk of Haventon. Small society was better than no society at all and keeping oneself busy was better than so much time given to contemplation.

Was this how her mother thought to sway her

decision in regard to the colonel? Was that what her father had meant? Isabel felt herself rise to the challenge. So that was their game, was it? Well, they would soon discover the strength of her resolve.

Isabel decided she should go inside as the sun began to fall over the horizon. The gold of evening bathed the earthen pathways and contrasted the stone carvings decorating the beautiful lawn. As she walked toward the manor, fine dust blew from the ground to surround her feet. Darkness came too fast, like the rapid clicking of time kept by an over-wound clock.

Isabel gasped in surprise at the abrupt change. Her heart pounded violently. She felt something growing around her, swelling up from the earth, awakening with the night. Spooked by the stillness of the grounds and the sudden eeriness of the evening, Isabel stared straight ahead of her. She didn't know why she was scared, but she began to run anyway.

Within moments, she was on the front steps and through the front door. She slammed it shut. She was unable to rid herself of the feeling that all wasn't well beyond the walls of the house.

Isabel darted to the safety of her bedroom. Changing for bed as quickly as she could manage, she crawled beneath the thick coverlet. The weight of it on her body comforted her, and she pulled the blankets over her head, leaving only a small space between it and the bed to peek out. She refused to move, and when she closed her eyes, she fell instantly into a fitful sleep.

8

Mist gathered in the night, creeping eerily over the tall grass of the field and winding around the tree trunks. The full moon shone brightly over Rothfield Park. The air was sweet with the scent of flowers, but, to some, another smell could be detected on the breeze, the acrid smell of burning wood.

Dougal felt an old presence gather in the misty darkness. Desperately, he searched through it, looking for movement within the fog. Occasionally he would detect a stirring so brief that it was gone before his eyes could make out the full shape of a hand, the flowing material of a sleeve, but he could tell that they were there—just as surely as whatever was there could sense him.

Following the path into the woods, he felt his

heart beat with dread and anticipation. He was too old to give credence to hope, but he felt the stirring of it inside of him. The speckled light over the path grew dim. Insects hummed, unafraid of what lingered. The limbs of trees sounded overhead, crashing their leaves in an orchestra of foreboding melodies.

"Margaret?" Dougal called softly. He stopped near the stream, trying to listen past the water for any sign of an answer. The wind grew fiercer. The stiffness of the breeze was a warning he tried not to heed. He detected the smell of roses wafting around him. He took a step. The mist grew thicker, as if warning him to turn back. He called out, louder this time, "Margaret!"

He felt that he wasn't alone. There was someone else on the path, and it wasn't Margaret. The mist hid its secrets well, for he couldn't see ahead of him. He knew he should turn around and go back to the safety of the house, but he dared another step. His heart thudded painfully. The mist began to choke him, growing weary of keeping him at bay.

A sudden slash of a tree limb disturbed the fog, curling it in waves, aiming for his head as if to crush his skull. Dougal paled, stumbling back. When he righted himself, he knew he couldn't go on. It wouldn't let him pass. It never allowed him to pass.

"Margaret," he whispered, heartbroken, beyond anger, and filled with frustration. With deep regret, he watched the mist clear while he slowly stepped away, and as the path opened before him once more, he was forced back to the manor.

9

Isabel shot up in her bed, startled by a terrible scream. Sweat coated her clammy skin. Gasping for air, she threw the coverlet from her legs. It was dark. Thin slivers of moonlight shone on the floor, and the only sound she could hear was the pulse beating in her ears.

She jumped off her bed and padded barefoot to the window. Beyond the chilly panes were the gardens, swirling with the fine mist of night. She pressed her face against the glass, her nose fogging a pattern as she frantically searched the countryside for signs of life. There was nothing. All was as it should be, silent and still.

The thudding of her heart lessened, and the tremor of her breathing calmed. Isabel giggled nervously. Berating herself for giving in to her bad dreams, she began to relax.

Another scream rent the air. Isabel jumped in fright and then fought to hold still as she shook in renewed terror. The sound didn't come from outside. Turning slowly, she carefully searched her bedchamber.

That scream had been real. This was no dream.

Detecting nothing within the shadows, she crept slowly to the candle on her dresser, striking the flint to light it. The orange glow of the small flame haloed her, casting her ghostly shadow in a globe of diminishing light. She lifted the meager flame high and looked around the room before hurrying to the door.

Isabel took a deep breath before cracking open the door to ease the candle through it. She listened intently for sound. The hall was empty.

Without letting herself consider the danger, Isabel rushed through the house until she reached the main foyer. It, too, was empty.

This time when the scream sounded, it was more of a loud moan, softer and childlike, followed by weeping.

Isabel hesitated, not knowing what to do. She'd give anything to have her sister with her, for the comfort of not feeling so alone. Even Mr. Weston, with his disapproving frowns, would be a welcome sight.

The voice came from outside and sounded close. Surely whoever it was would be standing on the other side of the door, waiting for someone to answer her. After glancing around the empty foyer, Isabel then eyed her long white nightgown. No one else had come to investigate, not even the servants.

The child continued to cry, not knocking to be let in.

Isabel set the brass candle holder on a table before pulling the door open enough to see out. No one was there. The crying grew louder.

"Hello? Who's there?" Isabel whispered. There was no answer. "Please, come forward to where I can see you. I won't hurt you."

The crying began to fade, moving around the corner of the house. The sound seemed to travel on the wind. Isabel followed the noise with her gaze and caught a glimpse of blonde hair formed into thick ringlets. Bright moonlight outlined the child, making her appear as if she glowed.

Isabel ignored the frantic pounding of her heart and raced after the girl.

"Wait," she insisted softly, going around the corner. "Where are you going? Come back. I can help you."

The child stopped. She turned around, her

head tilting impishly to the side. Isabel stumbled to a stop.

The trick of the moonlight faded as the girl stood in the shadow of the house. She stepped closer. The brightness of her clear, green eyes struck Isabel. A smile formed on the child's mouth, the look instantly replacing the tears that should have occupied her rounded features.

The girl's yellow dress was old, the tight sleeves and stiffly formed bodice fitting snugly to her thin frame. The skirt flared like a bell, swinging back and forth as if it would ring. The child giggled, lifting her skirt ever so slightly to show an abundance of petticoats beneath.

"I can help you," Isabel said.

With a small shake of her head, the girl took off down the flower garden path.

Isabel followed her. The child appeared to glide rather than bounce with each step. Unable to gain on the child, Isabel remained several paces behind. She raced through the garden until the child was out of sight. Breathing heavily, Isabel slowed her pace and walked down the path that the child had led her to.

Isabel tried to be quiet, listening for footsteps other than her own. As she came around a small shrub, she found the girl sitting demurely on the stone bench where Isabel and Mr. Weston had talked days before.

Isabel stopped to watch. The child buried her face in her hands.

"Hello," Isabel said.

When the girl looked up, tears streamed down her face. Picking up a shawl from the bench, the girl pulled the material around her shoulders, then stood and started to turn away.

"Wait," Isabel insisted, lifting her hand to stop her. She took a step forward.

The girl turned and tilted her head to the side.

"Why do you cry?" Isabel asked.

The child sniffed. "I'm lost."

"I can help you." Isabel drew nearer. "Where are you from?"

The girl glanced up at the sky and then over her shoulder. The girl's pale skin was translucent, and her bright eyes glowed strangely in the moonlight as she searched the distant trees. Again, her face turned to the moon as if to see the time in the mystical globe.

When the girl didn't answer, Isabel inquired, "What is your name?"

"Have you seen my mother?" the child asked suddenly, her tone changing. The sweet voice carried like a whisper on the breeze. The words were hollow, as if they had echoed before reaching

Isabel. "Have you seen my father? I am looking for him."

"No, I don't believe I have. Who is your father?" Isabel dared another step forward.

The girl, seeing her advance, stumbled backward down the gentle incline of a small slope. Her face scrunched as if she might again weep.

Isabel stopped, not wanting to frighten her away.

"Are you my mother?" the girl asked. "I cannot remember her."

Isabel hesitated. The question sounded oddly familiar, but she couldn't place it. Uneasily, she shook her head in denial. She couldn't speak.

The girl again looked around as if searching. Then, staring off into the distance like she'd detected something in the darkness, she shook her ringlet head and muttered, "He wouldn't like it."

"Who?" Isabel followed the child's gaze. That's when she saw him again—the figure on a dark horse, waiting in the distance, watching them. At their attention, the rider nudged his horse forward. The horse's hooves stirred the mist. Going to the child, Isabel asked frantically, "Who is that? Is that your father?"

"No." The girl bowed her head as she walked to meet the rider in dejection. She didn't try to run from him as he came for her.

"Wait," Isabel demanded, the loudness of her voice sounding harshly out of place. "You don't have to go."

The child turned with a sad smile and didn't answer. She waited as the rider approached her. The horse moved slowly, at a comfortable stride, but covered more distance than his pace should have allowed.

Isabel's heart thudded in warning. She wanted to run but was torn between her fear and her concern for the child. Unable to look away, she watched the rider as he neared.

Isabel eyed his medieval attire, wondering at the knightly costume. He was a large man with shoulder-length black hair that flowed around his tunic-covered shoulders. His black eyes were cavernous pits sunken in his face.

"What do you want?" she asked.

The man looked at her, his face expressionless as he studied Isabel carefully. Then he silently reached down to the child. His fingers curled, motioning her to hold his hand.

"Don't touch her," Isabel ordered. Her words were weak, but she bravely lifted her jaw into the air.

The man again glanced at her with something akin to curiosity.

Isabel turned to the girl. "You don't have to go with him. Stay here with me. I will protect you."

The girl didn't hesitate as she held her hand up to the man. The man pulled her before him onto the horse. The child wiggled until she was comfortable in his arms. She sat sideways on the animal's back, her head leaning against the broad expanse of the man's chest. Her sorrowful eyes stared at Isabel.

"Who are you?" She saw the child was unafraid of the man who held her.

The horse pawed the ground. The man and child continued to watch her with intent gazes, as if she was the one intruding, not they. Their eyes grew brighter—too bright for the reflected moonlight.

The man urged the animal toward Isabel, and she lifted her hand as a weak barrier. The mist swirled around her, creeping up her legs. Trembling, Isabel began to cry. Where she would have expected coolness, the fog instead burned her flesh. The tears streamed down her cheeks.

Isabel couldn't run, couldn't swing her arms to fight as the man came closer. His hand reached as if he would grab her and take her with him. She screamed in terror.

At the high-pitched sound, the horse startled, rearing in the air, its forelegs flailing. When the stallion struck the ground once more, the faces of the riders changed.

The child's yellow dress singed, the soft material scorched with the flames of a past fire, growing dark with ash and soot. Her features crumpled, wrinkling into a red and black mass of scarred flesh, the lips discoloring like dying roses against her skin until the tightened lines pulled back from her teeth. Her golden curls melted away until only the oozing mass of her bloodied skull showed. Her green eyes stared from the depths of her lidless eyes.

Isabel tried to scream again, but her voice stuck in her throat. Her stomach clenched at the grotesque sight. The image burned into her mind.

The man's transformation was less horrible. His face grayed with the stark, waxen pallor of death. His lips tinged with blue. A hole opened in the man's chest, exposing the still remains of his bleeding heart, once impaled but now a gaping wound that would forever seep.

Dragging in a ragged breath, Isabel forced a yell. The vibration of her voice jerked her legs into action, but before she could run, the thick mist wound around the man and the child, enveloping them. They disappeared.

Still screaming, Isabel turned, running along the dim pathway. Clouds drifted over the moon.

The land became dark—more so now that the mist curled toward the trees. Her heart pumped faster. Suddenly, she bumped into an unyielding chest.

"Let me go!" She fought the arms that tried to restrain her.

"Isabel," Mr. Weston commanded with a hard shake. "Isabel!"

"Let—" She stopped as the tone of his voice sank into her harried senses. Staring at him with wet eyes, she managed, "Spirits."

"What?" Shoving Isabel behind him, he started down the path whence she'd come.

"No, Mr. Weston, please." She grabbed his arm, tugging him to stop. "There are ghosts in the garden. Horrible—"

"Where?" He turned to her. His hand lifted to her cheek to calm her. She stiffened at his touch but didn't fight it. There was something familiar in his hold. His fingers ran down the side of her face and over the frantic pulse in her neck. He demanded, "Where did you see them?"

"In the garden by the stone bench, but please, don't go there. I think the mist swallowed them. They vanished—I…I…" Isabel shrugged helplessly. "Don't leave me."

Drawn by his light touch and the worry in his eyes, Isabel buried herself against his chest. The steady beat of his heart thumped against her reassuringly. She needed to feel something tangible, something real. She needed to know that he wasn't like the others in the garden.

Even with her fear, she was well aware of how different his skin was to hers, how warm his body felt against her chilled flesh. She was no fool. She felt his stiffness, knew he was uncomfortable, but she couldn't let go.

❧

Dougal held his breath in surprise at her sudden embrace. He kept his hands wide, away from her, refusing to hold her in return. Regardless, she clung tightly, her slender arms wrapping around his waist, holding him. He felt her tremble. Even as he'd been affected by the look of her form swathed in the voluptuous folds of her nightdress, his body wasn't immune to the press of her softness against him.

He stood for a long, spellbound moment, afraid that if he startled her she'd pull away, afraid of what it would mean to him if he held her, afraid of the memory that would haunt him afterward if he were to feel her flesh beneath his flesh-starved hands. These feelings were wrong, for so many reasons. His lust couldn't be explored or reciprocated. He couldn't lay voice to his passions. His loneliness couldn't be redeemed. They could *never* be together. Their paths were crossing for a brief moment, and soon the intersection of their lives would end. And he would never see her again.

After several frantic heartbeats, she began to pull away. Dougal could take it no longer. He wrapped his arms around her shoulders. How could he deny her comfort, even knowing the pain this memory would cause him later?

"Isabel." The word was tortured. His caress was stiff, brief, and he knew that it was wrong. He forced his arms to release her.

"No, don't go," she begged, not letting go of him. "Don't leave me alone. I'm not crazy. I know what I saw. The ghosts are real. It was the marquis. It had to be. He was in costume like he'd been to a ball."

"How—?"

"I just know."

Dougal studied her. In many ways, she was so vulnerable and innocent. The way she looked at him drove him to distraction. He'd been hard-pressed to keep his desire at bay since meeting her. Only now did he realize how close to the surface they bubbled. In that moment, he knew the fates plotted against him. And they were very cruel indeed.

Isabel still didn't understand what was going on

at Rothfield Park. Dougal wouldn't be the one to tell her. Where would he even begin? And, without that truth, there was nothing between them but her innocence waiting to be crushed. He wasn't the monster to do it. He needed her more than she could realize—for more than the fulfillment of his body. He needed her to complete the search for his soul.

❦

Isabel gazed into Mr. Weston's eyes, then over the strong line of his nose, and the small birthmark beside it. The worried crease on his brow deepened until he appeared to be displeased with her, but she didn't feel that tension when he held her. His arms had been tender, gentle, caressing. An unfamiliar sensation made its way over her body.

She needed his comfort. It centered her in a world that made little sense.

Isabel pulled him close and held tight. He made a small noise before holding her. His fingers kneaded her nightgown, causing it to lift and fall with each gentle stroke. She felt like she was floating, and at any moment, he would sweep her across the earth and sky, into the starry night.

Isabel forgot the ghosts, forgot that she was scantily clad in the arms of her tutor. She forgot her parents and the servants sleeping within the manor. Her mind didn't warn her of how wrong her actions were, for her body cried out with approval. Licking her lips, she glanced at his mouth, her attention suddenly drawn there.

"I—" She couldn't finish. Lifting on her toes, she pressed her mouth to his. He stiffened in surprise at the bold action. The sound didn't stop her. Nothing could stop her once her lips felt the firm pleasure of his.

A light plea escaped her throat. Her hands lifted to his face. The stubble of his chin scratched her, but she didn't care. Not knowing what possessed her, she opened her mouth. She needed to get closer, feel more. His breath fanned over her, and she inhaled him. Unsure how to end the torment of her flesh, she pulled back and peered into his stunned eyes.

Taking her hands in his, Dougal pulled her away from his face. Shaking his head, he said, "No."

"But I—"

"No," he ordered more forcibly. "You're distraught."

"But I thought that you…that I—"

"You're confused," he stated, his voice becoming more controlled with each passing moment. "You're tired."

She pulled angrily away. "Quit treating me as if I were a child!"

"Then don't act like one," he answered. "You're not thinking clearly. Tomorrow—"

"Tomorrow?" She backed away from him, fists balling at her waist. "Quit telling me what I am, or who to be, or what to do."

"Quiet. You forget what's out here," he warned. "Would you draw attention—?"

"You high and mighty…" She struggled to find an insult. "You think that just because you're my tutor, you can order me about? I'll have you know I didn't even want to kiss you. For a passing moment, you looked like my dear, sweet Edward, and I thought I was kissing him. If it weren't for the ghosts that gave me such a terrible fright, I wouldn't have…" Her words trailed off. She trembled as she remembered why she'd been running in the first place. "There are spirits in the garden."

"What did you see?" he demanded. Grabbing her arms, he gave her a little shake. "Tell me what you saw."

"Let me go! You have no right to give me orders."

His tone softened, but his grip remained tight. "What did you see?"

"A ghost," she said.

Isabel thought of her sister. Jane knew all the

stories. She needed to write to her, find out who the ghosts were and what they wanted. What had happened to the poor child? The burned face worked its way into her mind's eye. Isabel grew nauseous.

"Let me go," she begged. "I want to go inside. Your touch is making me sick."

As if realizing he hurt her, he looked at his hands on her arms and instantly released her.

She stumbled away from him. Rubbing her arms, she sniffed back tears. Her jaw jutted into the air. He opened his mouth to speak, but she cut him off with a dark look.

Turning, Isabel ran to the house without a backward glance. She found the candle where she'd left it, still lit, and grabbed it with trembling hands. Panting for breath, she hurried to her room.

❦

Dougal watched Isabel leave. He didn't like the pain he felt at her words, but he'd expected nothing else. Seeing her safely inside, he closed his eyes.

Determined, he rushed through the gardens. As the darkness consumed him, he whispered into the wind, "Margaret. Margaret. Where are you, my sweet Margaret?"

10

The next morning found Isabel lost between embarrassment for her inexcusable behavior and her fear over what she'd seen in the garden.

Were there ghosts? she wondered over and over again. *And did I actually kiss my tutor? Whatever possessed me? Or was it a nightmare?*

Not one to sit around, and feeling reasonably safe once dawn illuminated her room, Isabel hurried to her writing desk to write Jane, in care of her Aunt Mildred's home in London. Sparing no detail, Isabel told Jane everything that she had seen and begged her to come home. When she finished, she made her way to the library and shuffled the letter into a stack on her father's tray for outgoing mail. As soon as a servant saw it, they would have it delivered.

She would have ordered the letter posted straight away, but that would have only drawn suspicion, and her mother would undoubtedly read what she'd divulged to her sister. The last thing Isabel wanted was to explain herself to the viscountess. Her mother only needed an excuse to have her committed. Isabel was determined not to give her one.

No, Isabel thought, *the ghosts will remain my secret.*

Well, she amended ruefully, *Mr. Weston's and mine. And soon, Jane's.*

She doubted her tutor would care to mention last night to her parents. If they suspected anything improper happened, he would be relieved of his position and his reputation ruined. He would never tutor in fine society again.

Mr. Weston wasn't in the library to greet her with his usually dismal self. Part of her longed to see him, but it was a small part she thought better to ignore. After her behavior, she wanted to fall into a hole and hide. The knowledge of her attempt to kiss him was almost worse than the knowledge of the ghostly marquis.

She could still feel Mr. Weston's lips, rigid and unmoving against hers. He hadn't returned her kiss but had instead stiffened in revulsion.

I'm such a fool.

Turning to leave, she jolted in surprise to find

Mr. Weston. She blinked to clear the image from her mind. When it became apparent he wasn't her imagination, she held very still and waited for him to speak. His expression tightened.

Wearily, he looked at the tray where she'd deposited her letter. It appeared as if he hadn't slept. Then, facing her, he gave a polite nod. "Miss Drake."

"Mr. Weston," Isabel returned a stiff curtsey. Propriety had never stung her as it did now.

Her hands shook. Isabel couldn't meet his eyes for long. Having nothing else to say, she made a move to brush past him. His hand shot out, grasping her elbow to stop her.

"You have a guest," he said quietly.

"A guest?" she asked in surprise. Isabel became aware of the pressure of his touch. She couldn't stand his cool indifference.

"Yes. A vicar."

"A vicar?" That did get her attention. "Not Reverend Campbell. He's a horribly disapproving man. I can't endure him today. I won't sit through one of his self-righteous sermons."

"No. His name is Reverend Stillwell."

"What does he want with me? Did you send for him to lecture me about morality?"

"No," he replied.

"Have we a new vicar at Haventon?"

"Yes and no," Mr. Weston said. With a frustrated sigh, he released her and moved away.

"Is he angry because my church attendance has been…irregular?" she asked pensively. "Has he come to lecture me?"

"I think you should talk to him. He'd be the one to tell you what he wants better than I. He's in the garden."

"Oh." Isabel sighed, reluctant to go to the gardens after what she'd seen.

Sensing her hesitancy, Mr. Weston asked, "Would you prefer I direct him somewhere else?"

"No, no. Don't be silly. The garden is fine… perfectly fine."

❊

When the door shut behind her, Dougal drew a deep breath. The scent of roses from Isabel's perfume lingered in the air. He couldn't think clearly when she was near him.

Her reaction wasn't what he'd expected this morning. He'd studied her face for any signs of affection and had been desperate to explain things, but he didn't know how.

At least she didn't run from him screaming as she had the night before. That was something, even though he felt the tension radiating off her.

Going to the letter tray, he stared at the stack. On the top was a payment of a bill addressed in the viscount's script. Dougal shifted through the messages until he found one made out to Miss Jane Drake. Taking the letter, he rearranged the other correspondences into a neat pile.

At the window, he watched Isabel cross the yard. Her smile as she politely greeted the vicar caused an unreasonable pang of jealousy in Dougal's chest. If she would but smile at him like that. He closed his eyes and took a calming breath. Then, regaining his composure, he broke the seal on her letter and began to read: *Dearest Jane, you will not believe what it is I have to reveal to you…*

11

Clouds blanketed the sky like splotchy white ornaments. The clouds diffused the sunlight, and hardly a shadow cast over the ground. Isabel straightened her straw bonnet, hoping she looked more pious than she felt. Her gloved hands smoothed the cream-colored fabric of her linen day gown.

On her way to the vicar, she peeked at the library window. For a moment, she thought she could see Mr. Weston watching her, but then decided she was mistaken. Forcing a cheerful smile, she approached the short man.

Without waiting for an introduction, Reverend Stillwell held out his hands in greeting, "Oh, Miss Drake! What promising things I have heard of you."

"Good morning, Vicar," Isabel said, bewildered by the compliment. She curtsied politely. The man's good humor seeped infectiously from him and produced a ruddy complexion. "You must be Reverend Stillwell. I'm sorry to say that I have only just now heard of you."

"Yes, yes, certainly. Young people have so much more to worry about than meeting an old man like me." The vicar gave a sweeping gesture befitting a man of the pulpit and urged her to join him for a walk. He chuckled, and his two chins jiggled as he moved his head.

"So, are you to take over the parish at Haventon?" Isabel asked politely. "Since we haven't met, I assume you're new to our town."

"No, not at all. I have lived here many years and have worked at the parish just as long," he answered.

"But Reverend Campbell…?" Isabel looked at the man in confusion.

"The good Reverend Campbell and I share the duties of the parish," the vicar laughed.

Isabel didn't get the joke but smiled politely, nonetheless.

"He tends to the church and the pulpit, and I tend to the old and sickly souls of the parish," he explained. "We keep out of each other's way."

"Oh."

"Mr. Weston tells me that you had quite an adventure last night," Reverend Stillwell said, turning his kind blue eyes toward the wooded area by the stream.

She didn't pay attention to where they strolled. Her mind focused on the vicar's words.

He didn't, Isabel thought in horror. *Mr. Weston couldn't have confessed such a thing.*

Noticing the vicar watched her, she swallowed nervously. "Well, yes. I suppose."

"You saw spirits," the vicar stated.

Isabel almost collapsed with relief, only to be overcome by embarrassment. She couldn't answer.

"I believe you if that helps you regain your tongue, dear." The man smiled. "I know for a fact that spirits wander this world just as the living do."

"You don't think I imagined it?" she whispered, her gaze fixed on the ground.

"There was a time when I would have," he admitted. "But I have seen them too. I see them often, in fact."

"What do they want?" she asked. "Why are they here?"

"It depends on what's keeping them bound to the earth. Some want to be helped. Some don't. Some don't even know they have died and only need direction to find their way."

"And you help those souls find their way to Heaven?" she asked.

The vicar scratched his balding head. "More or less. I help them find peace if they don't already have it, and for those that do, I help them find their way."

"They have spoken to you?"

"Some," the vicar answered. He guided her closer to the forest. "Usually only the ones who don't know they're deceased, and only if they're generally at peace. But, occasionally, there is a soul that needs my help, and, by the will of God, I help them in whatever way I can."

"I don't think the two I saw were at peace. I don't know what happened, but their faces melted into something terrible." Isabel shuddered at the remembrance. She hugged her arms around her waist, feeling a chill sweep over her skin.

"Hmm," the vicar mused. "Did you startle them?"

"Startle *them*?" Isabel returned with a laugh of disbelief. Seeing his serious expression, she said, "I screamed. Their horse—"

"Horse?" the vicar interrupted. "You saw a horse with them? An actual animal spirit?"

Isabel wondered at the man's tone. His face stayed cheerily the same, but his voice dipped in concern, which he was hard-pressed to hide.

"Yes, one of them was riding it. I think it must have been the Marquis of Rothfield, although he dressed like a knight. I heard they used to hold costume balls here." Isabel frowned. "Why? Are animal spirits rare?"

"Yes, indeed. I have never seen one, only heard rumors. Honestly, I didn't think they existed."

"They do," Isabel assured him.

"As a knight, you say?"

"Yes. At least, I think he was a knight. He didn't wear armor but a tunic shirt and breeches from long ago. For some reason, I got the impression he was a knighted man. And I seem to recall a sword at his waist." Isabel paused, finding the exact details unclear. "He was very proud and handsome in a ruffian way."

"Proud? How so?"

"Just his carriage," she said, still unable to explain. "Do you know of him?"

"Were those the two you saw?" he asked. "The horse and the knight? Did you say that there was another with them?"

"Yes, a young girl." They'd neared the small alcove of trees. Isabel stopped and lifted a hand to her cheek. She felt sick to her stomach. "May we turn around, Father? I don't want to walk in the woods today."

"Are you afraid?" he asked, lowering his eyes to his black smock.

"All this talk of spirits is making me weak," she said. "I should like to stay near the house."

"All right, child."

As they retraced their steps, Isabel had the distinct impression that he was disappointed in her decision.

Changing the subject, he asked, "Do you ever ride, Miss Drake?"

"Yes, often." She smiled.

"Hmm. When was the last time you went out to ride? We have fine weather for it, have we not?"

Isabel tried to recall.

"I have been very busy," she said at last. "Surely, I have gone within the last week. Truth be told, I can't remember."

The vicar nodded as if it was no consequence. They walked in silence until they were back in the garden.

"A young girl, you said?" the vicar prompted her to continue her tale.

"Yes, perhaps eight or nine years. She had golden hair and the brightest green eyes I have ever seen. When I startled her, her hair melted off her head, and her skin became all…wrinkly. Tell me, do you know who she is? Is she the marquis' daughter?"

"Maybe," the vicar said. "I've never seen her."

Isabel glanced up at the library window, wondering if Mr. Weston was still within it. Blushing slightly at the thought of her tutor, she looked away. The vicar caught the look but said nothing.

"Tell me, why are they showing themselves to me? I have never before seen them, and we have lived at Rothfield now for nearly seven months. My sister has often claimed she can hear them walking about. If anyone should see them, it would be her. She believes in them. I do not...did not." Isabel paused to study the vicar earnestly. "What do they want?"

"Some people are born seeing them."

"But that is not me," Isabel protested.

"It's natural that you would have a lot of questions," he said.

"Before yesterday, I've never believed in them. I never *wanted* to believe in them."

"These things are not a matter of want." He smiled kindly. "Sometimes, when a person comes near death, they become marked by it. Afterward, they begin to see death."

Her eyes narrowed in thought. She knew there was something she couldn't remember. "But why me?"

"The ghosts may not want anything to do with

you. Perchance, you merely stumbled upon them. Death is a great mystery. I've heard that different spirits can dwell within the same place and not even know the other is there." The vicar motioned for her to continue around the side of the house. Isabel followed his lead. "They pass each other by, never even feeling the other's presence. You were probably in the right place at the right time. Perhaps your mind opened in some way, or it was how your heart was feeling."

"Is that why you've come this morning? To reassure me?"

"Yes, I suppose that's why," he answered. "Mr. Weston mentioned you'd seen a ghost. He worried you might be having a hard time with it."

He was worried? Isabel thought. Her heart fluttered in tentative pleasure. "Then, Mr. Weston sees them also?"

The vicar smiled. "Not so many, but yes, he has seen a few. So you see, my dear child, you're in good company with us."

Isabel started to go up the steps to the front door and then stopped when she realized the vicar wasn't planning on coming in with her. "It was a pleasure to meet you, Reverend Stillwell. Please feel free to visit whenever you wish. And you must have supper with us soon. I'm sure the viscount will be most pleased to receive you—though I wouldn't mention this business of spirits if I were you. The viscountess doesn't like to hear of such things."

"I'll be sure never to utter a word to them," he said diplomatically. "Now, if you'll excuse me, I'd like to speak with Mr. Weston. I think it best if I set his mind at ease and tell him you are adjusting quite well. As you may imagine, he's aware of how unusual an experience this can be for someone."

"Yes," Isabel agreed. She did indeed feel better after talking to the man, although she couldn't help but wonder why Mr. Weston didn't tell her personally of his experiences.

Taking her leave, she made haste to her bedroom. She overflowed with emotions—most predominately confusion. Why was Mr. Weston so concerned about her? Could she dare to hope he felt anything above the general, dutiful affection of a tutor to his unruly charge?

Isabel flung her weary body on her bed and closed her eyes. Though it was morning, she felt exhausted. She slid her arms around until she found the softness of her pillow and then hugged it to her stomach. Within moments she was fast asleep, dreaming of ghosts in the mist and one man standing solid amidst it all.

12

"Reverend." Dougal stood from his chair. He'd been waiting anxiously to hear what the vicar had to say. "Did you take her to the forest?"

"I tried," the vicar answered. "She wouldn't go."

"Did she remember her accident?" he insisted. "Is that why she's scared to go there with you?"

"No," the vicar said. "She just wouldn't go. And when I asked her about her last horse ride, she couldn't remember. Maybe you should get her to go riding with you? Take her over the north field and then see if you can race her into the trees. That one has a wild spirit in her. I think she might meet a challenge if issued right."

"I don't know that such a thing would be possible. She's angry with me," Dougal admitted.

"Make it up to her then," the man ordered. "*Apologize*."

"I did nothing wrong," Dougal said before adding, "not really."

"It does not matter when it comes to women. I know you have not pursued the fairer sex for some time, but surely you can remember that much?" The reverend laughed. "Apologize and get her out on the horse. Take her on a picnic, just the two of you. You're her tutor, aren't you? She won't think twice about being alone with you. If you do this, perhaps then she will recall what we need her to. She might even remember what spooked her."

"And what saved her," Dougal whispered. Reaching behind him on the desk, he grabbed Isabel's letter. He held it up for the vicar's inspection. "She wrote to her sister."

"Really?" the vicar asked in surprise. "About this?"

"She wrote about what she witnessed. She told Jane everything." Dougal dared not hope. "She saw Margaret. I know it."

"Are you sure?" The vicar reached for the letter. He scanned its contents, then mumbled awkwardly, "She mentioned seeing a child and a knight on a horse, but there could be hundreds of children—"

"A black horse," Dougal broke in, pointing at the letter. "I know it's Margaret! It's all there, Margaret's yellow dress and her golden curls. It has to be her."

"Even her burns," the vicar murmured, his gaze traveling over the letter.

Dougal nodded, fighting the decades of pain that rolled over him. He went to the window and peered out over the expansive lawn. "Yes, even her burns. It's Margaret. It's my daughter. It has to be. And Isabel is somehow the link between us. She's talked to her. She's talked to both of us."

Dougal's fervent whisper carried over the library. He stepped back to the vicar. "Isabel saw her and the man who holds her prisoner. She's the only one who can bring Margaret back to me. Can't you make her remember what happened? Can't you make her understand that I need her to remember? She's my last hope. She's the key to ending this torment."

"I can't force her to remember until she's ready," the vicar said. "You know that, Dougal."

"But..." Dougal knew the vicar was right. "Should I tell her my secret? Perhaps that will help her come around. I can't abide lying to her. Every time I see her face, so trusting in me, I grow ill with my deceits. I just want it to end."

"No, it's too soon for that. For whatever reason, she's comfortable with you as you are. Stay her tutor for now. When the time is right, she will discover the truth on her own." The vicar glanced once more over the letter. Silently, he held it out. Dougal didn't take it.

"But will she accept me as I am?" Dougal wondered aloud. He didn't expect, nor did he receive an answer. He hated feeling helpless. He hated being out of control. He wanted his daughter back. He wanted his life back—a chance to redo what was already done. "What if it takes her years to come around?"

"Right now, she believes that you have also seen a few spirits. In that, she will feel connected to you. It might enable her to trust you, to talk to you about it," the vicar offered as a small comfort.

"She thinks I'm alive. She believes it. She touches me as if I'm a real man of flesh and blood, and I feel her as a real man feels a woman. I would tell her the truth," Dougal said. "I would stop lying to her. Until I do, she has no reason to trust in me."

"People believe what their minds wish them to believe. Her mind wants you, *needs* you to be Mr. Weston, her tutor and new friend. Aside from you, she's very alone right now. Think about it from her view. Her parents aren't speaking to her as a sort of punishment. Her sister's been banished. The servants are ordered to avoid her. That isolation plays in your favor. You're all she has at the moment. If we tell her too soon before she's ready to hear, it might frighten her and hinder her in some way." The vicar motioned soothingly to Dougal, not trying to touch him because he knew he couldn't. "There have been those in my care who have gone mad from the realization. She's strong and has handled the idea of the spirits better than I could have ever hoped, but she's not ready for everything. You must wait. You must be patient. You must be her friend."

"But what if it's too late? What if the knight takes Margaret away from me? I can't find her without Isabel." Dougal sat wearily in the chair. He rubbed his forehead, knowing he had no choice but to play along with the woman's little fantasy. The crease between his eyes deepened. The vicar offered him the letter again. Dougal shook his head and held up his hand in denial. He couldn't read those damnable words, the horrible description of his little girl in the hands of a monster. This was the first sign in a long time that Margaret was still around, and it was grim. "I wish she would tell me what she saw the day of her accident. Something frightened her horse in the forest. She saw into the mist."

"She'll tell once she remembers." There was no way the vicar could know if the words were true. "She sees you for a reason."

"We shall see," Dougal mumbled.

"It's better if her sister doesn't get this." The vicar took the letter and threw it into the fire. They watched the flames eat up the edges until it disappeared into ash.

"Thank you for coming." Dougal tried to smile and failed. His had been a hopeless journey, but now there was the promise of Isabel's memory to reunite him with his daughter. If her mind didn't hold the key, he knew nothing ever would. "Thank you for speaking with her. Maybe it helped."

"It's always a pleasure to see you, Marquis," the vicar answered with a polite bow.

"It's a burden to be seen," Dougal answered.

The vicar gave a wry laugh and nodded as he walked from the room, leaving Dougal to wallow in his own agony.

There was nothing the vicar could do to lift the man's burden. It was a sorrow the Marquis of Rothfield carried with him from life into death, and it had haunted him for the last fifty years. Dougal's unrested spirit had been doomed to roam the manor and gardens of Rothfield Park, searching for a daughter who wouldn't be found and might never forgive him. No one could lift the burden of such a curse, perhaps not even the woman who held within her the only dim ray of hope.

13

Isabel winced as pain radiated down her head. Gingerly rubbing her scalp, she examined it for lumps. It was smooth, but the ache didn't lessen. This wasn't the first time she'd felt it. The pain was most persistent the moment she awoke, and it had become harder to ignore.

"It's because I sleep too much," Isabel reasoned. She had been sleeping more.

Since it still looked like morning, Isabel walked to the library, anxiously wanting to see Mr. Weston. She needed answers.

The pain eased as she touched the library door. She sighed in relief. Throwing it open, she went inside.

Mr. Weston looked up from his book in surprise. Isabel's heartbeat sped a little to see him.

She paused, waiting for his demeanor to harden. To her disappointment, it did.

"Miss Drake," he said at length when she didn't speak. "I've been wondering where you went off to."

"Oddly enough, I napped. Last night left me overtired." She quickly averted her eyes, not knowing what to say.

After a long moment, Mr. Weston stood under the pretense of putting away his book.

This man was her mentor, sent to polish her for marriage—a man whom she could never dream of pursuing. To do so would ruin her. Tutors were poor, a high-ranking servant at best. Her father would disown her. If her parents were outraged over Mr. Tanner's station in life, they would be livid if they discovered she had any feelings for Mr. Weston.

Isabel took a deep breath. "I must apologize for—"

"Don't think it," he said sternly. "You were distraught. I'll never mention it."

"Yes, I was distraught," Isabel agreed, though she didn't mean it. She wanted to cry with the knowledge that he could forget the feel of her mouth more easily than she could forget his. "However, I feel I must apologize."

Gaining her nerve, she lifted her head. His

gaze met hers. For a moment, she was lost in the clear depths of his green-gray eyes. They were the color of a field, shadowed beneath the clouds of a gray storm.

With her need to explain, she rambled almost incoherently, "I didn't mean to be cruel. I know that nothing could come of us. And in fact, I wish to make you understand that I know such a match like ours would be futile at best—not that I'm saying we would be matched. You're a poor man, and I the daughter of a nobleman. I'm expected to be with a man of a certain status in life—as you know, because you're here to prepare me for him. I can't very well go about kissing servants, can I? It's not done. And I promise not to do it in the future. So please, let it be our secret."

None of that came out the way she meant it to.

Moving to the settee, Isabel sat down before she fell over. He didn't reply, which meant he must agree with her. She tried to hide her disappointment. All it would have taken was one word from him for her to forget everything.

Just one word…

He said nothing.

She trembled beneath his watchful gaze. "So, having explained, I do apologize for making you uncomfortable. It wasn't a fair position to put you in, Mr. Weston. I promise never to do it again."

Dougal's expression didn't change. He felt like she'd kicked him with her candidness. What she said, in essence, was correct. They couldn't be together. However, the fact she thought him beneath her was insulting. She rejected him on the basis of his presumed lack of wealth. If ever he had thought she could come to care for him, he stood corrected. She might feel an attraction, but she didn't favor him enough to defy the standards of society.

Inwardly, Dougal cursed. What was he thinking? Even if she would defy the will of her parents, they couldn't be together. Why was he being so sensitive? Position and wealth didn't matter in death. And the attraction and love she hinted toward *could* not matter in death. The time for love had passed.

Dougal wanted to reach out to her. He knew he could entice her into his arms. He was still a man, after all. And being a man of vast experience, he knew when a woman was attracted to him. Dougal knew how to manipulate that attraction, but he held back, unwilling to take unfair advantage of her. Everything she understood about him was a lie. Nothing could ever come of their feelings.

"I suppose I was acting out of spite," she said at length.

He wished she'd stop trying to explain. Each attempt made him feel worse.

"Forget it," he answered.

"I wanted to thank you for sending the vicar to me."

"He's a wise man. I hope he was able to help you."

She abruptly stood. Her gaze focused on her hands as she picked nervously at the tips of her gloves. "Yes, it would appear so. Have…?"

The sound of her pained voice tore at him. He ached to reach out to her, but he knew he couldn't. Slowly, he put distance between them, taking a seat in the viscount's chair.

Isabel peered at him. Appearing all too exposed standing before him, she reclaimed her place on the settee.

"What is it?" he asked.

"Have you really seen the ghosts too? Is that why you were not surprised when I told you I saw them?"

"Yes." He forced himself to remember the vicar's words. "I have seen spirits."

"Here? You've seen them here?" Isabel asked.

He nodded, not elaborating.

Unable to stop the flow of words, she rushed

on, "What do they want? Am I to help them? Should I be afraid? I think I should be, but I'm not —not exactly. There is a general shock, which is the least to be expected. Beyond that, however, I only feel as if I have acquired a new, living acquaintance. Well, except they're a bit scarier in appearance at times."

At that, Dougal pressed his lips together to keep from answering. It would be so easy to blurt out the truth, to tell her what he longed to say. Reverend Stillwell was sure they shouldn't rush her to remember too quickly. If he tried to rush it, then all might be lost. He'd tried to force her once, in this very room. He'd wanted to make her remember that day she'd fainted into his arms. For a moment, she had accepted the truth, albeit numbly. Afterward, she'd gone to bed only to awaken without memory of the whole evening. If he tried again, Margaret might be lost forever. He couldn't chance such a grave error.

No, for now, he must remain silent.

"Nothing," he said. "My guess is most of them want nothing from us. And we shouldn't be afraid of them."

"Most?" Isabel gasped. "How can you tell the difference between the *most* and the others who *do* want something from us?"

"I can't say for certain the minds of others. We

must remember all spirits were once human, and from that, we can logically assume they still carry feelings and desires that keep them here. And, being once human, their numerous traits and motives must vary. So I say, fear them no more or less than you would a living being. Distrust them no more or less."

"That would be the logical way to see it, wouldn't it?" Isabel replied. "But what if I were meant to help them? Do you think I should seek them out? Should I try to talk to them?"

Yes, Dougal desperately wanted to cry out. Instead, he said, "Perhaps, if you see them again, you should try to see what they want. Maybe you can help them find peace. They may not know they're dead, and all you need to do is tell them."

"Don't know they're dead?" Isabel asked in surprise. "They fade into the mist. How can they not realize they're dead, Mr. Weston?"

"Forget the ghosts, for now, Miss Drake. If they wanted to hurt you, they would have done so already."

"I'll try," she allowed. "Though I don't know what could take my mind from it."

"What about a picnic?" Dougal recalled the vicar's advice. If he could get her on a horse, then maybe she would remember on her own. He'd be there to help her fill in the gaps.

"A picnic?"

"Yes, a picnic." When she tried to protest, he added, "I'm your tutor. I shall tell your father that I'm taking you out to practice the names of the local flora. It's quite a noble pursuit to know of landscaping."

"And will we learn about plants?" Isabel appeared a little breathless.

"Yes. I don't want to lie." Dougal stood. Smiling at her, he held out his hand. As she took it, they stood transfixed with each other for several moments. Taking a deep breath, he regretfully let her go.

"I shall ready the horses," Dougal said. With a quick bow, he rushed from the room before she could protest the ride.

14

Hooves thundered over the northern field, racing through the tall summer grass. Isabel felt strands of her hair loosen from its coiffure, haphazardly blowing around her shoulders. Urging the tan mare onward, she tried to catch up to her tutor. Mr. Weston glanced back at her. A smile formed on his lips, and a competitive glint filled his eyes as he galloped faster.

Isabel smiled, basking in the diversion of his company. His shoulders lost their rigid pull as he rode farther from the house. Mr. Weston was an experienced horseman. She couldn't resist slowing her mare to ride behind him just to watch the way he seated the brown stallion. It was a truly wicked thing to do, but who could resist such a view?

Isabel sighed in appreciation even while she tried to catch up to him.

Suddenly, he changed directions and headed toward the forest. A strange lethargy fell over Isabel's limbs, filling them with a prickling sense of trepidation. She nudged her mare and finally managed to pull up alongside Mr. Weston. He glanced at her curiously. Hiding her anxiety, she called out, "No, Mr. Weston. I know of a much better place. Come!"

Without giving him time to answer, she took off in the opposite direction.

❧

Dougal cursed under his breath, glancing toward the trees with longing. The horse responded to him as it would a living man. He risked much in taking it out. Should the stable lads find the horse missing, they would instantly search for the runaway beast.

With a troubled sigh, he raced after her. Isabel's skirts fanned out over the animal, and when she urged her mount to jump, the wind picked up the hem, displaying a fair amount of ankle and calf. Dougal jerked his head up to keep from staring. His grip tightened on the reins. She didn't wear hose, and the intimate peek of her flesh appeared quite fetching in the sunlight.

Isabel led him to a tree away from the woods where he needed her to go. Its long, willowy branches hung down toward the earth. Close by, an oak tree provided the perfect shade. Slowing her horse, she waited for him.

"What about here?" she asked, gesturing to the ground.

"Perfect." He glanced toward where he wanted to take her. He would have to think of another way to lure her to the forest path.

Forcing the worry from his expression, he dismounted. When he looked at her from the ground, he had himself under control. He managed a tight smile.

"Help me down," she said, holding her hand out to him. He went to her, catching her by the waist while she slid from her horse. Her hands glided onto his shoulders for support.

Isabel's smile faded as she looked up at him. Deliberately, her hands slid down the front of his chest to rest above the steady beat of his heart. Her breath became deep to match his.

Isabel's beauty and spirit entranced him.

"I believe I won the race past the hedge," he said, trying not to grin too widely.

"I would have beaten you if you'd given me a better saddle. I say we have a rematch. Only this time, we switch horses. You can ride on that lady's perch."

He laughed. "I shall do no such thing."

❧

Isabel didn't want to move and debated on whether or not she should pull away. Mr. Weston held her waist. She felt the heat coming from his strong hands. Luckily, he decided for her and let her go.

She hid a shy smile as he hastily busied himself with the basket tied to his horse.

"I should've known you'd prefer to ride astride," he said. "But what sort of tutor would I be if I allowed it? I'm supposed to show you how to be a proper lady."

"Oh, most assuredly," she answered in a serious tone, but her expression of feigned penitence couldn't last. The day was too brilliant, and Mr. Weston's smile too warm. She was drawn to him and couldn't resist the magnetic call of his nearness.

"I would not like to see you relieved of your post because of my audacity. Nevertheless, I must tell you that my father already understands that such things are the fault of my character. He would undoubtedly believe you if you told him my impulsiveness was beyond repair. Already I have outwitted some of the best governesses of our time."

At that, he turned. The side of his mouth lifted at the admission. "But I am a man."

"Yes," Isabel answered breathlessly, "you are."

"Are you of a mind to match wits with me?"

She froze, wondering at the challenge in his gaze.

"How will you best me, Miss Drake? By reciting the social pages?"

"I—" Isabel began, heat filling her cheeks. "You know, don't you? You know I was trying to fool you. How?"

"I have my ways, Miss Drake. You'll have to try harder to outwit me." His gaze roamed over her face before he caught himself. Turning, he slid the blanket from the horse's back.

"No, not there," she said when he headed toward the shade of the tall oak. "Let's sit in the sunlight."

He spread the blanket in the sun as she'd asked. She grabbed the basket he'd set on the ground and carried it over to the neatly arranged blanket, pulling out the light picnic lunch while Mr. Weston tethered the horses to a low-hanging branch to let them graze.

They ate in silence, enjoying the gentle afternoon breeze. When they finished the fare of cold meat and cheese, she cleared their plates and arranged everything neatly in the basket. Mr. Weston watched her in silence. She caught his small smile and flashed him a modest one in return.

"What shall we do now?" Isabel set the basket on the grass.

"Do you forget your lessons or just hope I have?"

"I was hoping you had," Isabel admitted. She turned away from the steadiness of his regard. "What a dunce you must think me if you insist upon instructing me further. Since you have already uncovered my deceit, I must tell you I don't need training. I have mastered my lessons long ago."

"Then why was a tutor sent for?" he inquired.

"Because I ran off my boring governess...*again*."

"You mentioned you'd had several."

"Yes, I have," she admitted, "but they're all so bloody boring. They insist on treating me like a...like a..."

"Like a what?"

She frowned. "Like a lady."

Mr. Weston noticeably wanted to laugh but refrained. He edged closer to her, and his voice took on a husky quality. "But you are a lady, Miss Drake."

"I know." Shyly, she watched him from beneath her lashes. "But that is not what I meant. Ladies are only expected to know of certain things, most of which I mastered by the time I was twelve—or at least as much as I was ever going to master them. I know I'm not destined to be a great pianist or painter, and there are only so many ways to set a proper table. Can you imagine what it's like to be forced to sit and listen to some old crone droning on about needlepoint and the proper way to arrange a nobleman's table? The duke sits here and the duchess here, unless they're estranged, and then they sit there. The head is reserved for the man of the house, and his lady may be placed at advantage—*ugh*."

"So, you ran them off?"

Isabel felt his low voice moved over her in a light caress. She shivered, unsure what to do with the feeling inside her. His voice was soft, but his body was as rigid and controlled as ever. This man confused her. She couldn't tell if he liked her or if he merely tolerated her because he was forced to.

The truth came out of her, unabashed by propriety. She told him things she'd never revealed before, not even to her sweet Jane. "Yes, I did. In the beginning, I would show them how well I could master their skills. That only seemed to aggravate them until they found fault after endless fault with all I did. Once I was forced to practice lifting a fork for hours on end."

Isabel shivered in repulsion, drawing her arms over her waist.

"And after mastering did not work?" he asked.

Isabel smiled sheepishly. "I would pretend to be ignorant, like with you. It drove them to distraction. I would stomp about improperly and recited endless lines of nonsense until they could no longer stand my presence. Miss Martens, my last governess, only endured a few months. They usually last longer."

"And what, pray tell, did you do to the poor woman?"

"I pretended not to speak French. I daresay her vocabulary was vulgar." Isabel turned red thinking of it. She couldn't meet his eyes.

"That is not all, is it?" he prompted.

"No," she answered, flustered. Isabel was unsure whether she wanted to laugh or run away in shame. Something in the easy acceptance of his tone urged her to continue. "I would purposefully say very improper things to her in French and pretend I didn't know what I'd said. Often she would curse at me and say mean things, thinking I didn't understand her. Once I told her that her backside must be…never mind, it loses something in the translation, I think."

"And what is it you're planning for me? Should I be on my guard?"

"I was sure I could have scared you away before now. You should have seen your face when I told you nothing existed outside English borders. I almost couldn't contain my laughter." Isabel giggled, thinking of it.

"Yes, very amusing," Mr. Weston said wryly. "I admit to having dreaded what might've come out of your mouth."

"Shall we call a truce and start over?" she asked. "I will promise not to play too many tricks on you if you promise not to make me recite the duties of a housewife and other such dreadful nonsense."

"All right. But then, what shall we study?"

"I was reading up on horse breeding," she admitted. "However, the dreadful Miss Martens burned my book in the fireplace."

"Breeding, eh?" Mr. Weston murmured, shielding his expression. His gaze wandered over her as she sat next to him.

Isabel lowered her chin and studied him while trying not to be obvious.

"I did say I would teach you of the plant life at Rothfield," Mr. Weston offered.

"I wouldn't want to make you a liar, sir," she answered playfully.

Standing, Isabel smoothed her skirts. Glad to have something to keep her mind busy, she strolled in the field.

❧

Dougal watched Isabel, not trusting himself to follow her. Leaning over, she plucked a couple of flowers from the ground. The folds of her long blue skirt covered her legs, but the material molded around her form in the breeze, and his imagination filled in where reality left off.

She turned her attention to the sky, and Dougal took the opportunity to study the long line of her neck. He was as captivated by her beauty as he was by her wit. He saw the top curve of her cleavage, soft and inviting. His hands ached with a hunger born of years of torment. With an inward curse, he squeezed his eyes shut and turned toward the distance. She had no clue what she was doing to him.

She turned back to the flowers. He didn't know if he would be able to keep from touching her. When she looked at him, her eyes were bright with innocence. She trusted him, and she shouldn't.

Angling a white clustered flower toward him, she inquired, "What is this?"

"*Conopodium majus*," he answered without hesitation. His eyes were distracted as he added, "Pignut."

"And this?" Isabel quickly asked, dropping the white cluster to replace it with a blue-petaled bloom.

"A meadow cranesbill," he answered dutifully. He waited until she held up another, and again he answered. Testing him several more times, Isabel smiled. When she finished, Dougal said, "You knew all that, didn't you?"

Leaning over, she picked another flower. She twirled it in her fingers, keeping it from view. "I was testing your knowledge."

"Did I pass?" he asked, careful to shield his eyes from her lest she detected his increasingly wicked thoughts.

She nodded before admitting, "I only picked ones I knew."

He chuckled at her honesty.

"But I don't know these two." She leaned over to pull another from the ground. He liked the proud tilt to her head when she glanced at him. She then hid the two flowers in her hand.

"Let me see." His tone came out sharply. She

shook her head, mischievously. Sunlight bathed her flushed skin.

Isabel swung around in merriment, cupping the flowers to her chest. "I love to dance. I would do nothing else if it were possible. Tell me, Mr. Weston. Do you ever go to balls?"

"Not for a long time." Grabbing a blade of grass, he twisted it in his fingers and followed the movements of her lithe body. She twirled her way back to the blanket. Stopping at the edge, she stared down at him.

"Then I shall insist that Father allow you to come with us the next time we are invited to one," Isabel said. He hid his frown. Dropping next to him, she asked, "Would you ask me to dance if we were at a ball?"

"Maybe," he murmured.

Isabel smiled. Trying to adjust herself on the blanket, she pulled on her skirts and arranged them properly about her legs. Then, with a dreamy sigh, she fell back. She gazed up at him and giggled.

Dougal couldn't turn away. The sun outlined his head, and his shadow fell over her features. Without considering the consequences, he leaned on his arm next to her, careful not to touch. He rested his arm over his knee and twisted the weed in his fingers as he forced himself to study it instead of her.

Isabel's laughter subsided. Coyly, she lifted one of her flowers and stroked the petals down his cheek. He stiffened but didn't move. Brushing it over his lips, she let it trail down his neck. "And what flower would this be, Mr. Weston?"

"Call me Dougal," he said, the words tortured. She dropped her hand to her waist and glanced away. He could see the pulse beating rapidly on her slender neck. His lips parted as he studied the thin thread of skin that would block the beat from his kiss.

"But such a thing is not done," Isabel said nervously.

"It will be our secret then." He gravitated closer to her. "We shall just have to break a few rules to keep us sane."

"All right, Mr. Dougal." When she met his eyes, he was unable to look away.

"No, just Dougal," he said in a soft, inducing trance. No one but his mother had ever addressed him as such, and only as a young child. Since his birth, he'd been "my lord," or "Lord Rothfield," or "Marquis Rothfield" to everyone else. Somehow hearing his given name formed so intimately on her lips sent a thrill through him. It made him feel closer to her than he ever had to anyone.

"All right," Isabel agreed. "Dougal."

She smiled tentatively, and a look of pleasure flitted through her eyes. She licked her mouth. He felt the heat of her body and saw the inviting texture of her lips.

"What kind of flower is this?" she inquired, never looking away.

Dougal drew his attention down to the pinkish heart-shaped petals swirled in a perfect circle. Taking it from her fingers, he said, "This would be the *silene dioica*, a red campion."

"And this one?" When she moved to touch him with it, he jerked his head back.

"That is bittersweet, a cousin to nightshade. It's poisonous." Dougal plucked it from her fingers. "It's also considered a flower of secrets."

"Poison and secrets," she said with a slight smile.

Dougal detected the subtle scent of rose on her skin, mixing with the breeze. Every fiber of his being begged him to take her, to taste her. He told himself that no one would see. What could happen to him if he gave her what she asked for? He was dead. No harm would come of it.

"I much prefer this one." He reached to the side and pulled a small blue flower from the nearby groundcover. "*Myosotis Sylvatica*."

"Forget Me Not," she translated.

"There is a legend about this flower. Long ago, a knight was picking blue flowers for his lady near a flooded stream. He loved her greatly with all his heart and planned to make her his wife. But fate wasn't kind to the lovers, and he fell into the water. Though he fought to return to shore, the weight of his armor overtook him. Before he drowned, he threw the flowers at the lady and yelled, '*Forget me not!*'"

"A beautiful story," she said, taking the flower from him. "I've always loved these."

"I know."

She laughed. "How could you know that?"

"I remember everything you've said to me." It was true. He did. Every moment of her was etched on his eternity.

His unintentional seduction worked. Languidly, her lids fell over her eyes as she offered her mouth to him.

Dougal wanted to kiss her, but he *needed* her to remember her accident.

When he didn't take her offering, Isabel became embarrassed. She pushed past him to sit up. Tears threatened her eyes.

"I'm sorry." She trembled.

"What about your Edward?" he asked, unable to forget her words of anger the night she'd kissed him. He wouldn't want her to repeat them, especially if he was going to kiss her again. He wouldn't have her claiming she didn't want to be with him after they finished. If they came together, it would be because they both wanted it. It would be because they both knew what they were doing.

"Who?" Isabel asked in confusion as he sat up next to her. "Mr. Tanner? What about him?"

"I won't be mistaken for him." He tilted his head to better study her expression. With a hand to her cheek, he forced her to look at him.

"I could never mistake you for Mr. Tanner. You're nothing like him." Isabel tried to smile but couldn't. "Mr. Tanner is lighthearted and merry. You're stoic and…and different from him. The way you talk, the way you…"

"The way I kiss?" he questioned when she faltered. He hadn't kissed her back. His lips hadn't moved.

"No," she said in surprise. "I have never kissed Mr. Tanner. I've never kissed any man before you."

"You don't have to say that," he said. "I don't expect you to."

"I'm not just saying it. It's true." At his doubtful look, she rushed on. "I've read about kisses. Maybe that's why I could, why I knew what to do. And once I saw a kiss between a maid and a man from town. They were behind the stables and didn't know I could see."

Dougal didn't answer. He saw the truth in her words. She pulled away, and he regretfully let his fingers fall from her face.

"You didn't like it. Is there something wrong with me? With the way I...I'm sorry." Isabel started to stand.

Dougal couldn't let her. He grabbed her arm. "Isabel." Then, with a moan, he pulled her against him. He could deny himself no longer.

Her lips parted with a rush of air as he held her passionately in his embrace. His hands instantly found the windblown strands of her hair. Delving his fingers into her silken locks, he met her parted lips with his own. His hands refused to release her when she moaned against the force of his passion.

Dougal's body lurched with desire. He wanted her. He wanted to take her, to claim her. Her innocent lips moved against his in hesitation. He pressed his tongue between them, parting them gently, but as he felt the barrier of her teeth blocking his entrance, he suddenly drew back.

Her lips were swollen from his touch, her eyes hazy. She was beautiful, but she wasn't his. He released an agonized breath.

Rising abruptly, he turned away from her. His body protested the unfairness of the situation. He closed his eyes as he regained his control. Control was all he had.

Dougal cursed silently. He was losing his mind.

※

Isabel watched Dougal, the stiff line of his back, the proud lift of his head. Her fingers itched to pull him to her once more, to press into the soft waves of his dark hair. She was about to venture a touch when he'd pulled away. Now she wished she hadn't hesitated.

He didn't want her.

Before he turned around, she could already see the damnable calm returning.

"Was this a test?" Her shoulders shook with the effort it took not to cry. She felt so alone. His rejection was a cold reminder of how ostracized she was from her family, how no one came to call on her, how even her own mother ignored her very presence. Jane had not even been allowed to write, or if she had, someone kept the letters from Isabel. The pain of rejection choked her words, but she managed to say, "Were you testing me? Is this what my father wanted? To see if I were of loose morals? Is that why he sent you to tutor me? What are you, some kind of doctor for the mind? To see if I'm unfit?"

He was too close, his scent too overwhelming. Her mind fought to concentrate.

Before he could answer, she ran past him toward the horses.

"Isabel," he pleaded.

At the sound, she stopped. Whipping around to look at him, her hands on her mare's reins, she waited. His lips pressed into a severe line.

"This cannot be," he stated.

"Because I'm the daughter of a nobleman, and you're a poor tutor."

"Yes," he began, "you're a…" But he didn't finish. His mouth opened, but he didn't form the words.

"I am a what?" she demanded. When he only continued to stare, she continued, "I'm a spoiled girl? No, that's not what you were going to say, was it? You think me something else entirely. I'm a job you have to do. I'm an unruly child that you must test and tease into ladylike submission."

His jaw worked violently. She didn't care.

"That's it, isn't it?" she demanded.

"No, you aren't a child," he said. "But you're beginning to act like one."

Dougal didn't want to give Isabel time to say anything else. "I shouldn't have kissed you. You, yourself, said I have nothing to offer you. I'm just a poor man." He flung his lies at her with greater ease. "Do you wish for me to continue? Should I deflower you? Would you marry me? Come away with me to live in some poor cottage? Or worse? Would you be happy above some dingy tavern, listening to the calling of whores while we slept in our one room next to our numerous, dirty children?"

"N-no," she stuttered, shaking her head as if to relieve it of the picture he painted for her.

Dougal sighed. She was attracted to him, that was all—pure physical attraction. The kind of feelings required for her to choose the life he described still wouldn't have been enough to bring them together. Nothing save divine intervention could make anything but the briefest of passion a reality. There was no hope for their future.

Isabel fought her tears. "Will you tell my father?"

"No." Seeing her anguish, he felt his anger slip. He wasn't being fair to her. She was confused, more so than he.

Although part of him wanted to scream at the unjustness of it, he needed her friendship more than her passion. With her help, he could find his daughter. That was all that mattered.

Regardless, his body protested its neglect. It screamed at him the number of years that he'd been alone and untouched by anyone—not even a handshake. And here before him was softness and warmth, begging him to feel.

Running his fingers through his hair, Dougal took a step toward her. He wanted to draw her back to him. But how could he explain himself? How could he live with himself for an eternity knowing what he'd done to her? How could he let himself get distracted from finding his daughter? Who knew what kind of agony his little Margaret's soul suffered in the hands of the deadly knight? He should be concentrating on Margaret, not rolling on the grass at a picnic.

※

Isabel hated Dougal's cruel words but knew he was right. Her father would never allow such a match. Was she ready to risk everything for a man who hadn't said he loved her?

She watched his tortured expression. There was more to this than her undesirable behavior. The pain in his eyes drew her to him, releasing her from her own anger and hurt.

"Can we forget this happened?" she asked, knowing that wouldn't be possible. She could never forget. "I would like us to be friends."

He nodded, noticeably relieved.

"Do you want to ride?" Isabel forced a smile. Her lips tingled, and she couldn't forget the feel of his mouth, but she could pretend.

"How about we walk the horses to the stream?" He avoided eye contact with her. "I think we should let them drink before taking them back."

15

"What happened?" Isabel's eyes fluttered open. Above her the library ceiling came into focus. She sat up in surprise, only to find herself face to face with Mr. Weston.

No, on the picnic he'd told her to call him Dougal. She ached to touch him but held back.

His brow creased with worry. He searched her face, as if desperate to read her mind. "You swooned."

"I don't swoon," she said, taking offense to the notion. Women like her mother fainted. Isabel did not want to be like her mother.

For a moment, his eyes softened, and he took her breath away. He chuckled. "You keep telling me that, right before you collapse."

"What were we doing?" She felt the back of her head for a bruise. A dull ache threatened her consciousness. She resisted the pull of darkness, not understanding why she should feel so out of sorts.

"You don't remember?"

"I remember that we…" Isabel stopped. She looked at his mouth. Uncertain, she amended her original thought. "Agreed to be friends."

Dougal hid his smile at the modest portrayal of what had happened. "And beyond that?"

"Did we walk the horses?" She furrowed her brow. All she could remember was the feel of his kiss, the tight hold of his hands on her hair, and the deep wretchedness of her spirit when he pulled away.

"Yes, we did. We walked to the stream in the forest."

"I don't remember the forest," she said with a delicate wave of dismissal.

He didn't speak. His brooding silence disturbed her.

"What happened in the forest?" She slid her feet from the settee, setting them on the carpeted floor.

"Nothing. I think you were overtired from the walk. You mentioned you haven't been sleeping well."

"That doesn't sound like me," she said, wondering why he might be lying.

His face hadn't changed when he turned to her. "I need to go. There are things to which I must attend."

"Oh," Isabel gasped, part in question, part in surprise. "Will I see you later this evening?"

"Maybe."

"I should find my father. Have you seen him?"

"He left for London with your mother," Dougal answered. "I believe your sister, Harriet, needs them for some reason."

"Oh, Harriet." Isabel chuckled. "No doubt she has run up her bill with the dressmakers again, and Father has gone to take her to task for it. I will never understand her fascination for ribbons."

"I couldn't say," Dougal replied.

"Then it's just the two of us?" she asked. "They have left us to our own devices?"

"It would appear so."

Before she could inquire as to his mood, he abruptly moved to leave.

"Good day, Miss Drake." He bowed and strode from the library as if he couldn't wait to be free of her.

"Good day, Mr. Weston," she said to the closing library door. When she was alone, she whispered, "My most darling Dougal."

❧

Dougal sighed in frustration as he left the house. There was so much he'd wanted to say to her but couldn't. He wanted to shake the truth from Isabel, to scream at her until she told him what had happened the day of the accident.

"What happened?" She'd asked him as if the answers weren't locked inside her head.

You turned pale and refused to go on once we heard the water. When I tried to make you, you grew weak and fainted. Come on. Remember. Tell me why you're afraid of the forest, he answered to himself. *Tell me what happened the day of your accident. Tell me what you saw!*

The sun shone over the garden. He hid his frustration behind a blank mask. What else could he do?

Then there was the obvious attraction he felt toward her. As they'd walked to the forest, he hadn't allowed her to seduce him again with the sweet offering of her lips, though she'd inadvertently tried. He knew what she wanted him to do. And, heaven help him, he wanted to do it to her, but these feelings must be denied.

Evening was upon him, and he knew what he must do. The responsibility slammed into him like a rock to the head. His heart ached in desperation.

Tonight he would search again for his daughter. And tonight he would again fail.

16

"You sent for me, my lord?" The cheery smile faded from Reverend Stillwell's smooth, ruddy complexion when he saw the marquis' hollow grimace. It clearly had been the vicar's greatest hope that all would be resolved. Coming around the tree to sit next to Dougal, the vicar waited for him to speak. He didn't have to wait long.

"There has to be another way. It's not working," Dougal said without preamble. "She's not regaining her memory. Every time she gets close, she blacks out. I never know when our conversation is going to restart or how much she will remember from the last time."

"Did you take her riding?" The vicar leaned his back against the oak, taking momentary pleasure in the cool shade.

"Yes. It's like you said. She avoids the forest. When I finally convinced her to walk the horses to the stream, she fainted as soon as we heard water. There has to be a way to make her remember. Should I just tell her who I am?"

"No. If you do that, she may be lost to us completely. You know as well as I, she must come to it on her own."

"But she seems fine knowing about my daughter and the man who holds her prisoner," Dougal insisted. "She admits they don't frighten her. Maybe she won't be frightened by any of it. She's strong."

"It's because she learned of it on her own when she was ready to learn about it. Her mind shall not let her take in more than she's prepared for. Her swooning is proof of that. And if you force it on her, bad things could happen. She could go mad." The vicar stood, pushing his weight up from the ground. "You're both in my flock. I won't favor the happiness of one over the other. I won't allow you to send her down into the abyss of insanity."

"I don't want that. It's just that I have to do something." Dougal became argumentative. "I can't stand this waiting. I'm losing Margaret. And we are so close to finding her, to getting her back. You read Isabel's letter to her sister. The demon has my daughter. He comes for her every night on his black horse and whisks her away. How long until he takes her to the fires of damnation?"

"Maybe it's not the demon that has her," said the vicar. "We can't know for sure."

"We can," he insisted. "It was a knight who killed me. And it's a knight who kidnaps my Margaret."

"There is no way of knowing for sure. We don't know how many spirits linger here. I've heard mention of over twenty, all not visible to the others."

"This you have told me," Dougal said. "And all claim they were killed by a knight. Margaret's knight."

"And some have mentioned that an unknown being protects them," offered the vicar. "If the knight wanted to take Margaret to damnation, would he not have gone by now?"

"Who can tell with demons?" Dougal countered. His helplessness made him bitter. "And we shan't know until Isabel remembers."

"Perchance, there is something else bothering the woman," the vicar mused, rubbing his jaw. "Maybe she's facing too much and needs to sort through things before she can handle remembering that day."

"What do you mean? What else is there for her to face?"

"There are things—" Stillwell began.

"Speak clearly, man," Dougal snapped. "I feel like I'm losing time. I know I'm losing my daughter. I'll do anything. Just tell me how I can help Isabel remember."

"All right, maybe she's having trouble with her feelings for you."

"For me?"

"Don't forget that she is foremost a young woman. And if her heart is confused, she'll need time and help to put it right."

"Did she say something?" An unfamiliar tremor spread over him. "Did she speak with you about me?"

"No," the vicar answered, undoubtedly sensing Dougal's affections for Isabel. He read well the hope the marquis tried to hide from him. "She said nothing, but I can see it in her. She's not unaffected by you. And perchance her preoccupation with you is keeping her mind from focusing elsewhere. If she were secure on that front, then maybe she would be more open on others."

You mustn't, cautioned his brain. *She's not for you.*

"Are you suggesting I take advantage of her?" Dougal demanded in disgust. He wouldn't use her for his own purpose in such a way. No matter how desperate he was, he couldn't purposefully mislead her. On that, he had decided. "Would you have me seduce her to have my way?"

"I'm suggesting you be honest about your feelings and not send her differing messages. Either show her affection or don't, but stay consistent." The vicar closed his eyes with a weary sigh. "Once she figures you out, she will be able to see the rest of it."

Dougal couldn't respond.

"Be careful, my son." Stillwell opened his eyes to stare pointedly at the marquis. "Do not take advantage of her. Do not make her love you if you don't return the sentiment. Love is a splendid burden. Do not burden her heart unless you are prepared to share in its suffering."

"How can you speak of such things? You know what I am, and you know what she is. There can be no love between us." Dougal stood. He spoke the truth but hated the words, nonetheless. His was a lonely existence.

"It's God's place to decide who shall love and who shall not. You would do well not to question his decisions."

"You still believe in him after all these years?" Dougal asked in amazement. "After what you've seen? After what you know."

"Yes, I still believe, more so than ever. And so

do you. You're lost right now, but you'll find your way." Rising, the vicar moved down the path whence he'd come. He called over his shoulder, "We all, eventually, find our way."

"But what if our path is one of heartache and loneliness?" Dougal muttered. He received no answer. The vicar hadn't heard him.

He watched the portly figure disappear into the distance. Dougal scratched the back of his head in frustration. Then, turning toward home, he followed the path to Rothfield.

17

The power of the night fog once again overwhelmed the land. It crept over the countryside, covering the gardens of Rothfield Park like a thick blanket. Shadowed by moonlight, the mist inched its way closer to the house until finally twisting and creeping like vines up the sides of the manor.

Drawn by a power outside herself, Isabel made her way through the labyrinth of halls toward Jane's empty room. She didn't think to question her path as her feet moved over the hard floor. In a dreamlike state, her eyes stayed fixed ahead.

From the holder clutched in her hand, candlelight flickered, threatening to blow out. Isabel lowered the flame to her side. The soft illumination cast over her white nightgown, causing it to look like it glowed. Outside, the world was dark and quiet.

With her parents gone to London to visit her sisters, she'd seen few people in the house. Dougal didn't return to be with her, and the servants kept away. Not even Charlotte stayed after delivering the evening meal to Isabel's bedroom.

Smoke met her feet as she turned the corner, curling as she disrupted it. Numbly, she watched it spiral from the base of Jane's door. Suddenly, the smoke was sucked back under the doorframe.

Isabel gasped and leaned to press her ear to the thick wood. The door trembled, seeming to come to life. She swallowed nervously, refusing to retreat while she listened. She heard movement within.

"What are you doing?"

Isabel jumped at the sound of Dougal's voice, nearly dropping the candle. His words broke through her trance. She spun around to face him. The motion blew the candle out, and she couldn't see him in the darkness.

"Dougal? Is that you?" she asked, fearfully.

"Yes," came his low response. "What are you doing? Why are you whispering?"

"I thought I heard something in my sister's room." Unconsciously, she moved toward the sound of his voice. She felt for him in the darkness.

Her hand came up against his chest and the beating of his heart. His body had warmed the fine material of his waistcoat. She shivered, mesmerized by the feel of him.

"Step aside," he commanded. "Let me look."

"We'll look together," she said, no longer scared now that he was with her.

Dougal stepped past her, and, finding the latch in the darkness, he pushed open the door. Isabel's hand dropped from him, but she stayed close to his side.

The silvery glow of moonlight streamed in from the window, falling over the cherry wood bed with its yellow coverlet. The room was cold and empty. The fireplace, built after the great house fire, was barren.

Isabel huddled close to Dougal's back. She rested her hand between the blades of his shoulders. He angled his chin toward her to whisper, "There is nothing here."

"Perhaps I imagined it," Isabel said, though unconvinced. She'd heard something—something that drew her from a deep sleep, something lured her to the room.

"Are you sure?"

As he turned, her hand didn't leave him. Her fingers glided over his jacket and rested on his arm.

She felt the firmness of his muscle beneath. She met his eyes. Weakly, she nodded, unable to speak.

"Isabel…" he began.

She glanced over the empty room, searching for a sign that something had been there before them. For a moment, she stiffened as she met her reflection in a mirror. Silvery light outlined the loose hair falling over her shoulders. Her skin shone, the moonlight glistening in her moist eyes. However, the shadowed outline of Dougal's body was harder to detect in the shadows.

"Isabel," he said again, his voice thick with longing. The hard length of him pressed against her. She lifted her face toward his, and she was lost in his nearness. She tried to smile and failed. Her gaze dropped to his lips. She smelled him all around her, invading her with his scent.

His hand trembled as he lifted it to touch her cheek. His fingers brushed softly over her skin. Tortured, he whispered, "I want to kiss you."

Isabel smiled insecurely at the admission. Seeing his eyes, the steadfast gray-green she trusted, she nodded. She wasn't afraid of him. She wanted him to kiss her—to do what he desired, for he already claimed her every waking moment. She would allow him anything. Closing her eyes, she lifted her lips to him.

❦

Dougal moaned, a dark sound that held no merriment. He didn't heed reason. With her, he could no longer think, only feel.

His fingers continued over her skin as he brushed the pad of his thumb over her offered mouth. Isabel waited. He balled his hand into a fist, pulling it stiffly away. He did his best to resist her, but his best wasn't good enough. She was a force beyond his control.

The smell of roses engulfed him, making him forget all about the woman before her. Suddenly, nothing else mattered but her nearness.

"If I kiss you," he said as he pulled off his cravat, "I won't be able to stop there. If I kiss you, you can't ask me to try."

At that, Isabel opened her eyes with a nervous flutter. She didn't understand his words, couldn't comprehend the depths of his emotion.

"Kiss me," she begged. "I want you to. I don't care that you're poor and that it shouldn't be. I want it to be."

Dougal closed his eyes in pleasure. "Sweet woman, you don't know what you ask for, but so help me, I cannot deny you."

Her expression brightened at his words, but she

had no time to answer before his lips crushed down to claim hers. This time, she didn't hesitate. Her hands climbed over his arms to wrap around his shoulders. Her fingers buried themselves in the warmth of his jacket behind the nape of his neck.

Her lips parted, allowing his tongue to lick between them. His kiss deepened, moving in languid desire. Thoroughly laying possession to her mouth, he found he couldn't deny himself the complete taste of her. Isabel's knees weakened at his deliberate force. A moan escaped her lips.

Dougal forced her back toward the bed. His hands roamed over her body, stroking over her shoulders, moving down her arms until they found a hold on her waist. Pulling her back, Dougal broke for air.

"Oh," Isabel gasped, unable to say anything else.

He released her to shrug out of the confines of his jacket. She saw his purpose and lifted her hands to help him. The material dropped on the floor. Instinctively, she began to unbutton his waistcoat. Her eyes stayed on his. He felt her fingers trembling as she worked the buttons loose. His hands found her, pulling at the back of her nightgown, looking for laces. His mouth once again claimed hers.

Isabel freed him of his waistcoat, gliding the

material off his arms. The linen of his undershirt fit against him like a second skin, molding to his form. Into his kiss, she moaned, "Your skin is so hot."

"Yes," he groaned. His hands became frenzied when they couldn't find the laces to her gown. Giving up, he pulled her hard against his chest.

Isabel gasped in surprise. His mouth trailed from her lips to her throat. Her body sought his warmth. "What are you doing?"

Dougal flicked his tongue over her skin, eliciting pleasurable sensations. "I'm going to have my way with you."

"Oh," she managed as he continued to kiss her deeply. "Can I have my way, too?"

Dougal stopped, pulling away to study her. A smile found his mouth as he forced her to step back. "I insist upon it, my lady."

His fingers pulled at his shirt, unfastening the buttons with urgency. Once free of the linen, his hands went to the buttons at his waist. Isabel watched his fingers.

"Get out of that gown, lest I rip it off you."

"I don't look like you," Isabel observed. She waited for his hands to move from his waist, so she could see the protrusion that pushed at her stomach.

"I should hope not," he said wryly.

"Can I touch you?" she wondered, her eyes still lingering on his waist. "I want to touch you."

"If you don't, I think I shall die," Dougal said. Seeing her attention fixed on his manhood, he grimaced with pleasure. He repeated more softly, "Take off that gown."

Isabel obeyed, tugging the laces at her shoulders. Dougal finally managed to undo the last of his buttons. The soft linen slid off her shoulders and sank silently to the hard floor. She stood proudly before him, a blush threatening to stain her cheeks. Her eyes widened to see the tip of his member peeking through his breeches.

"Touch me," he insisted.

Instantly, Isabel reached for his manhood. She cupped him boldly, her fingers wrapping around his length. He groaned, his hips flexing into her palm.

"On the bed," he commanded. He couldn't hold back much longer.

※

Isabel didn't mind his forceful ways. She liked being controlled by him. He was a controlling man. Only now, even as he ordered her about, she had the feeling it was she who commanded him.

His words were too desperate, his urgency too visible.

Falling onto her back, she then moved up to the pillow. She pressed into the soft coverlet as she waited for Dougal to kick off his boots. When he was completely naked, he followed her. With determination, he crawled over her. His gaze swooped possessively over her skin.

Closing his eyes, he lowered himself against her. Their bodies met for the first time, free of any barriers. The softness of her thighs rubbed against him.

Instantly, his tongue trailed hotly to her breasts, taking a solid nipple between his lips. Her back arched. A passionate cry escaped her. He moaned, noticeably pleased with the desire she showed so freely.

Next, he explored her waist. His hands discovered the untouched peaks of her body.

Her skin was on fire with his caresses, and Isabel was no less bold in her exploration of him. She ran her hands over his chest, his sides, urging his lips onward when he would linger, only to draw him back. Unable to stand the curious fire in her body, she began to push at his shoulders.

Hoarsely, he muttered in surprise, "I told you before that I can't stop. Don't ask it of me. I want you too badly."

It was Isabel's turn to be surprised. Her eyes shone with innocence consumed by passion. "If you stop, I swear I will kill you myself."

"Then—"

"I want you on your back," she commanded. "I told you I want my way with you."

Dougal couldn't deny her while she forced him to roll to the side. Her legs threaded around his thighs, holding him prisoner under her silken guard. The heat of her sex pressed into him, growing moist as he rubbed his leg up against her. Her lips lacked his precise skill as they roamed and tasted his body, but she easily found ways to return the pleasure he was giving her.

Dougal cupped her breasts, massaging the tips with his fingers. His flesh was smooth, but for the hair-roughened stretch of his legs and arms. His thigh pushed more frantically against her as she struggled against him, seeking an end to the torment of her body. The stiff length of his arousal pressed into her stomach.

"You must end it," she gasped, licking up the side of his neck. She laid herself fully against him. "Please, I don't know how to end it."

"Sit up," he ordered. His hands wrapped around her waist. "Straddle my waist as you would a stallion. I shall show you how to put an end to it —how to put my end into it."

She did as he commanded, though she didn't fully understand. Being separated from him only brought a new agony. Her skin begged her to lean back down. When she would fall against him, his firm hold stopped her.

"I was meant to fit inside of you." He groaned when she would protest his restraint. "You were meant to take me inside of you."

To prove his point, he lifted her by her hips. Isabel shot him a look of utter confusion. Dougal saw her hesitation and knew she didn't understand. With a moan, he flipped her on her back.

"No, wait!" Isabel gasped in protest, her hands flinging wildly to stop him. "Don't go."

He paused only to kiss the worry from her brow. He positioned her body beneath him. He drew his hand under her knee, lifting her leg to hold her still. Nuzzling his nose to hers, he whispered, "Next time I will let you control it, my little vixen, but for now…"

She felt his member rubbing against her opening. She gasped again. Her calf stirred uselessly in the air as he held steady. He took her breath into his mouth while he placed a light kiss on her lips.

"…for now, it will be easier if I just show you." And with those heated words, half-whispered, half-groaned into her mouth, he thrust himself inside.

Her eyes widened at the forceful entry of his conquering hold.

Dougal gripped her knee and the coverlet by her head. He kept his forehead to hers, barring his hips from their naturally sought rhythm as he waited for her to adjust.

"Could...?" Isabel began in breathlessness. The sharp pain of his entrance took her by surprise. However, it quickly subsided, to be replaced by a wave of fulfillment.

Dougal slid his hand from her knee, down the side of her thigh, before gripping the rounded curve of her buttocks. He hooked her leg on his shoulder and adjusted his hips more comfortably on top of her.

She gasped, "Oh, yes. Do that!"

His measured stroke was slow and deep as he pushed boldly toward her core. He expertly ignited a fire within her. He took his time, enjoying the bittersweet temptation of a climax as he held back, wanting their touch to last forever.

Isabel's hands fitted around his shoulders, falling to his chest while he raised to control his movements better. Grasping her free leg, he lifted it above his waist. His hands gripped her thighs, using them for leverage and control as he deepened his powerful thrusts. Isabel thrashed in the senseless web he wove around her thoughts. The pleasure built before erupting in a crescendo of gratification. Dougal stiffened. He was everywhere —above her, at her sides, within her. He was everything, and as his hold on her loosened, she was oblivious to anything but him.

18

A SIGH ESCAPED Isabel's lips. Her mouth formed into a dreamy smile as she slid her hands over the soft linens of her sister's bed. Her arms discovered the vast expanse of the mattress, not meeting with flesh as she swept her hand over the crumpled bedding. She frowned. Again, searching blindly for Dougal. He wasn't beside her. Sitting up, she pulled the yellow coverlet up to hide her naked body.

"Dougal?" she called. Her head whipped around in nervousness. The tousled length of her hair flowed down her back in tangled locks. But she received no answer to her summons. He'd left her.

For a moment, she wondered if their lovemaking had been a dream. If so, she willed herself back to sleep, for she never wanted to wake up again. However, when she moved, she felt a twinge between her thighs. The night had been real, and her body very sore from it.

Contented, she assumed he must have left her for the sake of her reputation. It wouldn't do for her parents to come home to the gossip of servants. Not that she cared, she assured herself. Nothing in her life had affected her more than being with Dougal—the sweetness of his touch coursed through her body, the smell of him lingered on her skin, the texture of his flesh had been branded onto hers. With him, she felt alive for the first time in her life.

After their lovemaking, he'd been quiet. She didn't mind. He was always quiet and reserved. For a long moment, he'd held her, stroking her hair from her face with an intense agony in his eyes. Then, kissing her forehead, he'd bid her to sleep. And she had obliged, falling under the spell of his tender words.

Slipping into her nightgown, she straightened Jane's bed. A momentary wave of guilt washed over her as she thought of her sister. She would just have to tell Charlotte to have all the rooms cleaned before her parents arrived home. Oh, how she wished Jane was here. She would love to talk to her sister, to tell her the feelings that poured out of her heart.

After sneaking off to her room to clean herself and dress in a gown of light linen, Isabel made her way to the library in search of her tutor. She skipped through the empty halls, pinning up her hair as she moved. The swing of her skirts bounced while she danced about. She couldn't stop grinning and didn't care to try.

To her disappointment, the library was empty. Sighing, she crossed to the window overlooking the garden. Her heart sped up as she saw Dougal strolling over the earthen path. Daylight outlined the subtle movements of his body, movements she was only beginning to appreciate. She smoothed her hair and pinched her cheeks, unaware that the natural flush that fanned her features added more life than the pinching ever could.

She grabbed a book from the shelves. Then, as she passed the empty fireplace, she stopped. She frowned as she noticed a charred corner of parchment. It was her letter to Jane, burnt in a fire.

"Mother," Isabel concluded in irritation. She wondered how the woman had found it. Panic threatened her as she imagined the viscountess reading the words it had contained.

However, not even her mother could spoil her good mood. Isabel shrugged off the concern and slid the burnt paper into her book. In moments, she'd forgotten all about it.

❧

In the garden, Dougal's mood was less buoyant. Guilt propelled his stiff movements. His night with Isabel had been sweet—sweeter than anything else in his life—or death—had been. When he closed his eyes, he could still see her response to his touch. The smell of her perfume lingered with him.

It should never have happened. Dougal had nothing to offer Isabel because he'd dedicated his whole existence to finding Margaret. And once he found his daughter, there would be nothing keeping him to the earth. It was the way of things.

Yet, for all the years he'd spent searching, he now found he wasn't as eager to leave as he'd once been. It was all because of her. Isabel bewitched him.

"Dougal!"

He froze. At the sound of her voice, pleasure threatened his good sense. He'd worked all morning, and most of the night, to steel himself for what must be done. With one call of his name, she destroyed it all. Closing his eyes, he took a deep breath. Slowly, he turned.

"Dougal," this time, her voice was nearer. He

refused to answer her—afraid the torment of his soul would shoot out of his mouth to curse her as it had him.

Isabel grinned, not stopping as she raced forward to greet him. A book dropped from her hands and landed with a thud. She flung her arms around his neck and pressed her lips to his.

Dougal gasped in surprise at the unhampered contact. He automatically wrapped his arms around her waist to keep from falling over under the force of her affections. Despite his turmoil, he returned her kiss, deepening it when she did.

"Mmm," Isabel moaned lightly against his mouth. She brought her hands to his face. Her lids drifted open to gaze adoringly at him, but when she saw his seriousness, she pulled back to study him.

Dougal's eyes met hers. He tried to harden his expression and failed. Her face was too beautiful, her happiness too contagious.

"Isabel, I…"

"I know you had to leave me this morning," she said, not letting him go. "But still, I missed you. I had to find you." Blushing a little, she added, "I wanted to see what other lessons you had planned for me."

Dougal didn't like the reminder of what had happened, and her words endangered his resolve.

He had to get her to stop. The truth of what he had become outweighed anything she felt for him. He untangled his hands from her back, pulling away from her.

"We shouldn't…" Unsure how to handle this, he looked around the garden for a place to sit.

※

"What?" Isabel asked, stunned. Why wasn't he smiling at her? What had happened to the sweet man who had held her so tenderly? As an idea struck her, she swallowed to get the feeling of her lodged heart out of her throat. "Oh, you're worried someone will see us, aren't you? I don't care. I want the world to know how I feel this wonderful morning."

"Isabel, don't." Guilt flowed through him.

"Don't what?" Her tone came out sharper than she intended, but a woman could only take so much coldness. "Don't be happy?"

"Just don't." He turned from her. "We can't do this."

"But why?" She wanted to strike his back and make him look at her. "Has something happened? Talk to me, and we'll fix it together. Is it because you're my tutor? Does that worry you?"

"No—"

"Are you worried about my father? I can handle my father. He will naturally be upset that I'm still refusing the colonel, but he can hardly find fault with your character—"

"Isabel," Dougal snapped to get her to stop talking. "You dropped your book."

"Oh," Isabel turned to pick up the volume from the dirt. Brushing it off, she noticed the burnt letter from Jane had fallen out. She picked it up.

"What is that?" he asked.

"A letter to my sister," she answered. "After I saw the spirits in the garden, I wrote to her about them. She knows more about the history of Rothfield Park than anyone does. I thought that Jane might know what the spirits want with me."

"She can't help you," Dougal said.

"Oh, I know, but I thought maybe she could explain it to me. You're not angry that I wrote to her, are you?"

"No, of course not." He started to walk away from her.

"Dougal, wait." She hurried after him. "About what happened—"

"It shouldn't have happened."

"Well, no, I suppose it shouldn't have happened like that, but I don't regret it." She tried to smile, but his hard stare stopped her. "It's all right. Truly, it is. You're so proud and honorable. That must be why you're so upset with yourself."

When he didn't answer, but to mutter something to himself, she took his arm and forced him to face her.

"That is why I have fallen in love with you," she said. Isabel knew he cared for her, could feel it in him.

"You don't even know who I truly am," he answered.

"Then tell me who you are." Lovingly, she stroked back his hair. "It can't be as bad as you're making it out to be in your mind this morning. I already know you're a poor man without the prospect of title or much property. If you're worried about supporting me, I'll just have to demand a large dowry from my father. He'll grumble and curse the both of us, but he'll see how right a match it is. And we can live here if we must or rent a small cottage near London if you would rather be by the city. I care not where we live—"

"I'm not the man you think I am." He jerked away from her.

"I know. You're so much more than a tutor. You're kind and gentle and honest," Isabel said. "I didn't mean to insult you. I don't care if you're not a rich man. You're a good man, and that is what I would have."

"What if I told you I wasn't that man you describe? What if my treatment of you has not been honorable?" he questioned. He hesitated before caressing her cheek.

"Oh, but you are honorable. If you don't see it, I do. A dishonorable man wouldn't feel such remorse as you feel now."

Dougal let go of her cheek and balled his hand into a fist. He paced away from her.

"Dougal?" she implored. "Talk to me."

"We shouldn't have come together. It was wrong."

"It didn't feel wrong." Tears pooled in her eyes. She wanted to reach out to him, erase his pain, but she didn't understand from where it was coming.

"It was," he said, more forcibly. "What happened between us can never be. It was a mistake. We were weak, and it won't happen again."

"So you just propose to throw me away like a stained handkerchief? I won't accept that," she argued. "I know you feel something for me. Why won't you face the truth?"

She smacked his arm in frustration, wanting to do much worse.

He grabbed her by the wrists, shaking her to get her attention. "*I* face the truth? What about you?"

"What about me?" Isabel demanded. "I told you how I feel about you. You're the one in denial. Tell me you love me. Admit it!"

"Love," he dismissed. "I speak nothing of that."

"So you won't say it?" The heartbreak his words caused was unbearable. "You're a coward."

"Love is not the denial I speak of, Miss Drake." Dougal's grip tightened. When he leaned near, she smelled a hint of mint on his breath as it fanned over her flushed cheek. His light caress sent prickles of awareness along her skin, breaking down her defenses as easily as his smile. But he wasn't smiling. "Why won't you go into the forest by the stream? What have you to fear there?"

"What? The forest? I'm not afraid of the forest. I've been there countless times. I've waded in the stream. I've ridden my horse endlessly over the pathways. I've fished there and...and picked flowers with my sisters."

"When was the last time you went? When was the last time you rode through there?"

"Last week? I don't remember the exact date," Isabel stammered, growing uncomfortable. Her temple began to throb, her body to sway. She felt like passing out. Dougal held fast to her, the sharp sting of his grip keeping her next to him.

"If you're not afraid, then come with me now.

Walk with me to the forest and prove it," Dougal pleaded, clearly desperate.

"I'm not the one with anything to prove, Mr. Weston." Isabel knew he cared for her. Not once did she doubt it, but she couldn't understand why he would deny it. "Now, take your hands off me."

❀

Dougal realized he held her arm in a bruising grip. Regretfully, he let her go. Isabel stumbled away from him. Accusation shot from her eyes. She gingerly rubbed her arm and glared at him.

The truth of his reality perched on the edge of his tongue. But how could he tell her now? How could he tell her who he was—a dead marquis searching for his daughter? How could he say he believed she was the key to finding his child? How would she react to being deceived from the beginning and that he tried to manipulate her still? How could he tell her that he was afraid his feelings for her were born of his desperation to find Margaret? And even if they weren't, what would keep her from coming to the same conclusion, anyway? These were not questions he could answer. He needed more time, time he didn't have.

"Isabel, come with me," he begged, gentling his tone. He reached out and motioned for her to take his hand. "Just walk with me to the stream. If you do, then we will talk about other things. I'll say anything you want me to."

"You're a coward. Do you really care so much about money and position? Do you think I do?"

He couldn't listen to more talk of propriety. Yes, if he were alive and money was their only issue, his heart would have sung with the strength of her feelings. But that dream was an illusion. He was dead. Money and property didn't matter to a man like him.

"I don't want to go anywhere with you." She shook with outrage at his callousness. "I don't see what you have to say to me that you can't say here and now. And if you get me near water, I might take it to mind to drown your irritating hide."

Furious, she stalked away.

Dougal let her go. There was nothing he could say to stop her. Reverend Stillwell was right. She would have to come to terms in her own time. He only prayed that it wouldn't be too late.

19

THE DAY PASSED in agonizing slowness. Time didn't lessen Isabel's pain or her feelings of betrayal. She didn't seek out Dougal again. The ominous tone of his words disturbed her as they repeated themselves endlessly in her mind. What was he hiding from her? What couldn't she know? And what was his silly obsession with the forest?

She examined what was left of her burnt letter to Jane and laid it on her writing table. Grabbing a quill, she set to writing to her sister again. Although this time, she would be more careful in what she revealed in case her mother intercepted the message.

The late afternoon fell into the approaching darkness. Isabel hid away in her room. She was confident Dougal wouldn't seek her there. He wouldn't risk being seen entering her chamber. If her father suspected what had happened between them, he would demand the tutor marry her by the end of his pistol. And Isabel didn't wish to gain a husband in such a degrading way. She would much rather be alone.

Isabel was watching the red and purple of the setting sun when Charlotte knocked on her door. She bid the maid to enter and managed to smile politely at her. Charlotte bowed silently, setting a tray on the table. As she turned to leave, Isabel beckoned, "Wait, Charlotte."

"Yes, Miss?" the timid maid inquired.

"I have a letter that must be delivered straight away. Can I trust you to see to it?"

"A letter, Miss?" Charlotte asked in surprise.

"Yes, to my sister in London."

"Yes, Miss."

"Thank you." Isabel picked up the letter from her desk and handed it over. "I prefer that no one else in the house knows of it."

"Of course," Charlotte agreed. "Will there be aught else?"

"No. Wait one moment. Yes, there is one thing," Isabel said. "Could you make sure that the bedrooms are cleaned, and fresh linens are put on all the beds before the viscount and viscountess arrive home?"

"Yes, Miss," Charlotte said. With a dutiful bow, she was gone.

Sighing, Isabel turned back to the window. She ignored the tray of food, having no appetite for it. As she watched the land grow darker, fear crept over her, for the mist always came with the night.

❀

Charlotte curiously fingered the letter. She couldn't read it and thus couldn't determine to whom it was made out. It wasn't her business. She knew that.

Moving soundlessly through the manor, she made her way to the oldest part of the house. Looking around, she knocked lightly on a tall door. Within moments, it opened. Charlotte curtsied.

"What is it, Charlotte?" Dougal asked. His eyes were brimmed with red, and his face sunken with grief. Stepping aside, he let her into his bedchamber.

Old, dusty furniture lined the walls. A large antique bed, which had been Dougal's in his lifetime, graced the middle of the room. Aged tapestries hung on the walls. In his human existence, he'd favored medieval things and had the tapestries made for his home. Sconces for torches jutted from the wall. They were not in use, but when he did light them, the room would brighten, and the dust would disappear as if he were still alive and lord of the manor.

"You asked me to inform you if Miss Drake tried to contact anyone outside the manor." Charlotte handed over the missive entrusted to her. "She gave me this and told me to tell no one of it."

"Thank you." Dougal was careful not to touch the maid, knowing he would slide through her like air. He took the letter, threading it into his fingers behind his back. "Is there anything else?"

"She bade me to have the family's bed linens changed, and their rooms cleaned afore the Viscount Sutherfeld and his wife arrived back at the manor."

"You can disregard that order," he said. "If she asks you, tell her it's done. She won't know the difference. And if she inquires after the letter, tell her it's sent."

"Yes, my lord." Charlotte curtsied obediently.

"You can go. I will deal with this," he said, holding up the parchment.

"Yes, my lord."

Dougal waited for the maid to leave. Then, breaking the seal on Isabel's letter, he sat down by a fireplace that lit itself in his room.

Dearest Jane, he read. *As I endeavor to write to you, I can only feel sadness in your absence. No doubt Mother has expressed her worry about me to all of London by this time.*

You must not listen to what she says until you have spoken to me. That is what I wish to plead to you. Please come home, dear sister. So much has happened to me that I don't dare to write about any of it. I can only say with certainty that I need your wisdom and guidance. If you ask her, Mother will let you come home. Tell her you wish to make me see reason in regard to the colonel. No doubt, she will be happy to have another ally against me. I wait breathlessly for your return.
Isabel.

Wearily, Dougal rubbed his head. Crumpling the letter in one hand, he threw it into the fireplace. He rolled his neck on the high back of his chair and stretched his legs as his gaze focused on the flames. This time, he would make sure the letter burned completely.

Sensing the late hour rather than seeing it, he rose from his chair. Dougal grabbed his jacket off his dusty bed. He gave it a hard fling to free it of dust and slid it over his shoulders. He lifted his hand to the fireplace with a weary sigh and smothered the flames with the breeze the movement caused.

Night meant one thing. It was time to resume his search—hopeless as it had become.

20

ISABEL WATCHED the creeping mist spread out from the garden and slither up the side of the manor. Her hand rested against the glass pane, feeling the unusual coldness of the summer night. She couldn't sleep, mindful of what stirred in the darkness. Surprisingly, she felt no real fear of it, just apprehension over what she was witnessing.

There was movement beyond the windowpane. Isabel couldn't see it, but she felt it as sure as she did the glass. Glancing upward, she saw a swatch of clouds hiding the stars like the isolating mist on the earth.

Suddenly, she felt a pull from outside her bedroom. With a curious melancholy flooding through her, a power outside of herself induced her to walk to the hall. It was the same feeling that had awoken her the night before, luring her to Jane's bedroom. She had an inexplicable feeling that she'd been meant to see something. That had been until Dougal came, and the spell had been broken.

Her heart began to pound. As she walked down the hall, she realized she was holding a candle. She didn't remember lighting it. She had little time to wonder about it as she made her way forth along the same path she'd been led the night before, past shadowed figures in their paintings, watching her with emotionless eyes. A haze overtook her mind, dulling her thoughts and emotions. Her heartbeat slowed into a comfortable thud. Her breaths became even and slow.

At Jane's chamber door, she leaned forward and listened. She wondered if Dougal would come to her, but this time her eavesdropping wasn't interrupted. Her hand trembled as she reached for the doorknob. The metal turn was solid and real against her palm.

Isabel paused. The sound of a child's voice drifted from beneath the thick oak, eerie and high, the song she sang a vaguely familiar tune. Swallowing, Isabel pushed the door open. Despite the late hour, the room was bright with daylight. She froze in the entryway, bombarded by the heat of the sun. The door continued to swing open on its own. She blinked, adjusting her eyes to the light.

The chamber wasn't as it should be. A small bed carved from honey-colored wood sat where Jane's larger one had been, its coverlet decorated with embroidered pink roses. Atop the bed were dolls, too numerous to count. A little table and chair were scattered beside the bed as if they'd been played with recently, next to a child's trunk. The fireplace stood on a circular platform, just like the one in her room. It wasn't the same fireplace that it used to be.

Beyond the window, past the rose embroidered drapes, Isabel saw a tree. Its buds were not in full bloom as they should be, but only showed the beginning signs of spring. The tree shouldn't be there either. The child's singing suddenly became louder and clearer, drawing Isabel's attention around to the far corner of the room.

On the other side of the bed, Isabel could see the top of a blonde head. She stepped hesitantly forward, recognizing the large curls and the yellow dress. The child sang her pretty song, stopping mid-verse to hum and make two of her dolls dance together.

"Hello," Isabel said quietly. The girl didn't move. Clearing her throat, Isabel said louder, "Hello. Do you remember me?"

The child looked up, a pout breaking over her mouth. For a moment, Isabel thought the child could see her, but the bright green eyes only looked through her.

"There now, Lady Margaret," came a soft scolding behind Isabel.

Isabel jumped at the sound, spinning to look at the door. Near it stood a portly maid. She placed her hands on her hips and shook her head. Isabel stiffened, realizing that neither the child nor the maid saw her. The maid sighed heavily, moving into the room. She passed right through Isabel, her body disappearing through her front and coming out her back, like a chilling breeze. With a nervous hand to her stomach, Isabel turned around in fright.

"Now, Lady Margaret, you know your father is expecting you to be on your best behavior today," the maid said.

"I know," the child grumbled, as if loath to put down her toys and thus end her fun.

"There now, off the floor with you. You don't want to wrinkle your new dress, do you?" The maid hauled the child up by her arm and began brushing off her little yellow gown. It was the same gown she'd worn when Isabel had talked to her in the garden.

"What is this?" Isabel asked, growing sick with

apprehension. She remembered too vividly the look of the child's burnt face. She didn't receive an answer.

Examining the chamber, she watched for signs of a flame. There was nothing.

As the maid turned to retrieve a stole from Margaret's trunk, the child wrinkled her nose defiantly at the woman's back. When the maid turned around, Margaret smiled sweetly.

"I do not want to wear this dress," Margaret pouted. "I want my green one."

"This is the one your father bought for you in Paris."

"He cares more about this house than he does for me. I doubt he would even notice if I didn't go to his fete at all," Margaret said sullenly. "I don't think he likes me."

"How could you say such a thing, Lady Margaret?" the maid returned, appalled. "Never have I seen a father dote more on a child."

"He blames me for Mother's leaving," Margaret insisted. "That is why he's never home."

"Your mother's leaving had nothing to do with you," the maid said. She gathered up the dolls and placed them roughly on the bed. Their porcelain heads bounced and clanked before settling over on their sides.

"I heard them fighting about me. Mother is

furious that Father made her have me. She said that I ruined her figure, and that Father destroyed her chance at happiness by moving her out to this barbaric countryside. That is why she moved away to London." Margaret didn't see the maid's pained expression as the woman turned her back on the child and faced Isabel. "She told me she would send for me as soon as she arrived."

"Now, now, enough of that," the maid said in annoyance. "Her Grace has been away from Rothfield Park for nearly two years now. You were too young to hear such things."

"I know what I heard," Margaret said defiantly. "She lied. She never sent for me. I saw a letter Father tried to burn in the fireplace. I couldn't read it all, but it was from her—"

"Now, Lady Margaret—"

"It said that she didn't want to see either of us again. And if Father wanted a male heir, he would have to have it himself."

Margaret shivered before lifting her chin with a regal air. Her little eyes carefully watched the maid for a reaction. The woman merely shrugged and said nothing.

Isabel wanted to hug the child and carry her from the room, and she wanted to slug the maid for her indifferent treatment of the girl's feelings. She again searched the room for signs of a fire, desperate to stop it from happening. She went to the maid and cried, "Take her out of here!"

The maid didn't hear her and continued straightening the room.

"Why doesn't Father have a male heir on his own?" Margaret asked. "I should like a brother."

"Lady Margaret, you know well enough that women carry the babies. I will hear no more of your nonsense, lest I have to inform your father of it." The maid needlessly slapped the coverlet free of wrinkles as she made her way around the bed.

Isabel wanted to scream until someone heard her. She balled her fists at her sides as she tried to stand in the maid's way, desperate that the woman should see her. The woman reached through her, picking up a glove from the floor.

Suddenly, a foreboding chill prickled its way up Isabel's spine. The maid passed through her again, and the air stirred over Isabel's flesh. The air did not settle, and it became apparent that the maid's contact wasn't causing this new sensation. At first, the draft was a slight tingle, but then it slammed into her like a stout winter breeze.

Isabel gasped at the suddenness of it. She heard the maid exclaim in surprise next to her. When Isabel glanced at the woman, the maid's eyes were rounded in horror. Isabel instinctively wanted to grab Margaret and take her to safety.

Isabel took a step for the child, but Margaret paled and backed shakily into the corner.

"By all the blessed saints," the maid uttered before she tore out of the room as fast as her feet would carry her.

"Mary, don't leave me!" Margaret screamed, her small hand reaching after the servant, but her cry went unanswered. Frightened tears flooded her cheeks.

Isabel tried to go to the girl, but mist curled from behind, binding her feet to the floor like shackles. Shaking violently, Isabel peered over her shoulder to see what Margaret feared. The child's crying echoed loudly.

The fire grew friskily in the fireplace, but she couldn't feel the heat. It had become as cold as death in the sunny bedroom. A dog began to bark violently, a loud, ugly sound that reverberated darkly in the chamber. The threatening sound extinguished Margaret's yell into frightened whimpers. Isabel heard the animal snarl.

Seeing movement, Isabel twisted her body around farther. The mist didn't release her feet. A knight stood behind her. He was tall and swathed in armor, the metal plates caked with blood. In his hand, a sword pointed maliciously into the air, the blade's steel clean and bright as it reflected the fire.

Atop his head rested a helmet, gruesome spikes

jutting out from the cheek plates. A narrow slit showed only the black gaze of his deadly eyes as they searched over the chamber and finally landed on the quivering child.

Margaret renewed her cry for help.

The mist released its hold. Isabel was propelled into action. Even though Margaret couldn't see her, Isabel rushed to the girl. She tried to shield Margaret's body with her own. The figure loomed forward, his breath coming in guttural pants. The knight, confused, said nothing as he looked around the room again. His dark, soulless eyes searched, only to rest finally on the now frantically screaming girl.

A growl escaped the knight's lips, its sound as fathomless as a bottomless well. His black companion's fangs dripped with spit and blood, the mist pouring from its mouth like an evil cloud.

Margaret's shrieks died into a terrified sniffle. She tried to burrow into the wall, scratching desperately at it.

Isabel felt the child shaking and knew Margaret was afraid and alone. Just like the child and maid, the knight didn't see Isabel. His eyes skimmed past her. It didn't lessen her fear. She wrapped her arm around Margaret, willing the girl to feel her. As the last of the monster dog's growl subsided into harsh breathing, the knight lifted his hand to the fire. He grabbed the flame from the distance, controlling it with his will. He pulled it like a serpent from hell.

"Come get me, Father. Come get me," Margaret whispered desperately, over and over. Her hands clutched frantically at the wall, her little bleeding fingers gouging the plaster, crumbling it to the floor. "I didn't mean it. I didn't mean it. Come get me."

With a swing of his arm, the knight threw the snaked flame at Margaret. Isabel saw it coming toward them. Her scream joined the girl's as the intense heat flooded their skin. She tightly closed her eyes, hearing the surrounding roar, drowning the sound of Margaret's screams from their ears. Melted flesh and rivers of blood dripped over Isabel's hands. She kept herself closed to it, not wanting to see.

When the roaring stopped, the child's sobs remained. Isabel felt Margaret stir in her arms. The texture rubbing against her flesh wasn't that of a smooth child. Skeletal hands pulled frantically at the front of her gown.

As Isabel slowly peered down, lidless eyes stared back at her. Isabel gagged at the reek of burnt flesh. Smoke curled from the variegated texture of Margaret's face and neck, whispering out of the two flat holes of her missing nose.

Isabel's first impulse was disgust. She wanted to push the child away and run.

The child wailed, the noise chilling and pitiful. Isabel pulled her closer, trembling as she forced herself to stroke the few chunks of melted curls that barely covered her bleeding skull. The soot from Margaret's skin blackened Isabel's gown.

"It's all right," Isabel whispered feebly. She tried not to breathe.

In truth, she didn't know if it was all right. She didn't know when the knight would come back for the girl. For come, the knight would. The ghost might not wear the full armor each night, but who else could it be? Isabel had seen him swoop the child atop his steed.

Isabel closed her eyes to the charred girl as she gently rocked her. "It's all right. He's gone. I won't let him hurt you anymore. I will protect you. Just stay with me. Don't leave. I will keep you safe."

Isabel opened her eyes as the tears subsided. The child's hand lifted, covered by the sleeve of the scorched yellow dress. The red and black mass of her scarred face began to fill, her lips growing around her teeth. Margaret sniffed, pulling away. The blood disappeared in a flash, and the soot melted from her gown onto the burnt floor.

"This is the part where Father comes," the girl

whispered. "I can't be here. He'll be mad that his house is damaged."

"No," Isabel whispered. "No one is coming. Stay here with me. I will protect you."

"I don't want to see him. He didn't come for me. He never comes for me. Always the demon comes, but never my father. When my mother left, he promised to take care of me. He lied." The child tore free of Isabel's arms to stand and back away. "I must go. He's coming."

"What do you mean? Go where?" Isabel asked. Glancing around the room, she saw that it was scorched. A breeze blew in from outside. The fire was gone from the fireplace, leaving a crumbling hollow shell in its wake. Isabel's arms fell helplessly to her lap. Margaret disappeared into the wind. Her body blurred as her spirit vanished.

Looking at her hands, Isabel took a deep breath. Her whole body trembled. She didn't understand why she was here, but she was unable to deny what she'd seen and felt.

Beside her was the corpse of the child. She detected the yellow gown peeking from beneath the ashes, her charred face but a skull with sunken features. Her tiny hands wrapped around the bony impression of her arms and legs curled eternally into a fetal ball. She was no bigger than a small trunk.

Isabel exhaled fearfully. The acrid smell of burning flesh was embedded in her clothes and on her skin. She tried not to inhale it in. Tears moistened her eyes, but she couldn't cry. She was too scared to make a sound. The ash didn't stir as she slowly climbed to her feet. Her legs swayed unsteadily. She looked around, unsure of what she should do. Isabel didn't know how to escape this nightmare into which she'd been brought, and she didn't understand why she was supposed to see it.

It was evident that Margaret had been lonely for her parents and needed comforting. Isabel could well understand. Although her own mother did not leave the family, she constantly reminded her oldest daughter how much she was to blame for all her life's unhappiness. Maybe their shared loneliness was the thread that connected Isabel to Margaret?

Isabel eyed at the remains of furniture. The fire the knight had started had spread through other areas of the house. Numbly, her gaze traveled over the bed. She saw the soot-covered faces of Margaret's dolls staring back from the rubble, mimicking the child's corpse.

"Margaret!" came a desperate cry from the direction of the charred door hanging on its frame. Isabel stiffened at the familiar voice.

She stared at the door in disbelief. Her heart

refused to beat, and her lungs stilled. And then he was there. It was Dougal, not as she knew him, but as a nobleman from the past. His clothes were fine and rich, from the silk stockings to the long coat with braided trim. The fashion was at least fifty years old, if not more. Grief strained his features as he stumbled into the ruins of his daughter's bedroom.

Isabel's tears spilled down her cheeks. She remained silent, wondering if Dougal would see her. He looked past her. Isabel quickly moved before him to block his view of the girl. She held up her hands to stop him from seeing the horror that awaited him. Bracing herself, she tried to push him back. His body, however, passed through hers. For a moment, she felt him inside of her, felt his pain as he passed over her heart.

"No, no," he said, pulling the powdered wig from his head. It dropped from his hands to the soot, the powder from it spreading the white flecks like snow. His voice was overwhelmed with grief.

"Dougal," Isabel whispered in mounting despair. She shook her head in denial, backing away from him.

He didn't see her—couldn't hear her.

"Dougal?" she insisted. "What's happening? Why are you here?"

He fell to his knees, gathered the charred

remains of his daughter's dead body, and began to cry pitifully. She felt his agony mixing with her confusion.

She slowly backed away. It couldn't be. She wouldn't allow this to be true. However, Isabel couldn't deny the evidence. Dougal was Margaret's father. Dougal was the late Marquis of Rothfield. Dougal was dead. He was a spirit.

Isabel was in love with a ghost.

"No," Isabel insisted, shaking her head in misery. Her lungs couldn't take air as she tried to draw in a stuttered breath. "Please, God. No. Not him. Not him. Why have you shown me this? Why have you shown me? Make it go away. Oh, Dougal, no. No!"

Dougal didn't hear her. Her stomach lurched. Covering her mouth with her hands to keep from retching, she turned to run down the hall. The burnt passageways of the past transformed almost instantly into the present. Isabel crashed blindly into walls as she made her way. She didn't care what happened to her. She wanted to faint. She wanted to die.

Dougal was a ghost. He was dead. And she was surrounded only by the sharp betrayal of her love.

21

A DAY PASSED by with the breaking of Isabel's heart. Her sorrow was more than she could bear. Yet bear it she must, and so she did with eyes that were hot from her tears. She cried until her body could weep no more and until her face grew swollen and red.

At first, she hid in her chamber, waiting for the sun to claim the land beyond her window, its golden rays forcing back the mists that brought nothing but pain to Rothfield Park.

Within the safety of the sunlight, Isabel crawled from the corner of her bed. She dressed. Her actions were more mechanical than those of self-will. Like a corpse walking lifelessly to its grave, she went through the halls. She saw nothing and no one as she found sanctuary in the library to wait for Dougal.

It was worse than if Dougal had unexpectedly died after they had come together, for then she would've had a chance to recover her heart and would have known his intentions toward her were honorable. But he was dead, and he had come to her under false pretenses. As a ghost, he didn't have to pay for the consequences of their actions. She most assuredly did.

And he had, quite possibly, used her.

Only too well did she remember his desperation the night she met with Margaret in the garden. Margaret had said she didn't want to see him, and he'd appeared frantic to know of her. Could it be that he searched for the child every night? Could it be that he believed Isabel could find the girl for him?

"Then why didn't he ask me?" she muttered bitterly, slapping her hands against the arm of her father's chair. "Why go through the farce of deceiving me?"

She nervously waited out the day in the library. She had no more tears to cry. Isabel forced herself to face him. She wasn't scared at the prospect of seeing him, just hurt that what she felt could never be. No wonder he was unable to return her sentiments of love. The knowledge that he'd never tried to trick her into loving him redeemed some of his honor. If she were honest with herself, he'd tried repeatedly to keep her at a distance.

The day turned to evening. Dougal stayed away. Isabel remained patiently in the library, watching for him in the garden. She wondered if he would ever come again. She fell back into her father's chair.

"He should have told me," she whispered, verging on bitterness.

"What?"

Isabel looked up in surprise. Her heart broke as she saw Dougal's handsome face. Pensively, he studied her, as if waiting to see if she would fight with him. He was even farther from her now than when she believed him to be a poor tutor.

He doesn't realize I know, Isabel thought in amazement. She turned her eyes away from him and said nothing. She couldn't speak. Part of her screamed that she was crazy, that she'd hallucinated the ghosts and the fire, but when she glanced back up, she saw that he was real.

"I want to say I'm sorry," he said at last. His eyes shone with the same steady kindness that first made her love him. The disarming dimple on the side of his cheek deepened as he smiled apologetically. "I never meant to hurt you. I was confused. There's much that needs to be said between us."

Isabel dejectedly thought of her broken dreams. She said nothing and fortified her emotions, lest she cry anew.

"Isabel, please, this isn't easy for me." He came into the room to stand before her. He shifted uncomfortably from one foot to the other.

"Why?" Isabel asked, staring at his boots. "What are you hiding?"

"I…"

Isabel studied his face. He glanced away in frustration and sighed, long and tired.

Dougal leaned toward her, his arms lifting as if he would hold her, but then he hesitated and pulled away again. She detected the rise and fall of his chest as if he breathed, felt the gentle stirs of that breath on her cheek. The fine texture of his skin, the birthmark beneath his eye, the crease of worry between his brows—it was all there and very real.

For a crazed moment, Isabel wondered if she'd dreamt it all, but as she continued to watch him, she knew it was true. He was dead. Silently, she forced herself to stand. Tears came to her eyes.

Dougal tried to smile. His arms widened as if he would take her into them.

Isabel opened her mouth, letting loose a piercing scream that sent a shrill echo through the library. Dougal jerked back in surprise. His skin faded. His mouth opened, and blood gurgled over his chin and neck. A long wound formed beneath his jaw, revealing a slit in his throat.

Isabel stumbled back in terror, going toward the window, desperate to put distance between them. Dougal's flesh faded to blue, his clothes turning to the linen of styles past. Crimson stained the white material as his life's blood spilled onto his chest. A frail hand lifted to stop her from leaving him. Falling to his knees, he held his gurgling throat.

Isabel watched, horrified. She wanted to go to him but knew there was nothing she could do to help him. Her heart pounded. She now had her proof, but it brought her no comfort. Unable to bear seeing him thus, she turned from him. Her hands fell against the windowpane, and she wept.

"Isabel," she heard at length. Sniffing, she lifted her head.

Dougal came up behind her. His body had returned to normal. She saw the impression of him reflected between her hands on the glass. Her thumb moved to stroke over his mirrored cheek. He didn't touch her.

Whispering mournfully, he asked, "Why did you do that?"

"I had to know," she answered. Wiping her face on her sleeve, she turned. Gently, she lifted her hand to touch him. Her fingers fell through him like his body was air. Her face contorted with pain as she whispered, "Who are you? What do you want from me? Why are you here?"

"Isabel, I wanted to tell you." He reached for her, but she slipped through his grasp, and he couldn't touch her, couldn't hold her.

"Then why didn't you? You lied to me. Everything you said was a lie. You're not my tutor. You're some dead marquis haunting me." Isabel swiped the tears from her face. It did no good. More replaced them. "Are you trying to make me crazy? Was it all a lie?"

"It's not like that," Dougal protested. He reached for her as he pleaded, "Please understand."

"I understand completely. You saw the opportunity to mingle with the living girl, take advantage of her," she said. "And there are no consequences for you, are there? But what about me? I'm ruined for any other man."

Ruined because I can never love anyone but you. Why did you have to make me love you?

"Isabel, no, I wanted to be with you. I still want —" Dougal again tried to touch her.

"Stay away from me. Get out of my house!" she yelled, pulling farther from him as he advanced on her. "You don't live here anymore. I would that

I'd never met you or any of your kind. And my one wish is that I could forget all of it. Take it back. Take all of it."

"No, wait, you must listen to me. If you believe that you can feel me, you shall. Here, take my hand. I'll tell you everything," he begged. "You must try."

"How often have you done this over the years? How many of us have there been?" Anger and hurt seeped into every word. "How many have you made fall in love with you?"

"No one, Isabel, I swear it. You're the first one to touch me since my death. And it was because you believed me to be real. I am real. Believe in me again. Take my hand in yours and let me explain. I shall tell you everything."

"It's too late for that," she whispered. "I want you to leave me alone."

"No, Isabel," Dougal begged. "Don't send me away."

"Go," she said more loudly. "Just go away."

Isabel lifted her chin in determination.

Slowly, he nodded. "As you wish."

Sorrow and pain crossed over his features, emulating her own. Deliberately, he faded until he disappeared into nothingness.

"I'm sorry," she heard him whisper. "I never meant to hurt you."

"Dougal," she tried to answer, but it was too late. He was gone. "I'm sorry, too."

Falling to her knees in anguish, she kneeled helplessly on the patterned rug.

Forgive me, Dougal. I love you still.

22

Reverend Stillwell flipped through the pages of his texts, searching for anything that might comfort those under his care. Dust drifted around him in the light as he looked. There was nothing new that he hadn't already learned long ago.

His candle flickered, dangerously close to going out, and the vicar looked up from his studies. Dougal appeared before him. Instantly, he saw the tortured lines and pallor of the marquis' face. The vicar stood and closed his book. Dougal looked around the sparse chamber in the back of the old church.

"Isabel knows about me," Dougal said. When he'd seen her pain, none of his other excuses mattered. He wanted her. He wanted to be with her. He wanted to turn back time to when he was alive and take Isabel with him to his living world. He wanted Isabel and Margaret to be his family. If only she'd been his wife, then his life would have been a blessed one. "She discovered the truth."

"Then she told you what happened in the forest?" the vicar asked.

"No, she still refuses to remember that much," Dougal said. He crossed over to the bed. "I have lost her. I have failed Margaret yet again."

"What happened?"

Dougal quickly explained most of what had transpired in the library, leaving out the details of their intimacy. When he finished, he added, "She commanded me away from her. I can't appear to her so long as she refuses to see me. She wouldn't believe in me enough so that I could touch her."

"Keep trying to reach her. Perchance, she will come around." The vicar looked out the narrow slit of his window. "I'll try to visit with her."

"There's more," Dougal said quietly

"More?"

"I'm in love with her. But after I find Margaret, I'll have nothing left to offer her." In pain, he whispered, "I have nothing to offer her now."

The vicar opened his mouth to protest, but the marquis faded from his chamber. He watched for a moment, hoping Dougal would return. When he didn't, the vicar sighed and moved back to his work with renewed purpose.

23

Isabel rushed through the dim hallway, unmindful of the late hour or the presence of those whom she might awaken. Her loud footfall pounded evenly throughout the manor. For the first time in nearly two weeks, she was happy. The sorrows of her ostracism were about to be lifted.

Jane had come home.

Isabel threw open her sister's bedroom door with a flush of excitement. She didn't bother with knocking, too eager for such etiquette. Instantly, she saw her sister unpacking the contents of her trunk onto her bed.

At the noise, Jane dropped her folded gown to the floor and spun around in surprise. Then she lifted her hand to her throat, taking an involuntary step back. She tried to calm herself as she stared at her sister in the doorway.

"Jane," Isabel squealed happily. She rushed forward. "I didn't mean to frighten you."

"Isabel," Jane gasped with a frail gesture of helplessness. She shook her head to clear her mind.

"Why, Sister," Isabel admonished, "you look as if you have seen a ghost. Aren't you happy to see me?"

Jane giggled nervously. "Of course I'm happy, Isabel. You startled me. Being back in this haunted room, I didn't know what to expect, and you made quite a noise."

"You should have known I would come straightaway," Isabel scolded lightheartedly. Her fondness for her sister shone too brightly for Jane to take offense. "Seeing you back, I feel more like myself. You can't imagine how lonely I have been."

Isabel leaned over to kiss Jane on the cheek before patting it. Jane fidgeted nervously, her gaze darting to the floor. Isabel smiled fondly at her little sister, eyeing her from head to toe. Then, moving to the bed, Isabel exclaimed, "I swear you've grown. Look at you. It appears Harriet got her claws into you and took you shopping. I wish I could have been there."

"Oh, yes, the gown," Jane mumbled, glancing down at herself. Self-consciously, she tugged at the low neckline of the green bodice, trying to pull it up. Then, with a delicate shrug, she opted for a shawl. Wrapping it over her shoulders, she said, "Harriet insisted that…well…I—"

"You look beautiful," Isabel said. "I'm envious of you. I have been so pale and sickly of late."

"How I have missed you." Jane changed the subject with grace. She moved to sit by Isabel and pushed her glasses up on her nose. "I'd started to think I would never see you again."

"I know the feeling," Isabel said, thinking of their mother. Seeing Jane frown, she forced a smile. "But you're home now. How was London?"

"You know about London?"

"Yes, I saw your carriage pull away when you left. Mother told me where you were going. Well, she didn't exactly tell me. She and Father are not talking to me these days. They're still upset over my impertinence." Isabel waved her hand as if it didn't matter.

"Yes, I know," Jane replied. "They took it pretty hard."

Isabel wrinkled her nose. If she thought of it, she would cry. She hadn't realized how badly she'd missed everyone. She was so alone at Rothfield.

It had been two long weeks since she banished Dougal from her. She'd even begun to wonder if she'd imagined their short time together. Every night as she stood in her room, looking out her window at the mist, she would start to call to him. She held back, knowing that if he were there, then she had best forget about him. And if he weren't real, then it was better she left the delusion alone.

"So, how was London?" Isabel inquired again, standing and moving away to hide her face from view. She didn't want Jane to see her tears. She didn't want to admit that her decision about the colonel's proposal was wavering. If she couldn't have love, then what did it matter if she married a tedious man? At least with the colonel, she would always have Rothfield Park, and her parents would let her out of isolation. "What news?"

"Mother made me go." Jane narrowed her eyes. "She thought it would be good for me. And I must admit that it was."

"How so?" Isabel dabbed at her eyes and turned to study her youngest sister's face. "You hate the London season, and you abhor high society."

"Yes, that's true." Jane hesitated. "But Colonel Wallace was there. He was very nice to me. We spent quite a bit of time together."

"Really? You and the colonel?"

"Oh, Isabel, you don't mind, do you?"

"No," Isabel said. "Why should I mind?"

"Good! I was hoping you harbored no ill will toward the colonel because we're to be married."

"What?" Isabel shook her head in confusion.

Jane and the colonel?

"I don't believe it," Isabel said. "You and the colonel? Shall Mother stop at nothing to get him in the family?"

"Oh, Isabel, don't be so harsh. It was our idea. You see, I love him," Jane admitted with a boldness Isabel had never heard in her sister.

"Then I'm happy for you." Isabel ignored the twinge of disbelief. Jane positively gleamed with happiness. In light of it, Isabel couldn't be angry.

Isabel thought of Dougal. Her heart squeezed in her chest, and she fought the pang of jealousy that tried to form. "When is the wedding?"

Jane didn't notice her sister's discomfort. "The marquis—"

"The marquis?" Isabel echoed, again thinking of Dougal. She pictured him in his silk stockings and powdered wig, standing frozen in his daughter's ashen bedchamber, *this* bedchamber.

Isabel shivered. She looked across the room to the unmarred spot where Margaret's body had lain.

"Yes. The Marquis of Rothfield, Wallace's uncle."

"Oh, that marquis," Isabel said, forcing her thoughts to the present.

"The marquis approved of the match. But, unfortunately, he passed away soon after his blessing. The wedding will have to wait until after the colonel is done with his period of mourning. You aren't mad that I will be titled?"

"No, silly girl, why should I be? Please pass along my condolences to Colonel Wallace." Isabel crossed over to the window and stared out into the evening.

"Oh, I shall." Jane hesitated. "Were you terribly upset to hear about Harriet? Is that why you're sad?"

"Who said I was sad?" Isabel asked, forcing a veil over her words. "I'm just surprised by your news and so very happy for you. Wait, what about Harriet?"

"You don't know?" Jane said, dismayed, clearly not wanting to be the one to tell her sister the news.

"Know what?" Isabel asked, growing concerned.

"Mr. Tanner and Harriet ran off to Gretna Green to marry. He was after the family money, and it would seem he succeeded. Apparently, Mr. Tanner is a bit of a gambler without a shilling to his name. Father is in London, trying to calm the gossip, and was put out enough to pay off Mr. Tanner's debts. And, naturally, Harriet couldn't care less about what she has done. It's why they left the manor so suddenly if you noticed." Jane joined Isabel at the window. "Are you upset?"

"Harriet and Edward?" Isabel said, stunned. It seemed everyone's lives were working out, and she was the only one left alone. All she had was the memory of a man fifty years dead. "How? When?"

"You're not upset, are you? I know how you favored him," Jane admitted.

"No, not at all. I have long stopped thinking of Edward," Isabel answered, knowing it to be the truth. The only man she could think of was her darling marquis—her darling dead marquis. Isabel forced her thoughts to stop lingering on him. She concentrated on her sister's words.

"I'm so glad. After your accident—"

"My accident?" Isabel echoed, drawing her consideration to Jane's expression.

"Yes." Jane's brow furrowed. "You remember your accident, don't you?"

"Jane, I think you're mistaken. What did Mother tell you? I've not met with any accident, save maybe bumping into a table when running in the hallway just now to see you." Isabel started to feel sick to her stomach, and her head began to throb.

"Isabel? Are you well? Can I get you something?" Jane asked.

"I didn't have an accident," Isabel insisted, her voice rising. Her limbs shook with fear.

"Maybe you hit your head too hard and can't remember," Jane explained. "The doctor said you hit—"

"My head," Isabel echoed, reaching for her skull. It felt uninjured to her. None of this made sense. "How, Jane? How did I hit my head?"

"You were upset. You went riding in the forest by the stream. Can't you remember? You were angry at your engagement to the colonel." Jane's words became a mere whisper. Her face paled as she studied her sister. "You must remember it."

"The forest," Isabel murmured. Her mind pricked with a sound she couldn't place. "Something happened in the forest. That's why he was trying to lead me there. I must have seen something."

"Isabel? Who tried to lead you into the forest? Father? You make no sense." Jane sounded panicked.

Isabel stood, moving blindly from the room.

Jane followed her. "Isabel, wait. Let me help you."

"I'm sorry, Jane," she called. She moved like a woman possessed. "I have to be alone for a while.

I'll visit you later, I promise. I want to hear all about your wedding plans."

Jane nodded helplessly.

Isabel rushed through the house, oblivious of the late hour. The long trail of her cream-colored skirts whisked behind her in a fleeting whisper. Running to the front door, she threw it open. It was the first time she'd braved the night since discovering Dougal's secret. She felt a presence beyond the door. She knew what was out in the mist. She knew that spirits roamed the earth at night, claiming the late hours as their own—even if she hadn't seen those spirits since sending Dougal away.

Without thought, Isabel ran toward the side of the house. She didn't bother to close the front door. She needed to find out what had happened to her.

The mist grew thicker as she charged around the house. Her steps hurried her over the garden paths. The full moon lit her way. Desperately she ran. Tears streamed down her face. She had to know.

Seeing a figure blocking her path, she stumbled on her tangling skirts. With a groan, she fell to the ground.

"Dougal," she began, pushing herself up. But, as her gaze focused, she saw it wasn't the marquis.

Black eyes stared at her. She froze in fear. It was

the knight. Gone was his armor, replaced by the tunic and breeches. His thick arms crossed over his chest as he waited for her to stand. Isabel eyed his sheathed sword at his side, the massive weapon glittering dangerously.

Her heart thudded until she felt as if she couldn't draw breath. "It's you."

"Where go you, m'lady?" The knight's voice crackled like the breaking of ice. The wind whipped his hair over his shoulder, the locks the same soulless color as his eyes. Isabel swallowed, unable to answer. The knight took a step forward, towering over her. Isabel cringed. The dark knight leaned toward her, and his tone changed, "Can you hear me?"

"Yes," she stuttered.

The knight relaxed as he watched her face. He straightened once more.

Isabel forced herself to be brave. "Yes, I can hear you. Who are you? What do you want?"

The man studied her carefully. He glanced over his shoulder down the path. A frown marred his features when he turned his attention back to her.

"He hunts," said the knight cryptically. "You should begone."

"Who?" Isabel persisted as she pushed up from the ground.

"The forest is no place to be at night." He

didn't move to help her. "You should go inside where 'tis safer."

"You're the only one to be feared," Isabel countered, thinking of the child.

"M'lady?" He tilted his head in confusion.

"I have to go to the forest," Isabel said. "Something happened to me there. I must know."

"Not now. 'Tis not safe in the mist. Go in the daylight."

"You're a murderer," she countered. In the moonlight, without his beast from hell, the knight didn't look as threatening. "That is why you try to stop me."

"Not me. My brother."

"Two knights are roaming the countryside? I don't believe you. You're lying. What did you do with Margaret? I'm taking her with me," Isabel said with feigned bravado. "Hand her over."

"She's my ward, not yours." He watched her charge him in defiance and faded from her path seconds before she could push him, only to materialize again behind her. Isabel tripped, tearing her dress as she landed.

"Who are you?" she growled.

"Sir Josiah of Merton." This time, he reached down to help her. Isabel had no choice but to let him. She wasn't expecting his ghostly hand to be warm. Josiah let her go.

Isabel studied the knight's face now that he was closer. True, his eyes were as black as starless midnight. However, she saw concern in them. It was a kindness the demon that attacked Margaret didn't have. There was mercy and pain in Josiah's gaze.

"What does your brother want?" she demanded. "Why did he kill Margaret?"

"'Twas a mistake. He was after the marquis, Margaret's sire." When he sighed again, the weight of his world showed on his face. Josiah motioned for her to walk with him down the path. Isabel followed. "Lady Margaret got in the way of things. She has the same blood as the marquis, and 'tis why my brother found her first. He would never have picked her intentionally. The innocent souls of children are more difficult to capture. They're too nimble and flighty."

"Dougal," Isabel whispered.

"Yea," Josiah acknowledged.

"Then why is Dougal not with Margaret if you have her? Why are you keeping them apart?"

"'Tis not I who keeps them apart. I found Margaret wandering the grounds, searching for her sire soon after she'd died. I can't find the marquis. His spirit is lost to me."

"But I have seen the marquis. I saw you look at him that day from your horse. You saw us." Isabel pointed to where Josiah had watched them from the trees.

"Nay, I saw you. Methought I saw you speaking to someone, but I couldn't see who. You say 'twas the marquis? You have spoken to him?"

"Yes, spoken to him, touched him." Isabel tried to hide her blush. The knight seemed too preoccupied to notice.

"Then maybe you're the key. You can see Margaret and her sire. 'Tis you that must join them."

"Me? The key?" Isabel shook her head uneasily.

"You must be the one meant to reunite them. My brother still hunts them. He can't find either of them. In death, their souls have proven elusive. However, soon I fear he shall succeed. Each eve he draws closer."

"What is your brother's name?"

"It cannot be uttered," the knight whispered. "To say his name is to summon him."

"You say he still hunts?"

"Yea, m'lady, he does."

"Can't you stop him?"

"Nay." The knight shook his head mournfully. "Wouldst that I could, but I did not stop him in life as was my duty. In death, he's too strong for me to try."

"How do you know you were meant to stop him in life?" She saw the pain on his face.

"Long ago, this was my family's holding. My brother made his pact with unholy wizards. They gave him power and riches beyond imagination. However, as he took his seat of power, the dark ones struck him dead. As payment for that which they had bestowed, he had pledged his afterlife to bringing them other souls. So long as he feeds their fire with others, they shall not take him." Josiah's expression hardened. "'Twas within my power in life to stop him. But I loved him too much and forewent my one chance. So now 'tis my destiny to roam the earth, trying in vain to protect others from him. My curse is to see the evil my hesitance caused."

"Don't say in vain. How could you have known the depths of his heart? You couldn't have known—"

"I should have seen him for what he was," the knight said bitterly. "My brother is lost. Now he's a demon who consumes souls."

Isabel shivered. "Then that is how we stop him. If he can't make the payment, they'll come to collect."

"I have tried. 'Tis why I intercept the souls of those he kills. That was how I came across Margaret. Many spirits are lingering here that I have saved, but he's too fast. By the time I find one, he will have killed another and taken them away. And each time he kills, he gets faster."

"And the spirits, they just stay here?" she wondered aloud. "Can't they move on?"

"Some do, once they unburden themselves," he answered. "I believe that Margaret stays because she is searching for her sire. My brother still wants her. Methinks, if you help her find the marquis, they can both find peace. So long as no other concern is keeping them here, they will be safe from the fires of damnation. It must be why you can see us all."

"Move on?" Isabel whispered. If Dougal moved on, she would never see him again. Selfishly, she wanted to refuse what the knight asked.

"Yea, we must reunite them," the knight urged. "'Tis only a small deed, but if we can save them—"

"No, I can't," Isabel said through tight lips. She shook her head in denial.

Josiah's eyes narrowed, irritated by her denial. "But—"

"I sent the marquis away from me," she said, torn between relief and sorrow. She fought her tears. "I can't see him anymore. I can't help you."

"Call him back," Josiah demanded.

"Will that work?" she wondered, trembling at the simple solution. He nodded.

Don't ask this of me. She wanted to scream at the unfairness. *Dear God, don't make me give him up completely. Don't make the decision mine.*

Isabel realized that so long as Dougal was near, there was a chance for them to be together. She'd refused to call out to him for fear he was imaginary, but he did exist, and now she was told she must sacrifice her love for him to save him. The pain choked her, numbing her with the agony of the situation.

"How long do we have?" she asked, a coldness coming over her words as she faced what she knew she must. She turned her back to the knight, trying to see the distance through the mist as it continued to swirl. The fog parted, and she heard Margaret's laughter. The child ran through the garden.

"He must give them a truly good soul about every fifty years when the moon is right. Meanwhile, he feeds the fire what souls he can gather—good or bad. He will need the marquis in a few days by my estimation." Josiah moved past Isabel, walking the way they'd come. He whistled for his horse, and the animal appeared out of the darkness. The destrier stopped to paw the ground.

"Will he be coming after my family next?" Isabel thought of Jane in her room. If she didn't find a way to stop him, Jane could be his next victim. Isabel couldn't think of anyone with a heart better than her sister's.

"I don't know. I never know until 'tis happening."

The knight swung onto the horse. He gave her a curt nod and without another word took off into the night. The animal thundered down the path.

Isabel watched as Josiah leaned over, darting his hand into the mist to grab hold of Margaret. The girl appeared from the darkness, swinging up into his arms. Seeing Isabel, the girl smiled, nestling into her protector's embrace. And into the mist, they disappeared.

❦

"Dougal," Isabel called, running through the halls. "Dougal, come out. I need to speak to you. Please, it's important!"

Isabel received no answer. She had searched the garden and now the manor. Dougal still wasn't speaking to her. Slumping against the hallway wall, she slid to the floor. Her head fell into her hands as she buried her face. It was useless.

With a groan, she banged the back of her head into the wall. Seeing the portraits before her with their dead eyes appearing to watch her, she grimaced. A man in a green tunic caught her attention. His arms folded decisively over his chest. The portrait was vaguely familiar. Shivering, Isabel crawled to her feet. She didn't like the depiction. As she backed away, she kept her eyes on the painted man. He didn't move.

Feeling the beginning of a bad headache, she decided to look for Dougal in the morning and wearily crawled into bed. Almost instantly, she was asleep. And while she slept, her dreams brought her no answers as she drifted through a black world of comfortless images.

24

The smell of hot tea banished the chill of the morning from Isabel as she made her way into the dining room. When she opened the door, she thought how odd it was that she hadn't been there for quite some time. Since her parent's punishment, she'd been taking her meals alone in her room. There was no one in the room, but the smell grew stronger as she entered.

Despite her desire for a cup of the potent blend, she denied herself the luxury and passed over to the library. She must find Dougal. Until she made amends with him and helped him, there would be no peace for her. And unless she helped him, there was a great chance the demon knight would send his and Margaret's souls into eternal darkness. Isabel trembled at the very notion.

At the window, she turned to face the room and carefully asked, "My lord, are you there?"

She received no answer.

Taking a deep breath, she closed her eyes and said louder this time, "Dougal. Come and see me. I must speak to you."

When she opened her eyes, Isabel saw the dark top of Dougal's head from behind the back of a chair. She sighed loudly in relief. At the noise, Dougal startled, spinning up from his seat to look at her.

Isabel wasn't prepared for how seeing his handsome face would affect her. Two weeks was too long to be parted from him. However would she manage the rest of her life? Choking on her emotions, she held still.

"Isabel." He moved to her, reaching as if he might try to touch her. "Are you really here? I have waited for you to come back. I've prayed for it."

"Yes," she said. "I've been calling for you. Didn't you hear me?"

"No, I...what's wrong?" he demanded. "What has happened? Are you hurt?"

"I'm just tired." She ignored the pain the lie caused her. He kept trying to smile at her, but she wouldn't encourage him. Stiffening her expression, she tried to wait until his face matched her hardness. It wasn't to be.

"Then, why have you called me?" he questioned, his expression hopeful.

"I must speak with you. But first, I have to ask you—"

"Yes," Dougal broke in, "anything."

"You're the marquis, aren't you?"

"Yes. I am the Marquis of Rothfield, or I should say *was* the Marquis of Rothfield. I'm sure someone else now bears that title."

"Is your name Dougal?" She refused to show her feelings.

"Yes." He gripped his hands together. "It is. Formally, I am Lord Dougal Weston. I have a long list of family names between those, but truthfully it has been so long I have forgotten most of them. Dougal Thomas…Anthony Montcalm—"

"Yes, fine," Isabel dismissed in distraction. At least he hadn't lied to her about that. "I understand, my lord."

"Don't," he muttered, his expression turning sad. "Don't call me by the title, not now. Call me Dougal."

"All right," she said, though she didn't say his name. Eyeing him, she wondered why it had taken her so long to suspect his nobility. He carried himself with a certain air.

"Did you miss me?" he asked.

"No," she lied.

He looked as if she'd slapped him.

Isabel moved away. "No more than I would miss the company of a dear friend."

"Then why are you here?" he asked.

"I was meant to help you find your daughter," she said. "But I don't know exactly how to reunite you. And I'm not sure you would see each other if I did get you to the same place."

"Isabel, that is well and good. But first, I must know," Dougal paused. His hand fell onto her shoulder and turned her to face him. Closing his eyes briefly, he sighed in relief when he didn't pass through her. "What about us?"

"We are friends, aren't we?" she replied candidly. "Other than that, there is no us."

"But, what about—"

"What?" she broke in, knowing she would have to say the words sooner or later. Before she lost her nerve and threw herself into his arms, she said, "You mean us coming together as we did? I suppose it shouldn't have happened, though it was…pleasant…enough, and I do thank you for the lesson."

That wasn't entirely true. Being with him was more than pleasant. And the weeks apart had only heightened her longing. She had missed his touch, dreamed about it until she awoke sweating in the night hours.

"I was emotional afterward, and I'm embarrassed about how I reacted. I was meant to help you find Margaret, not lie to you and myself. I should never have told you that I loved you. Thank goodness you were smart enough to realize it and not return the silly sentiment, lest we be in even bigger—"

"Then you don't love me."

"No," she said, glad that the lie was finally out. She could see he believed her. How easy it would be to take the word back, but she couldn't. "I don't love you. I was confused. Now I know what I must do. I will reunite you with your daughter, and your spirits will be released from the earth. You'll be able to move on."

"And you?"

"What about me?" Isabel shrugged as if it were of no concern. "I will live out my life. My sister Jane is to marry the colonel, and I will marry Edward. He's the man for me. I have always loved him."

"Edward?"

"Yes, we are the same. He will take me away from Rothfield." Isabel stared at him pointedly. "I hate it here. I can see why your wife left it."

Dougal frowned at her deliberate strike, and she was instantly sorry she'd taken it that far.

"Who told you of—?"

"It doesn't matter now," she said. The look in his hurt eyes was almost too much to bear. "I only meant to say that I'll be happier elsewhere. This country is no place for a woman of society. I need the excitement of the city life to...to be alive."

"No, Isabel, you must not..." Dougal moved to touch her again. Isabel artfully dodged his hand and skirted past him.

"It's my life to live," she stated.

"But that is what I mean, you mustn't—"

"I won't discuss it with you. You're dead. You have no possible say in my life. Now tell me how I can help you reunite with your daughter." Isabel waited for an answer.

His face became a blank, emotionless mask. She was glad for it. If he smiled at her, all would be lost. His soul would be lost. As she looked at him, she was cast into anguish, knowing his pain was partly her fault.

"I don't know," he stated after a great length. "Have you been to the forest?"

"I tried." She was glad to be off the subject of her feelings. "The knight stopped me."

"The knight?" Dougal asked with mounting alarm.

"You can't see him. I can," she replied. "He can't see you. He has been taking care of Margaret."

"Isabel, I don't understand. What has happened?"

"It's too hard to explain." Isabel tried not to think of the child's animosity toward her father. She couldn't imagine what it would be like to spend the years as he had, endlessly searching. Dougal didn't need to know Margaret blamed him for not protecting her. The two would have to work that out later.

"Try," he insisted.

"All right." She moved to sit on the settee, wondering just how much of the story she should tell him.

❧

Dougal couldn't look at her. With her, for the first time since before his death, he'd felt an emotion that wasn't born of pain and suffering. With her, he'd felt happiness. The emotion had been so foreign to him that at first, he didn't recognize it. But after she'd banished him, he had realized that only with her could he be whole. Isabel and Margaret were his existence. However, Isabel didn't want him. She didn't love him. And she still didn't understand.

He seethed with jealousy at the mention of Edward Tanner—an emotion he perceived he wasn't justified in feeling. Dougal forced his feelings aside. He had to focus on finding his daughter. He would have an eternity for self-pity.

"Tell me," he prompted when she didn't explain.

Still, she hesitated.

"Don't mince words," he ordered. "Tell me."

"When Margaret died," Isabel paused, sighing, "Sir Josiah found her."

"And?"

"I'm trying to think of how to say it."

"Tell me."

"It's his brother, an evil demon-possessed knight, who's been killing everyone. It has something to do with a pact the man made with the devil, and souls he needs to collect." Isabel frowned. "How are you? Do you need a moment? Should I have not told you?"

"Josiah told you all this?" Dougal inquired skeptically. He'd never seen a knight such as she described, but he'd heard rumors of the evil that lurked around the estate. And he knew that it was an evil that most likely had held his daughter captive.

"Yes, and I believe him. I have also met Margaret."

Dougal dropped into a chair. He couldn't

speak. He'd known she'd seen Margaret, but for her to say the words aloud was too much.

"She's well." Seeing his reaction, she softened her words. "She misses you."

His eyes became moist, but he didn't cry.

"Something happened in the forest. I had an accident." Isabel frowned at the words before rushing on. "Something must have frightened my horse. I fell and hit my head, and that is why I can see you. Reverend Stillwell told me that sometimes a traumatic accident could make people see the dead. It's how he came about his power and obviously how I came about mine."

"He told you that?" Dougal asked in disbelief. It didn't sound like the vicar.

"Yes." Isabel leaned forward, placing her hands on her knees. "So, when I fell, I must have triggered a part of my mind that allows me to see you. I'm supposed to help you."

"How will you help?" he asked.

"I'm not sure. I thought that maybe I could get you and your daughter to the same place at the same time. That would be a place to start."

"I mean, how will you help if you can't remember what happened in the forest? If you don't know what frightened...your horse? It could be the answer you're searching for. Shouldn't you go and find out?" Dougal insisted. "Are you still scared of going?"

"No," she said.

He saw the look on her face and knew she was lying. "Would you like me to take you?"

"No, I can do it." When he arched a brow in doubt, she hurriedly added, "I *will* do it—today."

Dougal nodded. Rising from his chair, he crossed over to her. Unable to resist, he touched her cheek. He again was relieved when his hand rested on her skin and didn't pass through. He felt her warmth and softness beneath his palm and began to caress her tenderly. When his fingers moved over her neck, he felt her pulse quicken. "I still think that I should go with you."

"No, I should go alone. It might not work if I get distracted," she replied. Her calm façade crumbled. "It might not work. It doesn't seem all that important. I merely fell from my horse. Who is to say anything else happened? I might not remember a thing."

"You will." With the tips of his fingers, he urged her to stand. She did, following his commands without question or thought. Her gaze moved to his lips. Her head fell to the side. Dougal knew the look on her face. She wasn't immune to him. She felt more than she let on. The realization gave him hope.

"Dougal, I don't think." His lips silenced her words. His body remembered all too well what his mind had been trying to forget. With a deep breath, she whispered, "We can't—"

"We already have," he persisted. "As you said, it was pleasant."

Isabel gave a light moan, and her hands found their way to his shoulders.

"Yes," she sighed. Her eyelids grew heavy as she leaned closer. "*Pleasure*. We might as well take some pleasure. It's not as if we can do anything at this moment. And it will mean nothing."

She spoke the words, but her actions proclaimed them to be a lie. The connection between them was more than a meaningless affair of the flesh. He felt it, and he knew she felt it too.

"Yes, Miss Drake, absolutely nothing," he agreed before deepening the kiss.

"And it's not as if we don't understand each other," she insisted.

"Oh, we understand perfectly. This is just pleasure—pure, hot pleasure." His hands wrapped around her, his fingers sliding to untie her laces. He was determined to make her feel.

"And—"

"Shh," Dougal hushed. His fingers continued to work on her bodice. He trailed his lips down her neck to the pulse that beat wildly for him.

"The door," she insisted.

Dougal went to the door even though he knew no one would interrupt them. He latched it and returned. "Locked."

"Where?" she asked. Her eyes moved past him to find a place to lie down. Her hands worked their way into his jacket, pushing the heavy material from his shoulders.

He successfully loosened her bodice. The material fell forward, exposing her chest. Instantly, his lips moved to taste her. His tongue lapped the sensitive flesh of her a ripened nipple. Isabel moaned in approval.

Dougal helped her undress him. His hands went straight to his breeches. His mouth claimed hers, kissing her as he turned her around. Freeing his member from the thick material, he backed up until his legs hit the settee. He dipped his head to kiss her naked chest and stomach.

Then, as he fell back fully onto the seat, he dug his fingers beneath her heavy skirts. She gasped as his head pressed near her waist. He places kisses on the material, sending chills over her body in the form of worshiping caresses. She threaded her fingers in his hair.

Dougal groaned in desire. He tugged her petticoats off of her. As the material pooled on the floor, he ran his hands over her thighs. She swayed, growing weak with desire when he found her center heat, moist and ready for him. She moved against his hand.

"Come," he ordered. Pulling her forward, Dougal grabbed her about the waist. And after artfully arranging her skirt, he lowered her onto him. She moaned as they joined. Her knees pressed into the padded seat on either side of him.

Eagerly, he thrust. She arched as he filled her. His mouth found the peaks of her breasts as they bobbed enticingly before him. She ran her fingers through his hair, over the fine linen shirt covering his shoulders.

"Ride me," he said against her skin.

Instinctively, Isabel obeyed. She pushed up only to come back down on him. They were rewarded with a wave of pleasure. She grasped the back of the settee for support. They made love, hard and fast, the desperation of their situation driving them with a mad, fervent passion.

He helped to guide her hips. The sweet scent of roses surrounded him. He died within the folds of her arms, lived within the heat of her center. She was life to his unyielding death.

Their bodies moved in harmony until they met with a heated release. Dougal felt her tremble with climax. Their moans joined in a song of perfect completion. She fell weakly against him, and his body remained joined with hers.

He saw the torment in her eyes. It tore at him. The hotness of her breath hit his neck as she pressed her forehead against his shoulder. He cursed himself for his weakness. He should never have made love to her. It only compounded an already complicated situation.

※

In the aftermath of pleasure came the pain. Isabel had wanted desperately to feel him again. Her heart bubbled over with love. She didn't ever want to let go. As her mind deflected the sweetness of these emotions with logic, she couldn't allow herself to dwell on it.

Isabel couldn't say all that she wanted to. She was going to lose him. This was their moment—their one last moment together, and she would take all of it with her into a lonely future.

Angling his head, he tried to study her face. "Did I hurt you?"

"Hurt me?" she echoed. Slowly, she shook her head in denial. His tender concern washed over her, more painful than any physical torment. "No, you didn't hurt me."

"Then?" Dougal pulled her back. "Do you regret—"

"Don't say it." Isabel tried to smile and failed. She stood and righted her gown. "Never even think it. I regret nothing."

Dougal watched her before straightening his clothes. When she finished dressing, he was sitting calmly on the settee. Only his eyes gave away the tormented drowning of his heart.

"You should go to the forest," he said, as if lacking the ability to say anything else.

"Yes, the forest," she said, taking a deep breath.

"Isabel, you must remember what happened." Dougal stood, touching her face. "It could be important."

"I know," she answered a little too abruptly. "I'm going."

When he tried to speak again, she held up her hand to stop him. Patting his chest lightly as she passed, she left him without a backward glance.

The aftereffect of their shared passion still raged in her veins. Her legs felt weak, and everything in her begging her to return to his arms, to forget what she must do, to insist he choose her, stay with her. But that was something she would never do. Margaret needed him. And he needed to find Margaret. It was the only way to keep them safe.

25

Isabel stared gloomily at the path ahead of her. She tried to get the courage to go to the forest but hesitated every time she looked at the tree line. Glancing up, she didn't see the vicar until he was well upon her.

"Reverend Stillwell," Isabel greeted in surprise.

"Miss Drake," he acknowledged as he joined her. "You look lost."

"Just my soul," she muttered.

"Miss?"

"Nothing." Isabel tried in vain to smile. "What brings you for a visit?"

"I come to see Mr. Weston," the vicar said.

"You mean the Marquis of Rothfield?"

"Yes, yes. Quite right." The man gave her a sad smile.

"He's inside. The library, I believe. If the servants give you trouble at the front door, inform them I told you to meet me there." Isabel peered off into the distance, growing sick to her stomach at the very sight of the trees. The closer she'd walked to them, the stranger she felt. "Maybe I should take you."

The vicar nodded, seeing her agony.

"There is something I should discuss with you, being as we're the same." Isabel turned back toward the house. Her thoughts mocked her for her cowardice.

"The same?" he asked, curious.

"Yes, being as we both met with accidents and can now see ghosts."

"Ah, yes." The vicar nodded. "What is it you need to discuss?"

"I need your help." Looking at the sky and then the garden, she motioned her hand to the latter. "Do you mind speaking with me here before we go in?"

"No, not at all, Miss Drake."

Isabel changed course for the garden paths. "I'm supposed to join Dougal and his daughter. I can see both of them. The knight on the horse I told you about is protecting Margaret. He agrees that we should get them together to save them."

Isabel quickly explained what the knight had

said of his brother before adding, "So tonight I want you to bring Dougal here to the garden. I shall get his daughter. Together we will make them see each other."

"But they have never seen each other before, and surely they have crossed paths."

"It is possible," Isabel admitted. "But we must try. It's a place to start."

"All right," the vicar agreed. They quickly decided the best way to go about their joint task. When the last detail was in place, the vicar declared that they should inform Dougal at once. Isabel agreed, glancing guiltily toward the forest.

What harm is there in putting it off for another hour or so? she told herself.

As they made their way up the front steps, the vicar said, "You say little about what is between you and the marquis, yet when you say his name, your expression changes."

"You're too perceptive," Isabel said.

"A hazard of the profession, I'm afraid," he answered. "Do you love him?"

"I can't love him. He would never be free to leave here if I held him back. If he doesn't leave, he and Margaret's souls will be lost. I lose him either way. Only one of those ways I can live with, albeit barely."

"Not necessarily."

"I won't risk it. If it were only my life and soul at risk, then I would fight. But I cannot endanger theirs. I can't hold on to him." Isabel fought back the urge to cry as she remembered the tenderness of Dougal's touch. She would never know another like him—dead or alive.

"You would sacrifice your love for his soul?" the vicar questioned.

"Yes," she replied without thinking. "I don't want to speak about it. If I think I shall lose my nerve. Promise me you'll say nothing to him. Dougal believes that we're friends. I told him I don't love him."

"Did you convince him?"

"Yes," Isabel answered with a certainty she didn't feel. "When it's time, he will be ready to go. And we must let him. It's why you must be the one to get him to the garden. I won't allow myself to rethink my decision. If I am alone with him, I might not be able to complete my task."

"Very well, Miss Drake. I will do as you ask."

26

"You didn't go to the forest?" Dougal turned in frustration toward the vicar. "How could you keep her from going? She *must* remember."

"I'm right here," Isabel said. "I shall go later—tomorrow. Right now, we have to find a way to reunite you with your daughter. I've told the good vicar what has happened…"

Dougal raised a brow, glancing at the settee. Isabel blushed. The vicar watched the interaction, not commenting.

"…and he has agreed to help us," Isabel finished.

Dougal didn't answer. What could he say?

"This is what you've been waiting for," the vicar said. "A chance."

"You are interested in seeing your daughter, aren't you, my lord?" Isabel asked.

Dougal stiffened at her formal tone. Of course, he wanted to see his daughter. Margaret had been his whole reason for being. "Yes, Miss Drake. I'm most interested in seeing my daughter."

"Then it's settled." Isabel hid her eyes under the veil of her lashes. "At dusk, just as soon as the mist rises, I'll look for Sir Josiah and Margaret. You and the vicar will await my word."

Dougal watched Isabel. She peeked at him from the corner of her eye. The vicar added his instructions, but Dougal wasn't fully listening. When the vicar finished, Isabel and Dougal nodded dutifully.

They agreed to the plan, and the vicar took his leave, telling them he wanted to review his books for a clue as to how to reunite father and daughter.

❖

Isabel tugged her stole around her shoulders. She watched the mist from the front door, wishing it were already morning, and she'd completed her task. She hadn't seen Jane since her sister's arrival. No doubt Jane had spent the day attending her friends in the country. Isabel would have sought her out, but knew it was better if

Jane wasn't around until this was over. Isabel didn't know how even to begin to explain what they were doing.

"Isabel." Dougal joined her. He glanced over his shoulder at the cloaked vicar. The man held a book of prayers to his chest. Leaning over, he whispered into Isabel's ear, "Let me come with you."

"No," she said. "I might not be able to find her if you accompany me."

"I don't like you going out on your own with a demon out there feeding on souls." At her determined look, he nodded. "Take care. If you see the demon knight, run back here."

"I will." She managed a sad smile. To the vicar, she said, "The sun has been set for a while. Wait here on the steps. I'll send for you somehow."

The vicar nodded in agreement.

Isabel went down the front stairs and walked down the familiar path through the mist, hating each step. As her agitation mounted, her stride became faster until she was in the gardens.

"Josiah?" she called out softly. With wavering steps, she walked deeper into the mist, past the buds of summer flowers. Lightly, she touched a shrub, tracing the top as she moved past it. "Margaret?"

She received no answer.

Fog coated the pathway. Isabel shivered despite

the warm night. She hugged the stole tighter to her chest.

"Margaret," she called louder. "Won't you play with me?" She tilted her head and heard the soft pattering of feet running through the garden. Encouraged by the sound, she tried again. This time, she hummed the tune the girl liked. After a few bars, she listened. Following a moment of silence, Margaret's sweet voice rang out, finishing the song.

Searching the fog, Isabel whispered, "Margaret, come to see me. I want to talk to you."

"You said you wanted to play," the child sulked.

Isabel jerked in surprise. Twirling around, she confronted Margaret.

The child folded her little arms defiantly over her small, heaving chest. Her blonde ringlets sparkled with silvery threads, and her rosebud lips curled down in a pout. Her cheeks flushed with red as if she'd run a great distance. "I want to play. I never have anyone to play with me."

"We shall play, darling, but first, we must talk," Isabel said.

The girl smiled at the endearment as she moved forward, pacified by the promise. "Very well."

Margaret threaded her hand into Isabel's. The girl skipped more than strolled as she led Isabel away from the house. Isabel followed the child's lead. Margaret kicked at the mist, swirling it with her feet, commanding it with years of practice to dance in various directions.

When Isabel didn't speak, Margaret asked, "Are you to be my new mother?"

Isabel hesitated. How could the girl know her secret desire so easily? Isabel shook off her surprise before responding, "No, I'm not. Although I do want to speak to you about your parents."

Margaret let go of Isabel's arm. Sinking to the ground, she leaned her face close to the ground. She lightly petted the petals of a flower before smelling it.

"Namely, your father," Isabel said.

Margaret stiffened. She tilted her head but said nothing as she continued to examine the flower.

"Do you remember your father?" Isabel kneeled on the ground, lightly touching the girl's arm. "He misses you. He wants to see you."

Still, Margaret didn't move.

"Would you like to see him?" Isabel asked.

Leaving the bud intact, Margaret slowly stood, her eyes wide and frightened. "Is he angry with me for the fire?"

"No, no," Isabel reassured her, smoothing her hair. "He knows it's not your fault. He was never angry with you. He misses you. He's been searching for you for a long time."

"You've talked to him?"

"Yes," Isabel said. "And I was sent to help you find him. Would you like that?"

"Very much," Margaret said, still appearing unsure.

"Good. Now I can't promise you'll see him right away, but I won't give up until you do." Isabel stood and took Margaret's hand in hers. She turned directions and led her back toward the house.

"What will happen?" Margaret gazed trustingly at Isabel.

A change came over the girl's childlike features, as if they matured beyond her round-cheeked years. Isabel didn't want to think about it, but she had to answer the girl. "Hopefully, you'll both move on to a better place."

"Like heaven?" the girl asked.

"Yes, heaven," Isabel said. "I bet your mother is waiting for you."

"No," the child returned, matter-of-factly. "She won't be."

"Still, you must want to go to heaven. I hear it's a beautiful place."

"I suppose I must." The child didn't sound too excited by the idea.

"What is it? Are you frightened?"

"Not really," Margaret said. "I never got to live. I have been stuck all these years as a child, but I don't feel like a child anymore. Well, sometimes I do. But mostly I don't. Do you think I will have to remain a child in heaven?"

"I couldn't say."

"Are you like an angel? Could you make me real again?" Margaret inquired with a hopeful smile.

The question broke Isabel's heart. "No, I cannot."

"That is what Josiah said." Margaret's green eyes lost some of their shine. "There is so much I want to do."

"Like what?"

"I want to grow up and go to a ball. I want to wear a beautiful silk gown covered in jewels. I want to be asked to dance. I want to play the piano again and sing for an audience. I want to…to have a…"

"What?" All the things Isabel took for granted, this child had never gotten the chance to do. Margaret had spent the last half of a century dreaming about what she'd missed.

"I want a gentleman to call on me. Not now," Margaret stated with a look of disgust down at her body, "but when I look as old as I feel to be. And I want a wedding—a big wedding here in the garden with lots of cake and white doves."

"I think that would be a fine thing to have."

"There's so much." Sadly, the child shook her head. It was impossible to list them all. "Plays, operas, travel. I've had many years to think about it. It's not fair. Why did that man have to come to my room?"

Isabel remembered too well the girl's burnt flesh.

Margaret saw her expression and smiled. "It's all right. Sir Josiah has told me all about it."

Isabel continued escorting her toward the house.

"Oh!" Margaret gasped suddenly. "I will get to say goodbye to Josiah, won't I?"

"Um, possibly." Isabel hadn't thought about it. "Where is he?"

"In the garden." Margaret pulled away from Isabel and ran. "I shall fetch him."

"Margaret, wait," Isabel cried, hurrying after the child.

"I'll meet you by the stone bench," the girl yelled before disappearing into the mist.

Isabel searched the mist, but the child was gone. She made her way to the front of the house. Dougal, seeing her, hurried forward. His eyes scanned the immediate area, anxious to find his daughter. Not seeing her, he asked, "Where?"

"She's not here," Isabel answered. His expression fell in disappointment, and she quickly added, "But I'll take you to meet her. She went to find Sir Josiah first."

"Is she…?" Dougal began, unable to finish. His voice trailed off into a tortured breath.

"She's fine." Seeing the raw emotion on Dougal's face, Isabel knew she was doing the right thing. Unable to help herself, she threaded her arm into his and led him into the gardens. She felt him tremble. Patting his arm lightly, she motioned for the vicar to follow. The man silently acknowledged her and kept several paces behind.

"Isabel…" Dougal studied her. The moonlight gleamed on his dark hair. The queue in back pulled the locks neatly from his handsome face. She refrained from lifting her fingers to touch his cheek, able to see the dimple forming in her mind's eye.

"You don't have to say it. I already know."

"What?" he questioned. "What do you know?"

"You wish to thank me for helping you." She looked away, torn between the need to memorize every line of his face and the need to escape the pain his leaving would cause her. No matter what, she knew his image was burned into her soul.

"There is more," he whispered, "that I would say to you."

"There is no need, Dougal. We are friends. There is no ill will between us. And I'm glad that I can help you with this. I only hope that it works."

"Yes, friends."

The word hardly seemed adequate to describe what she felt.

His hand covered hers, and he squeezed gently. "Whatever happens, I know that you've tried. And for that, I thank you."

"Maybe someday, many years from now, I'll see you again. Only, you must remember me young, for then I'll be an old woman, and you might not recognize me."

"It would not matter," he choked out.

"Then I expect to see you the second I get to heaven." The command of her voice hid the agony she was feeling.

"It's a promise," he returned. "I will throw a grand ball for you, and we will dance over the clouds. It will be the angelic event of the century."

Isabel laughed. It was a nice dream—one she could spend a lifetime picturing. Truthfully, she knew she would probably never see him again, not even after death. For who knew what was to come for any of them?

Isabel realized they were nearing the stone

bench. Letting go of Dougal's arm, she motioned him forward. "We're to meet them here."

"Do you see her?" the vicar asked, coming forward to join the couple.

"Not yet." Isabel tried to smile, but it was a weak attempt. "No, wait. I see her coming."

Isabel watched as Margaret joined them, dragging Josiah by the hand. The knight nodded in greeting but said nothing. His features were drawn and tight.

Dougal stared at Isabel's face. Following her eyes, he scanned the distance. "Is she here?"

Isabel frowned, realizing he couldn't see her.

"What's happening?" Margaret stopped in front of Isabel. She let go of Josiah to place her hands on her hips. "He decided he didn't want to come, didn't he?"

"No, that's—" Isabel began.

"It's not her?" Dougal sounded discouraged.

"She'll come," the vicar said.

"Yes." Isabel agreed.

"Then he doesn't wish to see me." Margaret looked in horror at Josiah. "I told you he's still angry about the fire."

"Nay." Josiah lifted a hand to comfort her. "The fire was not your doing."

Holding up her hands, Isabel demanded, "Wait. Everyone stop talking."

All eyes turned to her. Margaret sniffled.

"Don't cry, Margaret," Isabel soothed. Josiah and Dougal began talking at once.

"What is happening, m'lady?" Josiah inquired.

"What is wrong?" Dougal demanded. Loudly, he shouted, "Margaret! Margaret, can you hear me!"

"The marquis—" Josiah continued.

"Quiet," Isabel snapped. "I can't think with all of you talking at once."

The men instantly quieted. Isabel took a deep breath. Turning to the vicar, she asked, "Can you at least see them?"

"No." Reverend Stillwell shook his head. "I see us three."

"Everyone is here." Isabel pointed as she spoke. "Margaret and Sir Josiah, Father Stillwell and the marquis."

Isabel reached out to Margaret. The girl took her hand. Turning to Dougal, she lifted his hand in her other palm. Bring her hands together, she asked, "Can you feel that? Your hands are touching."

"Is this a game?" Margaret asked.

"No, Margaret, this is not a game," Isabel answered.

Dougal concentrated on where Margaret stood, even though he couldn't see his daughter.

"Can you feel each other?" Isabel asked.

Both shook their heads. Dougal's eyes bore forward, and she knew he willed his daughter to appear.

"Reverend?" Isabel asked helplessly. She pulled at her hands, trying to force the two of them together. Though they were solid to her touch, they drifted through each other like air. To Josiah, she asked, "What do we do?"

The knight peered at her hands and frowned. He shook his head to indicate he had no answers.

The vicar began to chant behind her. She couldn't understand the Latin words he read from his book. Keeping quiet, she glanced from Dougal to his daughter. A soft glow came over their faces. Isabel glanced from one to the other.

Isabel dropped their hands and stumbled back, waiting for them both to disappear. Her lungs heaved for breath, and her heart pounded terribly. Soon it would be over, she told herself. This was it. They were moving on.

27

Dougal saw an image waver before him. Margaret's small body became outlined as if by a million little stars. Its radiance spread around him. Isabel's hands fell away. He kept his hand outstretched, afraid to move. Flesh formed in his palm, molding into fingers.

Green eyes appeared where there had been nothing. The vicar's words continued, fading softly against the blood rushing in Dougal's ears. Seeing the yellow gown he'd bought fifty years ago in Paris, he fell to his knees.

The girl wasn't as quick to recognize him. She blinked heavily, confused by what she saw.

"Margaret," he whispered, not daring to release her hand. He needed to touch her, to confirm that she was real.

Hearing her name, Margaret threw herself into his arms and began to cry.

Dougal held his daughter to his chest, smiling gratefully at Isabel.

The vicar took Isabel's arm as his words stuttered to a finish.

"Goodbye," Isabel whispered.

A moment passed and then another. Dougal and Margaret remained in the garden, not ascending to their next plane of existence.

"Why are they not going?" Isabel asked the vicar. "What's wrong?"

"I don't know," the vicar mumbled, turning to his book. He leafed through it.

Dougal whispered several declarations of love to his daughter. Margaret smiled, returning his sentiments. Gripping Margaret's hand, he stood. That is when he noticed the tall man watching them.

"Father." Margaret jumped in excitement. "Can you see him now? This is Josiah."

"Sir Josiah," Dougal acknowledged, holding his hand out to the knight. Josiah shook it. "Thank you for looking after my daughter. I'm eternally in your debt."

Isabel faced the vicar and placed her hand on his book to get his attention. "What happened? Why are they still here?"

"I don't understand it. I was sure this would be all they needed." The reverend scratched his head. Closing the book, he lowered it to his side. "Maybe they were meant to avenge their deaths. Though it does not make much sense. Usually—"

"No, they have to leave. Please, this suffering can't be drawn out any longer," Isabel insisted.

"Can we all play now?" Margaret asked. "All of us?"

Isabel ignored the girl. To Dougal, she asked, "Why are you still here? It's not safe."

"I don't know," he answered. It was a lie. He did know. He was there to be with her. He hugged his daughter to his waist, happy to have found her.

"Dougal," Isabel said. "You must leave. Take her and go!"

"Don't you want us here?" Margaret asked.

Isabel tried to control her shaking. Seeing she frightened the child, she said, "Yes, but—"

"Maybe this is heaven," Margaret said innocently. "I almost feel as if I'm in heaven."

Dougal frowned. He would have thought Isabel would've been happy to have him stay.

"Dougal," Isabel pleaded. She came close to him, keeping her tone soft so Margaret wouldn't hear her. "You must go. Your work here is finished."

"I cannot." He saw the torture of his soul

mirrored in her gaze.

"There is nothing to keep you here," Isabel insisted.

Josiah bowed behind them, turning to leave. Margaret let go of her father, running to the man to give him a big hug. She begged Josiah to stay with them.

Dougal glanced after her to make sure she was all right. He didn't want Margaret out of his sight, but he also didn't want the child to overhear his conversation with Isabel.

"You are keeping me here," Dougal whispered.

"No, don't say such things. You must not think that," Isabel said. He lifted his arms to hold her. She pulled back. "Save yourself. Save your daughter. You're done here."

"Maybe I'm meant to help you."

"I don't need your help. You must go. We'll deal with the demon once you're safe," she pleaded. "Josiah and I and the vicar will take care of it. Your duty is to protect Margaret. Please, you must let go of this world."

"I can't leave." Dougal cupped her cheek. "I'm in love with you."

"No, you're not. You're grateful to me." Closing her eyes, she lied, "I don't love you. I love Edward. We shall be married. So you see, there is nothing for you at Rothfield Park."

"No, you're not in love with him. You can't be."

"Leave," she ordered weakly. She was quickly losing the fight. "Take Margaret and—"

"I'm not leaving." Dougal's lips twitched at the corner. She looked at his mouth as if she would kiss him. Only Margaret's interruption pulled them back to their senses.

"We don't have to go, do we?" Margaret asked. "I don't want to go."

"No, we're not leaving," Dougal stated, not taking his eyes from Isabel. Her lips worked in protest, but his determined look stopped her from speaking. She might deny her feelings, but his affections had to be founded since he still stood before her.

Dougal had felt the pull of something greater the instant he held Margaret. And though his head told him to go, to protect her, his heart had chosen otherwise. And so they stayed.

Glancing down at his daughter as she tugged on his hand, Dougal said, "I wish to stay here also. There is much we need to do."

"Can we go inside now?" Margaret inquired happily. She grinned at Isabel. Isabel stood helpless against their decision. She looked from father to daughter and then back again.

"Yes," Dougal said, "we most certainly can go

inside. It's our home."

And without another word to Isabel or the vicar, he swung his daughter into his arms and carried her joyfully toward the house.

※

"Will she be my new mother then?" Isabel heard Margaret ask her father. The child's happy laughter rang over the yard. Margaret certainly was single-minded.

Although Isabel's ears strained, she couldn't hear Dougal's reply. She silently watched until they disappeared. Looking around, she realized the vicar had left.

"'Twas a good thing you did this eve, m'lady," Josiah said. "A very good thing, indeed."

"What now?" she asked. "They're still here. Your brother still looks for them."

"I know naught, m'lady. Methought it would work to bring them together. But, maybe, their work is not done."

"Vengeance," Isabel determined darkly. "It must be that they seek vengeance. It's the only reasonable answer."

"Perchance." Josiah bowed before fading into the night, leaving her to wonder at his ominous mood.

28

THE NIGHT PASSED TOO QUICKLY, but with more happiness and joy than either Dougal or Margaret could have imagined. They did not rest. Their bodies didn't need it. Margaret chattered incessantly about all she had seen—only darkening when she told her father of her death, but the mood didn't last long when she again turned to happier things.

Dougal was amazed at the changes in his daughter. The years hadn't aged her sweet, innocent face, but they had educated her mind beyond her years. Except for the occasional wish for her mother's presence, she didn't appear to be the same girl he'd lost.

Dougal noticed that many of her tales concerned Sir Josiah. And, although he knew he owed the man much for rescuing and caring for his daughter, jealousy seethed every time Margaret mentioned her hero. Worse than the jealousy was the self-loathing that it should have been he who had saved and protected her all these years.

❦

Isabel stayed away, going to bed although she wasn't tired. Her mind raced, trying to find ways to make Dougal and Margaret understand that they must leave. All the time, she knew that they wouldn't listen to her. No, the only way was to make Dougal understand that he must not wait for her. She was living. He was dead, and there was no hope of it being otherwise. She wouldn't kill herself to join him. Suicide wasn't an option, for if she committed that gravest of sins, her soul would be lost forever.

If the demon knight didn't consume his soul, Dougal would have to wait until she died. And if she grew to be an old woman, it would be torture to look at his eternally youthful face and see her reflection wrinkling and deteriorating next to it. She couldn't bear to see his admiration fade with her beauty.

As the morning dawned, Isabel was still awake. Wearily, she pulled herself from the bed, dragging her feet while she dressed slowly. She chose an empire waist gown of light blue linen with a dark sash and a matching stole of cream lace. Her hair took more time, as the dark locks didn't readily obey her fingers. Finally, she managed to get the unruly tresses into a suitable coiffure adorned with a silver clip her sister had given her.

As she opened the door to the library, Dougal smiled happily at her before turning to look out the window. Isabel came up beside him, placing her arm naturally next to his on the windowsill as she leaned toward the garden. Margaret was picking flowers, stopping to wave at her father to make sure he was watching her.

"She appears happy," Isabel said. Realizing her nearness to Dougal, she leaned away to put distance between them.

"Yes," he agreed. She could feel the tension between them.

Her mouth became dry. "I think you should go."

He didn't answer her at first. He refused to let go of his feelings. Finally, he stated, "No."

"Don't stay out of misguided gratitude or duty," she whispered. "You owe me nothing. I expect nothing."

"How can you say that after what I did to you?" he asked.

"You did nothing."

"I took your," Dougal paused, then finished weakly, "your maidenhead."

She had the feeling that he had wanted to say something else.

"Yes, you did," Isabel said. Stepping away, she added, "But I gave it to you freely. The loss of it's my own doing, my lord."

"My lord," he grumbled bitterly.

"What?"

"Then if you care nothing for your reputation—" Dougal stopped, realizing how ridiculous he was being. Things like reputation didn't pertain here.

Isabel realized it too. "What would you do to redeem mine? Marry me?"

His eyes narrowed at her voice. She watched him skeptically.

"Dougal, I'm fine. Aside from your sense of honor—"

His scowl stopped her words. All his honor and pride shone in his expression, mixed with helplessness. She saw his good breeding, the dignity and nobility he still carried. He took a deep breath before trusting himself to speak.

"Yes," he said. "I have honor. I may be dead, but I have honor. It's one of the few things I still possess in this world. Don't scoff at it."

"I—"

"What is stopping you from admitting you care for me?"

"Edward—"

"No!" Dougal seethed. "Don't say you love Edward. We both know it's a lie. Edward married your sister. He's just an excuse to hide your feelings." His fingers curled into a fist.

Isabel froze in mortification. It had never occurred to her that he would know.

"So I ask again. What is keeping you from caring for me?" Dougal came around the desk as she backed away.

"I'm alive," she whimpered. This man before her wasn't what she was used to. Never had Dougal acted so forcefully. She could see it in his eyes and feel it sparking off his skin like fire. "And you're not. What other reason is there?"

"And yet here we are."

"What do you think will happen when it's discovered I'm speaking to you? My family will have me committed. Or would you have me kill myself to be with you?" she demanded. Tormented, she lifted her hand weakly to him. She wanted him. She couldn't deny it, couldn't hide her feelings.

"No," he said. "I would never ask that."

"You were married once," she said, desperate

to change the subject. "Don't you want to join your wife?"

"Marianna is not my wife. The vows I swore ended with death."

"And what of love? Does it end with death?" she asked.

"You surely know that marriage and love rarely have anything to do with each other. My marriage was arranged. I met her for the first time a week before our vows. She was a terrible mother, an unfaithful wife, and an untrustworthy friend. She was vulgar and vain. There is nothing I miss about that woman. Margaret was the only thing of worth that came from her and leaving us was her only kind act."

"Oh," Isabel said. "Why are we even discussing this? You have completed that which you were meant to do. You found Margaret. You found your daughter. And now it's time for you to move on. You have to go. If you stay here, you'll be killed —*again*. I don't know how else to say it. The knight is after you. Don't you understand?" As his expression softened, she laid a hand on his cheek and ventured, "Don't you realize you have to move on?"

"I won't leave you to face him alone. I'm not a coward," he answered.

"I know you're not. It has taken bravery to be

as you have—alone for so long." She let her hand fall to her side, but she didn't back away.

"One does what one must," he said in return. "Do not ask me to be a coward."

"It's not cowardice, but prudence that I ask of you," she entreated. "What of your duty to Margaret?"

"Margaret is now a grown woman," Dougal said thickly, the words sounding strange in his ears. "She's still my daughter, but not as I knew her. I have truly lost my little girl and have gained a mature woman. The years have passed knowledge to her. She knows what is out there. It's also her decision to stay, and it's her decision that I must also respect. Out of anyone, her life was cut the shortest. She has lost the most."

But how do you—?" Isabel's voice trailed off.

"Have you been to the forest?" he asked pointedly. "I thought not. I shall make you a deal, Isabel. If you go now, right now, straightway to the forest and try to remember what happened to you—"

"But—"

"No, listen." Dougal lowered his face close to hers. As he spoke, his words brushed in whispers across her cheek to her neck. Isabel shivered. In a low tone, he continued as if she hadn't interrupted him. "If you go, I shall leave if you ask me to, but you must try to remember what happened to you."

"It may be nothing," she protested, not wanting to admit her fear. She could feel her body weakening to him. She could feel the pulse in her throat quicken. Her knees became like water. Swaying, she looked away. "I don't see why you all fuss about the forest."

"It may very well be nothing," he admitted. His lips brushed the side of her cheek. Despite what he'd said, she could see that he knew. Bringing his lips to hers, he whispered, "Something happened to you. You must discover what it was."

"You know, don't you?" she said in amazement. She jerked her head back when he tried to kiss her. "You know what I saw that day. You know why I have forgotten it. Tell me."

"No," he said sharply.

"But you know what happened. Tell me."

"You must see for yourself."

"Are you trying to hurt me?" she inquired in growing apprehension. "Am I to be punished?"

"How can you even ask that?" He pushed his fingers through his hair in frustration. "No. I don't send you to get hurt, merely to remember what you have forgotten."

"All right," she said at length. "I shall go, but as

soon as we learn what happened to me, you have to leave Rothfield Park. Forever."

"If you ask me to leave you, then I shall go."

Isabel studied him for a moment, her heart breaking. She bowed her head and then moved to leave. His hand on her arm stopped her.

"Oh, and Isabel…"

"Wha—" Isabel gasped,

Dougal swung her around on her heels. Instantly, his lips sought her mouth tenderly. His hands went to her jaw, the fingers spilling roughly over her neck and ears.

Isabel moaned, her hands crawling unbidden to his neck to explore. Dougal brusquely pulled her head away. She moaned in protest, and her hands dropped to his chest. Her fingers centered over the beat of his heart. When he was with her, he felt so real, and Isabel could almost forget what she needed to make him do. She could see the passion in his eyes, the longing he didn't try to hide from her.

"Now, go," he murmured, turning back to watch Margaret. "All of our futures could depend upon it."

29

Margaret made her way happily over the garden paths. She smiled with dreamlike abandonment as she again looked up at the window. Giving her father a jaunty wave, she skipped around a shrub out of his view. She began to run through her familiar playground only to skid to a stop. Her smile faltered. A change came over her features, the innocence of play fading from her eyes to be replaced by wisdom.

"Josiah," she whispered. Her bright eyes watched him somberly. "I'm so glad you've come back."

"Yea, child, I told you I would never leave you," he whispered. A cheerless expression fanned over his face. "How fares your father?"

"He is good," she acknowledged. She had long

noticed the sadness in him over the years when he would watch her play. Recently, his sorrow had become more intense and more frequent. Crossing over to him, she lifted her hand to him. Josiah sank to his knees. Margaret's fingers went to his cheek. Her small hand barely covered it as she patted him lightly. "I am nearly fifty-nine years of age, and I wish that I looked at least twenty."

Josiah studied her childish rounded face. However, her eyes held more knowledge than the lines of her complexion should have allowed. She was right. She was an old woman trapped within the spirit of a child. Only sometimes did her innocence take over her, compelling her to laugh and run. It was the only time she found any peace. At other times, she would cry—wretched, frustrated tears at her ensnarement. He'd once stopped her from trying to tear out her gentle locks and mar her beautiful face.

Josiah patted her hand in a loving caress. If he closed his eyes and listened to her voice, he could imagine her older. However, he knew of her as a child, and the image he carried could never be. Opening his eyes, he managed a smile for her. Yet he didn't kiss her. He never kissed her—not since the day he'd found her spirit wandering the garden, alone and scared. Then she'd been a girl, and he'd kissed her forehead in comfort.

Margaret breathed slowly before nodding. They never spoke of what they felt. For in a small part of them, they knew it wasn't right—that it wasn't meant to be. She dropped her hand, stepping away from him.

Over the long and twisted years, they were companions. They knew each other, understood each other. They discussed books, read plays, and sang songs—old ballads he remembered from his youth. When they were together, alone and buried from the world, they were happy. But then the happiness faded to be replaced by Margaret's frustrated tears, and Josiah would tell her to go and play—bidding her run in the garden so she may forget her torment for a while.

"Why have you not moved on?" he asked at last.

"I couldn't." Tears filled her eyes. She turned away from him. Pressing her small childlike hands to her chest, she seethed in anger. She hated her hands, hated her body. She hated being caged in innocence. If she could rip her limbs from her torso, she would have. "I couldn't leave you to face—"

"Nay," he commanded. "Don't even think it!"

"Josiah," she pleaded softly. "Please—"

"Nay, m'lady." He clutched his chest. The gaping hole over his heart had begun to open and seep. Josiah fell to his knees. Her lips worked as if she would speak. No sound escaped her. Shaking, she went to him. She tried to run her fingers through his hair. He pushed her back. Through blue lips, he gruffly ordered her, "Run!"

"I won't leave you," she denied in agitation.

"He's coming," Josiah gasped. Falling onto his back, he writhed in agony. His body thrashed violently upon the dirt. His muscles strained as he struck his own chest.

Margaret still didn't run. She watched helplessly as the man she loved folded in on himself. She saw the death coming to his pallid features. The fine mist invaded the daylight, curling like a smoking fire. Drawing near him, she held his hand tightly. Through her tears, she whispered, "I will never leave you."

"Go!" Josiah agonized over the bittersweet joy of her words. He drank in her comfort but couldn't endure losing her to save himself. His dark eyes filled with pain, looking past her head. Feebly, he managed, "Margaret, 'tis too late. He's here."

30

Isabel took a deep breath as she faced the forest. Leaning over, she patted her mare's tan coat. She rode bareback. It was the way she preferred, and if she ever were to have an accident, it would be on one of her wild rides of anger.

The mare became skittish. It pawed the ground as she slowly directed it into the trees. The animal's head nodded in agitation, pulling against its reins. Isabel didn't let the beast turn back. Nudging the horse in the flanks, she forced it slowly forward.

As she crossed over the threshold toward the stream, a fine mist showered from the sky, instantly fogging the pathway. Isabel fanned her arm before her, trying to clear the air and see where the mare instinctively led her.

Without warning, the horse sped up. Isabel

pulled frantically on the reins. The mare however ran faster, its hooves pounding hectically on the ground. Her heartbeat thundered in her ears, the only sound in the mist. She'd wanted to take the journey steady and slow. The mare didn't let her. Falling forward, she lost the thin straps of leather and was forced to grab the animal's mane to keep from tumbling off its back.

Suddenly, the horse's hooves skidded to a nervous stop. Before her eyes, the mist grew. It expanded and thickened until she could no longer see the trees in front of her. The pathway disappeared, claiming her feet with it.

Isabel felt as if she were possessed. Her body acted on instinct, pulled through her frantic motions like a puppet. Her eyes rounded in terror. Her head snapped to one side and then another, controlled by a will outside herself. The water grew louder until she could no longer tell from which direction it came. She was lost, and she was helpless to stop what was happening.

The palfrey turned around as she led it with possessed hands. An unseen force urged it to move forward. At first, the mare resisted, pawing the ground. However, the desire to run became strong, and the mare took off.

Isabel gripped its mane. Suddenly, her possession lifted, and she could again control her arms.

She lay down close to the horse's tan back, willing it to gallop home. She changed her mind. She didn't want to discover what had happened to her. She could feel that she wasn't alone anymore.

The fog thickened, growing heavy on her limbs. The horse's movements became slow and cautious, and she hugged the mare's neck. The animal's ears twitched to attention, and its head bobbed in agitation.

Isabel trembled. The flesh on her neck prickled. She hugged closer to the skittish horse. She could feel the animal's hot, sweaty flesh pressing into her gown. The white fog blinded her to the distance. A tree limb appeared close to her face. She jolted in surprise.

And then she heard singing, the sweet, haunted song of a child's voice, echoing in the trees. It started behind her, but the bearer of the sound ran through the mist, gaining on her. As the horse moved faster, it was beside them, keeping pace.

"Play," the child whispered near her ear.

"Margaret!" Isabel screamed. She recognized the child's voice. Tears poured over Isabel's cheeks. She bit her lip to keep from crying out in panic. The fog became so dense she couldn't see her hands on the mane.

"Play," the voice demanded again.

"Margaret?" She felt the mare shake and jolt

with each ring of laughter, each start of an eerie ballad. "What are you doing here? Run home to your father. It's not safe here!"

Suddenly, the laughing turned to crying. The mist seemed to press into Isabel's skin. She breathed it into her lungs like the smoke from a fire. Her skin burned. Coughing, she wheezed, unable to catch her breath. Her fingers released the mane to pry at her throat. She was choked by fear. Tearing at her neckline, she fought for breath.

"I want to play with you," Margaret called out sulkily. The sounds of her words rang hollow, and Isabel recognized the roaring of fire. She'd heard it when Margaret had died in her arms. Isabel coughed harder, desperate to escape the fog. Sweetly, the girl asked, "Are you my mother? Are you the girl from my bedchamber?"

"No!" Isabel yelled. She kicked her horse in the ribs, urging it forward. She felt the dark presence with her, taunting her. Frantically, she urged, "Margaret, run. Find Josiah!"

The horse raced faster. Isabel saw a hand shoot out from the fog, trying to stop her. The masculine fingers reached for the reins. She saw the ruffling of a shirt.

"Dougal," Isabel screamed, reaching for him, but the mare was too fast. Isabel grabbed for the reins, sitting up as she searched for them. She glanced behind for Dougal. There was nothing but mist all around.

With a frightened pant, she righted herself. They had to be nearing the end of the trail. Her fingers found the mane, but as she looked forward, a branch materialized out of the fog. Isabel's eyes didn't have time to focus. The thick limb struck her across the forehead, knocking her back with a sharp crack. Her eyes filled with blackness. Her head hit the jolting movements of the galloping rump. Her feet loosened their hold, and she flipped over the back of the horse. As her head struck the earth, the blackness faded, and the white mist turned to an enveloping bright light.

Isabel lay stunned on the ground. Her temple throbbed violently. She couldn't move her limbs. She was frozen. Only her lungs clamored noisily for breath as the mist dissipated and cleared.

"Get up!" Margaret's command came from the side.

Blinking slowly, Isabel glanced around the brightness while it faded and dimmed until finally, she found herself lying on the forest floor, surrounded by the normal look of trees. It was as if the mist hadn't been there at all.

"Hurry," Margaret commanded again. The child leaned over her. "Get up before he comes for you. Go!"

Isabel tried to speak, but she only gurgled a strange sound. Her body burned and ached, and her neck felt as if it had snapped. She couldn't move.

Margaret, panicking, looked down the path. Isabel realized her horse had continued without her.

"Get up now," the girl screamed in terror. Agitating her hands, she began to vanish.

Isabel convulsed, imagining how scared she must have been the first time this happened. She lay, looking up at the trees, wondering what was to happen next. She twitched her little finger. The feeling slowly returned to her hands.

From behind her head, she heard the crunching of footsteps on the forest floor. Isabel sighed with relief; sure she was to be rescued. The footfall grew louder. She heard sinister laughter behind her head. Isabel choked on her terror. She couldn't see the man who laughed, but she knew who it might be. The creepiness of his tone washed over her, prickling her skin.

Suddenly, the malevolent beast-dog stood over her—snarling viciously. Isabel willed herself into the ground as it neared her face. She recognized the animal from Margaret's room. It could only mean the beast's evil master was there too.

Does the demon come for me as he did for Margaret? she wondered in horror.

Isabel blinked, unable to turn her head away as the dog's foul breath wafted into her nose. The mist poured from his nostrils, suffocating her. Her throat tightened, and she couldn't scream. Her pulsed hammered violently. The heated fog came from the dog's mouth as the animal barked, hitting her skin in blistering surges. Appallingly long fangs bit through the air, inches from her nose. Spit flew from its mouth, splattering her face with the foul substance.

And still, Isabel couldn't move to fight the beast off. She could barely lift more than the tips of her fingers. All she could do was lie motionless while the animal decided whether or not to devour her.

Her lips trembled, but she couldn't yell.

"Back," came a guttural order. The beast did not obey.

The dog's dark eyes began to radiate a fiery red and orange. Looking into their barren depths, Isabel could see a black eternity within the animal's deadly gaze. It wanted to devour her soul. She felt herself being pulled into the void. She felt the pain of worlds colliding. She felt the death of millions living forever within the fiendish beast. It wasn't a dog that stood above her. It was a demon, a portal into hell.

Within demonic eyes, she saw what torment and anguish could be. The beast had no mercy, no feeling or heart. It exploited every fear of his victim, used it, magnified it, and fed off it until the soul was completely drained into nothingness.

Isabel's heart pounded loudly in fear, ringing in her head as her eardrums began to bleed from the loudness of the barks. Blood trickled from her ears, her throat, her nose, her eyes, pouring over her, mixing with the animal's slobber. The beast wanted her. It had come to scoop up her soul, and she knew that she couldn't resist. It wanted her to join in the agony.

Isabel coughed in protest, the force lifting her shoulders from the ground in a shallow jerk. It was a faint sound, but it drew the beast back. Her body was trying to hold on to life. The pain was unbearable.

"Back," the dog's commander ordered viciously. The animal crouched away, snarling lowly. She felt the coolness of air bathing her skin, drying the saliva from her flesh.

Isabel saw the demon knight before her, his face hidden behind his helmet. His eyes were swallowed up by blackness, and though she couldn't see his mouth beneath a plate of metal, she felt as if he smiled at her. There was no joy in his pleasure as he leaned closer to her face.

"Where is the child?" he asked. His tone rumbled as if impeded by gravel. A gauntlet clad hand reached to touch her cheek in a caress that belied tenderness.

"No," Isabel muttered. "You...have...to kill me first."

The man chuckled, unamused by her show of bravery.

"Do not fret, little one," he whispered. Lifting his fingers to his nose, he smelled her blood. The black, soulless gaze glossed over until it shone like polished metal. "I will come for you soon enough when you're ready. Right now, I want the girl. Where is she?"

"I do...not...know." Isabel felt some of her strength returning. Yet, even in her strongest days, aided by numerous weapons, she couldn't have thwarted the creature before her.

"Then that is your misfortune," the demon answered. His gauntlet hand slipped beneath her head to lift her to meet his face. He pressed himself next to her cheek. She felt the spiked plates of his helmet against her skin, scratching her as he spoke. Isabel moaned as she felt herself sucked into the bewitching spell of his heated body. Within his hold, there was no escape.

31

Dougal frowned. He looked out onto the gold-tinted garden. The sun had journeyed over the blue sky, working its way toward a gentle evening. He couldn't see Margaret. He waited for her to emerge from the pathways hidden from his view.

Loath to leave the library in case one of them returned, Dougal reminded himself that Margaret had changed from the child he once knew. She looked the same, down to each dimple and fluttering eyelash, but inside she was grown. He'd noticed it the moment he'd sat her down to talk.

Sighing resolutely, Dougal turned from the windowpane and grabbed his jacket off the nearby chair. He couldn't abide waiting much longer. Isabel had been gone nearly an hour, and his daughter a bit longer than that. His first impulse had been to run after Margaret and to scold her, but he knew that she wouldn't take kindly to him treating her like a child, as she'd been willing to point out to him each time he'd tried. He'd forbidden her from leaving his side until she'd laughed playfully and told him not to be foolish.

"I have lived in this world longer than you." Margaret had chuckled impishly. "And I know more of it than you. I shall come back to you with the dusk."

Reluctantly, Dougal had agreed.

Knowing Margaret should be able to find him anywhere, Dougal determined to walk to the forest in search of Isabel. She was gone far too long.

Reaching for the library door, he pulled it open as he shrugged his jacket onto his shoulders. Looking up, he gasped. Isabel stood before him silently staring at where the doorknob had been. He wondered how long she had been there.

"Isabel," Dougal said.

Oh no, he thought to himself. *I have pushed her too far.*

❀

Isabel blinked at the sound of Dougal's voice. Her eyes moved to his face, staring blindly at him. She knew he was there; she looked at him; her gaze traveled over his familiar features, but she didn't really see him—couldn't comprehend what he was doing before her.

"Isabel?" This time there was panic in his voice. His fingers hesitated near her cheek.

His face slowly swam in Isabel's vision. Her body ached from her fall. Her mind stung from the demon man's probing eyes. Yet, even as she thought of it, the distinct lines of the evil knight's face blurred as Dougal's manifested in his place.

Flinching as Dougal moved to touch her, she leaned back. He dropped his hand.

"Isabel," he whispered. "Can you hear me?"

Lethargically, she stepped around him, coming into the library. She stared at the fireplace—unable to feel its heat from across the room. A chill worked over her body. Dougal didn't reach for her again. Quietly, he shut the door before coming around to look at her ashen face.

Isabel didn't take her gaze away from the flame. Almost soundlessly, she murmured, "I fell."

"Isabel?" he inquired, desperately wanting her attention.

"I had an accident." She blinked, the fire reminding her of the dog. The image tried to fade from her mind. She let it go. "My horse threw me. I walked back from the forest."

"Isabel, that was a year ago," Dougal said.

"No, it just happened. Could you fetch a physician? My head hurts." Finally, she glanced at him.

"No, it was a year ago." Dougal turned from her and crossed over to the viscount's chair. Grabbing the London paper off the small table, he brought it to her. "Here, look at the paper. Read the date."

"But…" Isabel started weakly. She took the paper with a trembling hand. Shaking her head in confusion, she read, "July the second, eighteen hundred and thirteen."

"Isabel," Dougal said when she continued to stare absentmindedly at the print.

Isabel's gaze darted to him. She dropped the paper. It fluttered noisily to the floor, and she backed away. "No. It can't be. What is going on?"

"You had an accident a year ago," Dougal said patiently.

"No, it just now happened," she explained. Swallowing, she tasted blood on her lips. Reaching her fingers to her mouth, she drew them away. They were smeared with crimson. "What are you trying to do to me?"

"Isabel." He made a move to hold her.

"No," she shrieked, holding up her bloodied hand to keep him back. "Stay away from me. You're confused."

"Think, Isabel. *Reason.* Why do you think

you're never hungry?" he asked gently. "When is the last time you talked to anyone but us spirits?"

"Charlotte," she put forth vaguely.

"Charlotte is a servant who worked here nearly a hundred years ago. She only materializes when you require her. All she remembers is how to serve as she did in life. She appeared to me soon after you," Dougal explained. Isabel could see the truth in his eyes but was unwilling to believe it. "She takes care of many here at the manor—many we cannot see."

"Stillwell?" she mumbled.

"Yes," Dougal said.

"No," she said weakly in protest.

"Isabel," he reasoned. "How is it everything you look for is right where you would have it? When is the last time you had to search for anything—a hair ribbon, a lost bonnet?"

"That proves nothing."

"Don't you justify things to yourself? When you first met me, you easily accepted me as your tutor without any real proof. You made me, as you would have me be. And every time you wouldn't deal with a problem, you fainted. Do you remember falling asleep too fast—only to forget later how you got to bed? You have been called to relive your death, as were we all for a time. Do you remember eating recently, or just looking at the food and then walking away?"

"I do remember eating," she proclaimed, "or at least I drank wine."

"Did you? And how did it taste? Did it taste like wine?"

"No, it tasted like my blood. I can taste it now. What have you done to me? You had Charlotte serve me blood?" Isabel asked in disgust.

"Of course not!"

"I spoke to my parents," she said suddenly.

"I thought you said your parents weren't speaking to you. Did they speak to you or through you?"

"I saw Jane," Isabel insisted. "I talked to my sister. And she talked to me. We had a full conversation."

"You did?" he said in surprise.

"Yes." Isabel nodded emphatically.

"Maybe her belief in you made her able to see you," Dougal answered, puzzled. His voice grew louder. "Your sister I can't explain, but you have to admit you only remember things that you can accept. It's time to face the truth. You need to face the truth. You are like me."

"But Jane," Isabel protested. "I talked to Jane. She heard me, saw me. She would have said something if I was a ghost."

"Isabel," Dougal said. "Look in the mirror. See for yourself. You're a ghost. You didn't survive your accident."

"I am not dead." Numbly Isabel walked out of the library, wanting to prove him wrong, wanting to make him stop talking. Dougal followed her. In the main foyer, she stopped by a wide mirror. She gazed at the floor, too frightened to look into it. She felt her bare feet on the hard floor.

"Look," Dougal ordered. He grabbed her by her arms and forced her around. "See for yourself."

Isabel slowly raised her head. Tears already poured down her cheeks. The image that met her was as unfamiliar as a stranger. Her dark locks were tousled about her head, sticking up in spots, falling flat with matted blood in others. Trails of dried blood ran from her nose, ears, and eyes toward her hairline where it had dripped when she lay on the forest floor. It matched the blood surrounding her blue lips. Her skin was no longer the creamy pale of porcelain, but more of the ashen gray of death.

The dried blood stretched down her throat in a red tattoo she knew might never come off. She was missing a kidskin glove. And her clothes had changed from the ones she donned that particular morning to a gown of fine muslin. The blue and cream dress was torn and tattered and caked with blood and dirt. The ripped skirt fanned out from just beneath her breasts. The torn veil of lawn left her skin exposed.

Seeing a lump on the side of her neck, Isabel touched it. She gagged in disgust when she felt the bony protrusion.

"You broke your neck," Dougal explained quietly, "when the horse threw you."

"No." She shook her head. The movement was stiff and awkward and unsupported. Isabel swallowed in disgust, her appearance grotesque. "This is a trick. I can feel that it is. You're making me see things. You lie to get me to stay with you."

"No, I would never play such a cruel trick. I think you know that."

"The demon that held back the dog…when I was on the forest floor…he didn't take me because I wasn't ready. I wasn't dead yet. That I know is true. He was hunting Margaret. He looked into my eyes, and I saw…I saw death. The dog wanted to take my soul to join the others, but I wasn't ready. I wasn't dead. I just couldn't move. I was stunned. I'm not dead. I walked back here."

"No, Isabel," Dougal whispered. He started to reach for her but held back. "It's true you were alive when the knight came by, but you did die. That is why you couldn't move. You were dying.

Only when you were dead, could you rouse enough to move."

"No."

"I found you in the forest, on the ground. You were so dazed. You couldn't speak. Can't you remember? I carried you home and put you in bed." Dougal placed his hand hesitantly on her shoulder. "I sat beside you all that night as you thrashed about. You didn't want me to leave you. And when you spoke, you said you had seen a demon. You said you knew who he was. You said the beast wanted you. Isabel, you said you knew how to destroy it."

"No," she repeated.

"Don't you see, Isabel? You faced the demon and survived. No soul has ever spoken to the demon and remained to tell about it. You told me you had looked into the beast's eyes. You said he would come back. You said you knew his secrets."

"No," she wept. Her shoulders shook. She didn't have the strength to throw off his hand. She turned toward her horrible image in the mirror.

"The next morning you disappeared. I looked for you but couldn't find you. Then, after about three months, you began to appear to me, but you never seemed to see me, and if you did, you never spoke." Dougal pulled her around gently to face him. Her face was horrible in death, yet he looked at her like he could still see traces of her beauty. "And then I came across you in the garden. I didn't think you could see me since you had been blocking me out for so long."

Isabel couldn't answer. Her gaze fell to his mouth to watch him speak. As his lips moved, she remembered the feel of them against her. Entranced by his words, she listened through the veil hindering her emotions.

"I tried to ignore you like before, but you motioned as if you saw me. I had never dreamt that you would speak to me again, but you did. Only you didn't remember me. You didn't remember what had happened. You just went about your life, convinced in what you believed was true." Dougal sighed heavily as he waited for her reaction.

Suddenly, she jerked from his grasp. "Why did you lie to me? If what you say is true, you should have told me earlier. But, no, you just let me believe I was alive. You're using me for your own gain."

"No, Isabel. It's not like that."

"If I'm dead, then it's you who killed me," Isabel said. "I shall tell you what I remember. I remember Margaret laughing and spooking my horse. I remember you trying to grab me and yank me to the ground. Well, maybe you succeeded after all. If what you say is true, then you killed me—you and Margaret. The demon only came afterward to see what you had done."

"Don't think like that." Dougal shook his head in disbelief. "You cannot blame me for—"

"You said that you would leave if I asked you to," she stated bitterly. "I held up my end of the bargain. I went to the forest."

"Don't send me away." His eyes pleaded with her, but Isabel was hardened to them. "Just give yourself time to calm down. When you're thinking clearly, you'll see that everything will work out. With what you know, we can defeat the demon, and with the demon gone, we can be together. There is no living and dead issue between us. All we need is each other. We shall be a family. Everything I have ever dreamt of will be right here—Margaret, you, me. We shall be together."

"I don't know any secrets. I don't know how to kill the demon," Isabel answered honestly. "And I want nothing to do with you. I had a full life. I had a family. You took that away from me."

"No, please—"

"I don't believe your audacity in suggesting you could ever replace them." The anger felt good. At least it was an emotion besides pain.

"If you planned to find a mother for Margaret and a wife to help ease the torment of your eternity, then you killed the wrong woman. If there be any shred of honor in you, you'll get away from me and never, ever come back. I hate you. I curse you. I curse the day I met you. Damn you, Dougal. Damn you to hell!"

Instantly, Dougal flashed before her outrage. There was no fading, no warning. Just instantaneously, he was gone.

※

Margaret shivered violently as a cold breeze swept over her skin. Looking around the shallow cave, she couldn't tell where she was. The cave wasn't familiar to her.

Her eyes pierced the darkness. She was alone. Along the stone wall, she saw what could only be described as ancient writing scribbled along the jutting rock. Past the scrawl was a thin veil of light.

Slowly, she made her way forward to escape the cave. But, as she tried to pass the writing, she struck an invisible wall and was thrown back onto the ground. Stunned, she realized she couldn't move. She was trapped.

32

Isabel pushed through Jane's bedroom door without knocking. Her sister jumped up from her writing desk. Isabel said nothing as she watched Jane's face fill with fright.

"Isabel?" Jane stepped back from her older sister, seeing Isabel's face. "I didn't expect you."

Isabel observed Jane's reaction. Taking a deep breath, Jane tried to smile. She pretended she didn't see the dazed and battered version of her sister before her.

Speaking as she had when Isabel first appeared to her, Jane said conversationally, "I'm glad you came, Sister. I must speak to you. Tell me, have you been taking out the horses? Mother is quite upset by it. She thinks that they keep escaping on their own and ordered locks placed on the stable doors.

When they escaped again, and the locks were still attached, she neared hysteria."

Isabel tilted her head to the side. She panted, a horribly garbled sound, while she listened to Jane's comforting voice. Jane always calmed her down. She felt the tension leaving her body. The pain lessened.

Jane sighed in visible relief. Isabel's neck began to straighten by degrees. Her skin blossomed with color until a hint of delicate pink roses replaced the ghostly pallor.

"It's very wicked of you to scare Mother like that," Jane admonished gently. She smiled at her sister to ease the reprimand. "I know you're angry with her, but really, do you think it fair to unnerve her so?"

"Mother?" Isabel questioned.

"Yes." Jane ignored the harsh, grating sound of Isabel's voice.

"She...here?"

"Yes, she's here," Jane answered. Isabel's tattered gown was replaced with a fresh green one of simple print. "I thought maybe you were letting out the horses to scare her."

"No," Isabel mumbled with a grim shake of her head. She crossed over to sit on Jane's bed. Her eyes were dazed as she studied her sister. Jane looked so fresh and beautiful, but Isabel looked older than she remembered her. Hearing her sister's voice, it would be so easy to forget what Dougal had said to her.

"Oh," Jane returned, but she changed the subject when her sister didn't speak. "I don't know if you've heard, but mother and father are moving back to London. They wish to keep an eye on Harriet and Edward. It seems there has been another most disastrous scandal. Edward was seen coming out of another woman's home very early one morning. I'm so glad you didn't marry him, though I feel sorry for Harriet. She, naturally, does not believe a word of it and is standing by him."

Isabel only listened, staring at her sister's moving mouth.

"The colonel and I shall move here soon after the wedding," Jane continued. "I insisted upon it and he, having admitted to always loving this estate, readily agreed to let me have my way. I do hope you shall stay here. I should love to have you around."

"Jane," Isabel finally broke in. Her gaze shifted from her sister's mouth to her eyes. "Am I dead?"

Jane gasped in surprise. Biting her lips, she looked away and then back again.

"Jane," Isabel repeated, her voice rising by small degrees. "Did I die?"

"There was the accident," Jane finally admitted. Tears came to her eyes. She was forced to turn away from Isabel's suffering.

"And—?"

"The investigator said you snapped your neck in a horse-riding accident and hit your head on the ground." Jane sniffed. "They said you felt no pain, and that it was quite sudden. It was, wasn't it?"

Isabel, seeing her sister's agony, nodded. She felt no guilt over the lie. Jane didn't need to know the truth.

"I'm so glad," Jane said in relief. "We searched for you after your horse was discovered. I had nightmares of you lying on the ground, dying for hours. I would swear you called out to me to help you. Mother became so distressed. She sent me away to Aunt Mildred."

Isabel stood, moving instinctively to hug her sister. She leaned over and wrapped her arms around Jane's shoulders. Her limbs fell through her. Isabel frowned, standing.

Jane gave her a sad smile. "So you'll stay, won't you? Last time you left in such a hurry, I thought that you might never come back."

"Yes," Isabel whispered in a daze. Her eyes were hollow and far off as she watched Jane. It was true then. Her death had been an accident. She could see that now. She could remember. It was as Dougal had said. Her reactions to Margaret had spooked her horse. And Margaret wasn't to blame. She was just a child searching through the mist for her parents. No one was to blame but herself.

Isabel's knees weakened. Dougal had tried to stop her horse. He'd tried in vain to save her life. After she'd fallen and died, he'd found her spirit and carried her to her bed. She could remember it now. His voice had been so caring, so kind. He'd stayed with her, holding her as she'd screamed in fear. Part of her had fallen in love with him that night.

"Fear," Isabel mumbled.

Jane cocked her head in confusion.

"I was afraid."

"Afraid?"

"What?" Isabel asked, looking blankly at Jane. For a moment, she forgot where she was. With an eerie calmness, she muttered, "No, Jane. Don't worry about me. I must go now. I will try to come back to you. And if not me, I will send you a message."

"A message?" Jane inquired, growing fearful at the ominous tone of her sister's words. There was too much of a finality to them.

"There are others here, sister," Isabel said with a kind smile. "Don't be fearful of them. They're as lost as I was. Speak to them if you see them. If they don't answer, then ignore them as they do you. However, you might not see any of them. It's hard to say or explain. Just know that I love you and that I shall make sure this house is safe for you and your husband."

"Safe?"

"Have no fears, sweet sister." Isabel felt herself fading. It was a strange sensation, but she didn't fight it.

"Isabel?" Jane rose from her chair. Her hand reached out to her sister. "I love you."

Isabel nodded, smiling brightly at her sister as she faded from view. "And I will always love you."

33

Isabel's spirit drifted instinctively through the manor and then the gardens, looking for Dougal. She glided effortlessly through walls and furniture, through bushes and trees. She could feel the life in everything around her. It was splendid and sweet. It was freedom. But with this freedom came a longing so great it nearly ripped her in two. For she would never again be a part of the beauty she passed.

Slipping once more into the library, she frowned. She couldn't find Dougal anywhere. And if he'd really moved on, she would have to spend eternity alone. Near the window, she felt her body form by the mere suggestion of her will, and then she called to Dougal as she had before.

"Dougal. I need you," Isabel said clearly.

Hopefully, she watched the chair, never doubting that she would find him, but he didn't appear. Louder, she demanded, "Dougal, come here!"

Striding across to the foyer, she stopped before the mirror. She hesitated slightly before looking at it. The hideous reflection was gone, replaced by the near-transparent image of her face, as she knew herself to be. Standing in the approximate place she'd stood when she'd banished Dougal, she ordered, "Dougal, come back to me now!"

She waited, breathless. Still, he did not come.

"I hate you. I curse you. I curse the day I saw you. Damn you, Dougal. Damn you to hell!"

Isabel stiffened, remembering her own words. Had she said all that? She'd been so confused and angry. Her body had ached so badly.

"Oh, no," she muttered. "I cursed him to hell. What have I done?"

Isabel fell to the floor, shaking her head. Frantically, she yelled, "Dougal? Dougal! Please come back. I didn't mean it!"

Isabel's breath caught. She waited. Time suspended. When nothing changed, she tried to fight through the grief flowing throughout her. Tears swam in her eyes. Taking deep breaths, she looked helplessly around. She could see no one.

"Margaret?" Isabel asked. "Reverend Stillwell? Are you there? I need you. Come to me!"

Isabel gasped as the vicar materialized in front of her. Leaning over, he touched her cheek. She stared up in wonderment.

"You," she began weakly.

"Yes, I am dead like you. We are ghosts. And I heard your call, Miss Drake."

"You did? How?"

"When you have been dead as long as I, you hear such things," he answered. "I know when I am needed."

"B—but?"

"I died nigh seventy years ago," he confirmed.

"The knight?" she wondered aloud.

"No," he chuckled. "Roasted mutton. I choked."

"I think I sent Dougal's soul to hell." Her eyes widened.

The vicar lowered his gaze from her pain. His hand fell to his side.

Isabel stood. "I can't find him."

"What happened?" the vicar asked.

"I cursed him to hell. I told him to leave. He's gone. Margaret is gone. Tell me, do you know if they're damned?" Isabel asked. "Do I have the power to do that?"

"No." The vicar smiled kindly.

"Then, did the knight get them?"

"I can't say. I have not seen them."

"Do you think Dougal finally listened to me and left here?" Hope warred with disappointment. "Do you think they moved on?"

"If they did, they would be safe," he answered. "Dougal is a fine man. He's not marked for hell, merely sought by it."

"I must believe that they're safe."

"And you, child?" the vicar asked. "Why do you stay?"

"I don't know," she said. "I never had the chance to leave."

"Then there is a reason for it," he answered. "What are you holding on to? What do you regret? Your death was an accident. You shouldn't be here."

"I," she began weakly. Tears came to her eyes as she studied the kindly man. "I still feel as if I belong here. I'm not ready to be dead. I want to live. I want my life. I want to be who I was the morning of the accident—never knowing about all of this. It was so simple."

Catching her likeness in the foyer mirror, she could see the opposite wall through the reflection of her face.

"And your feelings for Dougal? Would you forget them?"

"I..." She didn't know how to answer, so instead, she threw out her hands helplessly. "I wish that he were a real man from my time so that I could meet him. That is the secret desire of my heart. If anything, that is what I cling to the most. And I would send the demon back into the hell whence it came."

"What you wish for is not possible, Miss Drake." Reverend Stillwell took her by the arm, leading her to the door.

"Which part?"

"You and Dougal cannot be corporeal again." The vicar opened the door, walking her through it. She was surprised by such an act. He smiled and explained simply, "We, who remain, try, for the most part, to live the semblance of a normal, living life. There is sanity in such real things as opening doors."

Isabel nodded. Had she not clung readily to her past? Hadn't she deceived herself into believing she was alive?

"Then what about the demon? I must focus on that," she replied. "I shall have an eternity to dream about the other."

"I will discover what I can." The vicar's image shimmered as he walked down the stairs and disappeared over the countryside.

34

THE SUN SET behind the horizon, leaving the land to those who would dwell in the moonlight. Isabel couldn't find Dougal or his daughter. She called out to him with every beat of her heart. He did not answer.

Choosing to walk, she crossed over the familiar garden paths. Her body ached for one last touch of Dougal's hand, one last kiss to sustain her. Dougal and Margaret had existed fifty years at Rothfield, the reverend seventy. How long must she roam here alone?

A sad melancholy settled over Isabel as she headed toward the bench.

What now? she wondered, as she gazed up at the moon. "What am I supposed to do now?"

"Fight."

Isabel turned. Her gaze instantly found Josiah. His features were pulled tight, and his eyes were haunted as if he were chased by hellfire. Something stirred in the pit of her stomach.

"Josiah." She rushed to him. He looked weak, sick. Touching his pale face, she ushered him to the bench. Wearily, he sat. Isabel joined him. Taking his hand in hers, she urged, "What happened?"

"My brother," he muttered. "He took Margaret from me."

"Margaret?" Isabel repeated numbly. "No."

"I couldn't stop him," he mourned. "I tried to fight, but he was too strong."

"Is she—?" Isabel couldn't finish the words.

"Not yet," Josiah said. "We have 'til the full moon hits the edge of the earth."

"Tonight?" Isabel demanded in horror. "But what can we do tonight?"

"That you must discover, m'lady," he whispered. "We lose time."

"Does he have the marquis?" Isabel pressed her eyes shut.

"I don't believe so," Josiah answered. "Why? Is he missing?"

"Yes," Isabel said. "What do you need me to do?"

"You know, don't you?" He looked pointedly at her. "You know you're dead?"

"Yes, I know."

"And you know how it happened?"

"Yes, an accident." Isabel swallowed, mildly embarrassed by the incident. Josiah didn't appear to notice.

"'Tis a good thing," he muttered. "Methinks that you are the one to stop my brother."

"What?" Isabel shook her head frantically. "Why me? I'm no one."

"You faced him and lived. You resisted his pull. You fought him. 'Tis more than anyone else has ever done. You do know that, don't you?"

Isabel nodded, uncertain. "It almost consumed me. There was so much hate and despair in him. I can't face that again."

"You might not have to," Josiah admitted.

"But why me? You're much stronger than I. Surely—"

"'Tis not with physical strength that you fight him. 'Tis with your mind, your heart. I have never been strong enough to control him. He knows my weaknesses too well." Josiah rubbed the back of his neck, sinking lower into the seat. "Methinks, you can banish him. You're not one of his victims, and because of it, he doesn't know your deepest fears. He won't know them unless you tell him. You died of your own recklessness and not by evil's doing. You faced him and survived."

"And if I don't?" she asked under her breath.

"Then he shall continue to kill whoever comes to live at Rothfield Park," Josiah said. "And we shall be able to do nothing."

"Jane," Isabel shivered in terror.

"Yea, m'lady, your sister. Methinks he might go after her next. She's a noblewoman and has a good, pure heart. With her marriage to a wealthy colonel, she will do many great things. Hers is the spirit the demon likes most to condemn. For if he's pluck in her youth, he'll prevent her future kindness. 'Tis the same reason they took Dougal. Ten years from the time of his death, in the year of our Lord, seventeen hundred and seventy-three, he was to enter parliament in London. His influence over the crown would have saved many lives. The Revolutionary War of the Colonies would have seen fewer tragedies."

Isabel wondered at the certainty of his revelation. "How do you know?"

"'Tis my brother's gift to see the future. And 'tis my curse to see the things he prevents. That is how I know where he'll strike."

"What is your brother?" Isabel grew determined. She must fight. Too many of those whom she loved depended on her. The beast already had Margaret and possibly Dougal. Isabel swallowed nervously. Her heart sank. And he might even take Jane.

"Evil," he answered.

"Does he only come with the mist and the dog? Are there any signs as to where he goes when he leaves?"

"I cannot say. I only feel when he's close. Evil can take many shapes—animals, humans, even statues in the garden. Who knows where he goes when he hides?"

"Paintings?" Isabel asked with an intense sense of foreboding.

"Assuredly, m'lady." He seemed reluctant to speculate. Isabel wondered if he still felt loyalty to his brother. Josiah had failed to stop him before. Would he be inclined to protect him now?

Isabel knew where the demon was hiding. She thought of all the times she'd roamed the halls. There was one place she was drawn to go—the portrait of a man and his dog. Once, she'd even suspected the subject in the picture had moved. It was worth a closer look. Jumping to her feet, Isabel said, "I think I know. I must go."

"Wait," Josiah called. "You must promise me something. Whatever happens—whatever it is you see—you must save Margaret. And you must kill my brother. Send him to hell."

Isabel wondered at the distraught words. She

knew there was more he wasn't telling her, but she didn't think it necessary to pry.

"Yes," she promised solemnly.

"I will help you in whatever way I can," he vowed, "though it won't be much." When she turned toward the house, he added, "And when I am gone, please tell Margaret I love her."

Isabel spun back to the pathways, but Josiah had disappeared.

35

Isabel crept through the halls. Her eyes scanned the numerous portraits. The aloof faces stared out from the canvases, their clothing ranging over decades. And when she saw a familiar medium-sized painting in the distance, she raced toward it.

At a glance, it was nothing special, not art that would linger in one's mind. The brush strokes were merely adequate, the frame of no spectacular quality. However, when she studied the figures, she saw that the dog had moved from one side of the man to the other, and the man's weight had shifted. The beast, she recognized immediately.

The hallway was too dim to make out much else. Coming close to the frame, she kept her gaze fixed upon his face. The dark eyes didn't move. Slowly, she reached out with trembling hands to grab the portrait from the wall. With a stiff yank, she pulled it down.

She tried not to jiggle the painting as she carried it through the hallway, lest she should awaken the figures within it. She watched them carefully, making it to the front hall without incident. Gingerly, she brought the painting to the light.

Isabel gasped. The frame plummeted to the ground, landing with a hard smack against the marble floor. Trembling, she shook her head. She knew the man's face—the dark hair, the black eyes, and the strong cheekbones. It was Josiah. It had to be. The face was too much like his—the wrinkles about the eyes, the crease beside the firm set of his mouth. This was no brother.

Unexpectedly, a rush of cold air came over her. Isabel froze. The foyer faded until she was standing before a memory, listening to Josiah as he spoke to her. She saw herself in the garden and watched herself answering him in kind. The words were fuzzy, growing louder as the memory became all the more real. The fog enveloped them, obliterating all but the cloud of the past conversation.

"He hunts," Josiah had said cryptically. "You should begone."

"Who?" she heard herself respond. Isabel ignored her own words, focusing on the knight. Walking around the two figures, she studied him. At first, what he said was harmless, just as she remembered. There was tenderness and concern in his words. And, as she watched his eyes, she knew she saw kindness in them. He couldn't be the man who had tried to trap her soul.

"You're a murderer," she'd accused.

Isabel watched the pain cross the knight's face.

"Not me. My brother."

"What did you do with Margaret? I'm taking her with me," Isabel had said. "Hand her over."

"She's my ward, not yours."

Isabel came close to his face. He did care for the girl—as a daughter, perhaps? His love as he'd said her name was there on his face. Isabel reached out to touch the memory. Her hand fell through his chest. Josiah glanced down briefly but didn't see her.

"Why did he kill Margaret?" she'd asked him.

Isabel froze, the chill over her body becoming more intense.

"'Twas a mistake. He was after the marquis, Margaret's sire," Josiah had answered. "Lady Margaret got in the way of things. She has the same blood as the marquis, and 'tis why my brother found her first. He would never have picked her intentionally. The innocent souls of children are harder for him to capture. They're too nimble and flighty and hard to hold."

And, as Josiah spoke, his true meaning became apparent, a voice tumbling over his past words in her head.

'Twas a mistake. I was sent after the marquis. My master tricked me into killing the child. I would never have harmed her. My brother is a part of myself.

Isabel stiffened. She turned toward her duplicate self in the memory. The past Isabel smiled at her, ignoring her conversation with the knight. The memory's lips didn't move, but Isabel heard the words clearly. The past Isabel nodded before returning to the discussion.

"Dougal," Isabel whispered, only to be mimicked by her shadow self.

"Why are you keeping them apart?" she'd asked. Isabel watched in a daze.

"'Tis not I who keeps them apart. I found Margaret searching for her sire soon after she'd died. I couldn't find the marquis in time. His spirit is lost to me."

I had to keep them apart. I knew the marquis searched for his daughter. If he found her and my brother found him, they would both die. I had to keep Margaret safe. I love her.

"Then maybe you're the solution betwixt them.

You can see Margaret and her sire. 'Tis you who must join them."

I knew father and daughter couldn't see each other. The demon that takes over me will no longer be satisfied with only Dougal. He wants Margaret too. He knows I have her. I must reunite father and daughter. But I need to get them to the same place at the same time. That is where you must help me. If you reunite them, I will lift the cloak of blindness I put on them.

"It can't be uttered. To say his name is to summon him."

I cannot tell you 'tis I whom you seek. To say it is to call the demon forth to hunt.

Isabel watched the conversation. The knight's voice quieted to a murmur, drowned out by the translation of his words in her head.

"Can't you stop him?" her past self had asked. Her attention once more fully on the knight.

"Nay," Josiah had answered with a mournful toss of his head. "Wouldst that I could, but I didn't stop him in life as was my duty. In death, he's too strong for me to try. Long ago, this was my family's holding. My brother made his pact with unholy wizards. They gave him power and riches beyond imagination. However, as he took his seat of power, the dark ones struck him dead. As payment for that which they had bestowed, he had pledged his afterlife to bringing them other souls. So long as he feeds their fire with others, they shall not take him."

I couldn't control the impulse in life. The dark worshippers tricked me. They promised me riches with no lethal consequences to me, or my family, at their hands. But, in the end, it was their voices that killed me and all those I love. I was stupid and vain to believe such was to be gained without a terrible price. Now, they demand I bring them souls. But, 'tis not me. 'Tis a demon who uses me to kill. I cannot stop him. I have prayed for redemption. I have prayed for the death of my own soul in place of the ones the demon hunts.

Suddenly, Josiah turned to the real Isabel, who froze. The image of her past self faded until only she and the knight were left. Seeing the flash of awareness in his eyes, she tried to back away. She was stiff within the memory. There was nowhere to escape.

"You fought me and won," he said. There was grim satisfaction and respect in the statement. "You can do it again. Destroy me to save Margaret. Kill me in my demon form and vanquish the demon within me. I give you this gift of knowledge. 'Tis the only way I can help you. If it is discovered that I have revealed this to you, all will be lost—including the souls of those you love."

With a flash, the image disappeared. Isabel fell to the floor, panting for breath. Her body felt weak.

Looking over at the painting, she saw Josiah watching her. His eyes held infinite sadness and pain. The portrait moved. Josiah bowed his head in shame and turned his back to her. The beast remained the same.

Without warning, the painting rose into the air. Isabel gasped, pulling back in fright. She blinked rapidly only to see her mother carrying the picture back to the hallway.

"If Lord Sutherfeld thinks he will bring this hideous thing to London, he's sorely mistaken," the viscountess fumed.

Isabel hastened to her feet. Chasing after her mother, she called, "Stop. Wait. Put the painting down."

The viscountess didn't hear her. Isabel began to reach for the painting, hesitating for a moment before yanking it out of her mother's arms. The viscountess screamed in terror. Her fingers flew to fan her cheeks as she stared at the floating portrait.

"My apologies, Mother," Isabel said. She reached over to comfort the viscountess but then stopped, knowing the woman couldn't see her. Helplessly, Isabel ran from the hysterical woman, carting the painting under her arm.

"Mother," Jane screamed, coming around the corner. She kneeled beside the woman, helping her to stand. Looking around, she saw no one. "What is it?"

"That horrible painting," the viscountess mumbled incoherently. "I think it wishes to come with us to London."

36

Isabel hefted the painting with her knee, trying to support the weight as she readjusted it in her arms. She refused to look at Josiah's likeness, turning the front away from her, and she was careful to keep her fingers off the paint, fearful of what might happen if she touched it.

She ran through the garden. The mist grew thick while she made her way to the forest. The fog always appeared to grow out from the trees, and she decided the woods were as good a place as any to begin her search.

At the tree line, she hesitated. The dim path was lightened as moonlight forced its way through the tree limbs, refracted in the misty pathway before her.

It wasn't easy to face the sight of her death. So

much of her wanted to take back the lost time. She cursed herself for her carelessness, for charging from the house like a spoiled, selfish child. How foolish she'd been to act with such audacity.

Her feet sped with purpose. The mist grew denser as she fought her way through it. She could hear the babbling water from the stream. The noise grew deafening.

Isabel shook. The painting dropped from her fingers, disappearing beneath her. Kneeling to the ground, she felt around in the dirt. She could see little beyond the tip of her nose. The painting was gone.

The mist came in from all sides to choke her, and she coughed violently. Isabel fell onto her back, lying with her face toward the sky. The world seemed to spin. Her body ached, and her neck cracked at the spine. She could feel her death creeping around her. She could feel the power of evil as if the demon knight was again before her, trying to claim her soul as he had the day she died.

Terrified, she began to whimper. Her purpose in stopping the demon slipped from her mind, and she couldn't think beyond the pounding of her fearful heart. She trembled as the mist grew thicker until it felt like smoke in her lungs. She clawed frantically at her neck as it constricted.

"Get up," came a whisper like a voice from the heavens.

Isabel gasped for air as the pressure on her neck lessened. Her eyes darted all around, but she could see nothing but the dense white. Weakly, she climbed onto her hands and knees. Her limbs were heavy and fought her progress. "What did you say?"

There was no answer.

"Dougal?" Isabel insisted, growing bolder at the sound of her own voice. As she stood, the noise of the stream lessened. She swiped her hands through the mist. Defiantly, she yelled at the fog, "You cannot stop me. I'm not afraid of you. I have faced what you are, and I have survived." And as she said the words, she believed them. Panting, she searched the ground to get her bearings. She resisted the fear that would waver her composure.

Isabel found the painting lying on the ground. She picked it up and tucked it under her arm. With solemn resolution, she continued forward.

Her journey became easier as the mist parted to let her by. Isabel glared defiantly all around her. She could sense movement beyond her reach.

All of a sudden, a cold chill ran up the back of her spine. The hairs on the nape of her neck stretched out in warning. Isabel stopped. Quietly, she whispered, "Margaret?"

Her answer was silence.

Taking a deep breath, she quietly hummed Margaret's song. She stopped midway to listen. A terrified whimper timidly finished the notes. Turning toward the sound, Isabel willed the mist to part before her, and as a trail opened up, she set off toward the child.

Isabel passed over fallen logs and rustling leaves. They crunched beneath her feet. The mist curved about her, to her sides, above her head like an arched passageway.

Isabel stepped along the fog, feeling it close in behind her. Abruptly, she stopped. At the end of the tunnel, several trees reflected the eerie orange glow of firelight. The light radiated down the misty passage.

"Help," she heard Margaret moan.

Isabel rushed forward.

Within a small clearing in the forest, the fire burned bright and high. Tall, old tree trunks formed the clearing's rough mossy walls, and their leaves the ceiling with only a small piece of heaven peeking through with starry eyes. Luckily, the forest hadn't caught fire.

Through the dancing flames, Isabel discovered Margaret, alone, cowering on the ground, her hands bound to a large stone with chains. Isabel hurried around the fire pit to go to her. Margaret's bright green eyes met hers. Isabel placed the painting on the ground and motioned for silence. Margaret nodded obediently.

Isabel grabbed the shackles on the girl's wrists and yanked until her hands scraped raw on the old metal. The chain wouldn't loosen.

Isabel winced. She dropped the rough iron.

"Isabel?" Margaret whimpered.

"Shh," Isabel hushed her, wiping her stinging hands against her gown. "I won't leave you. Where is the key?"

"He has it," the girl whispered

"Who, Josiah?"

"It's not Josiah. It's the demon," Margaret persisted. "Josiah tries to fight it, but the evil is too strong."

Isabel nodded. Josiah or not, it was he whom she must stop. Even the knight understood that much. Margaret's already pale face became pallid with fright.

In mounting dread, Isabel asked, "Where did he go?"

"Ah, m'lady, how good of you to join us." The bark of his dog punctuated Josiah's voice. "The fire will be most pleased to receive you."

Isabel felt the terror once again rack her body. The dog growled a dark warning. Spinning on her heels, Isabel rose and blocked Margaret from the creature's view.

Josiah wore his armor. The silver plates gleamed in the firelight. His helmet hid all but the mercilessly black orbs of his eyes. It was no longer the Josiah she knew. The man was gone, replaced by a monster.

The dog at his side growled, and its eyes glittered a fiery red. Blood dripped from its long, yellowed fangs.

"I told you I'd return for you, m'lady," Josiah said. The knight slowly drew out his sword. Angling the tip at her, he tilted his head to the side, daring her to run.

"Josiah, please," Isabel pleaded, hopeful that the man inside the demon could hear her. Her flesh would be no match against the steel of his blade or the bite of his dog.

Frantically, Isabel scanned the ground for a weapon. There was nothing overly useful. Grabbing a fallen branch, she turned back to him and held it before her like a sword, widening her stance to match his. Taking a deep breath, she waited for him to attack.

Josiah's laughter was mockingly cold, but his sword arm never wavered, his eyes never turned away. Isabel swallowed nervously. Her heart thudded crazily throughout her chest. Her stomach clenched into knots.

"Let Margaret go," she ordered.

His dog barked violently. Isabel recoiled. The knight's gaze hardened, and his laughter died.

"You cannot fight me." The knight stepped forward. The firelight moved over his armor's polished steel plates, and the orange contrasted with the blue-tinted metal. The dog took a menacing lunge forward, and his mighty jaws snapped. The knight ordered him back with a wave of his hand.

"Let the child go," Isabel said.

Margaret whimpered, cowering against the rock.

"I cannot," he growled. "Her father is lost to me. I heard you say he was gone. I cannot spare her."

"She's just a child. Let her go and face only me," Isabel pleaded, sensing that the man inside the demon might be wavering.

"Why spare one when I can take two?" The demon laughed.

Her arm was growing fatigued under the weight of wood, so she dropped the branch, knowing it would do her no good. She stepped away from the child and took his attention with her. "Josiah, I know you're in there."

"Ah!" the knight shrieked. His mouth opened at the sound, displacing his helmet as his jaw stretched beneath the edge. His face tilted toward the sky while he warred within himself. The demon was too strong. The helmet fell from Josiah's head to the ground. The demon within him rushed Josiah's body forward. He lifted his giant sword above his head and swung it through the air.

Isabel ducked, scurrying away from the blade. Her feet tangled in her skirts as she tried to step over her discarded branch. She landed on the hard earth. Her shoulder jerked in shooting pain. Her raw hands ground into the dirt.

Scrambling to her feet again, she cradled her arm. She'd barely looked up when another whoosh of the blade sang past her ear. The demon charged forward, chasing her around the fire. His canine companion barked at Josiah's heels. The knight swung again and again. His blade hit the fire, sending it sparking over his prey. Isabel screamed. Burnt embers showered her arm and head. They chafed the side of her face.

"Josiah," she tried to reason. "This is not you. You don't have to do this."

"Yea," he growled, taking another swing at her head. "I do."

"Demons come from the fire," she whispered, dodging another blow. She recognized the sound of the roaring flames from her memories of the demon knight. Every time she watched him appear, these horrible sounds would follow him.

"What?" the knight howled.

Having circled the fire, she glanced at Margaret, who now pulled at her bonds, her feet planted against the rock. One of the girl's hands slid free from the shackles. Next to the child lay the portrait.

"That is his haven," she muttered in sudden clarity. "I must send him home."

Grabbing the painting, she turned just in time to see Josiah and his dog marching around the flames. Isabel tugged it weakly to the fire pit with little help from her injured arm.

"No," shouted Josiah, his command chillingly loud.

Isabel saw the glimmer of his blade as it swung at her. When she lifted the portrait to block his attack, Josiah struck the picture. Isabel froze, waiting for the thrust of the blade that never came. The painting jerked from her hands. The blade glanced off of the canvas as if the material were made of stone and flew from the knight's hands.

"Give it to me," the knight ordered, ignoring his fallen blade. Isabel pulled the painting from the ground. She held it before her like a shield.

"No," she spat. The demon charged forward.

His hand lifted to wrestle the frame from her. Isabel knew if he captured her, she couldn't win. Her strength would be no match.

"Josiah," Margaret called.

The knight stiffened at the terrified sound. Isabel saw the hard black pit of his gaze soften somewhat at the call. Both their heads snapped toward the child. The dog had her trapped beneath him, his paws on her shoulders as he growled into her face.

"Nay," Josiah yelled, but the animal didn't listen. With a lunge, Josiah forgot his portrait, forgot Isabel, failed to protect himself. He flew through the air, his arm shooting over Margaret's throat to block the dog's bite. The beast's lips found flesh, tearing and ripping with abandonment. Josiah screamed in torment.

Margaret's bonds dissipated into the mist, freeing her. The girl screeched in horror, crawling away from the dog's attack.

Isabel didn't hesitate. She tossed the portrait into the fire pit. The flames sparked, growing so hot as to blister all those who stood within its light. Margaret fell into a ball. Isabel turned to block the heat. The dog let its victim go—howling painfully as its own painted image was scorched.

A flame shot out, lassoing the beast with a supernatural force. The dog tried to resist, striking its large paws defiantly into the dirt, but the flames dragged it howling to his death.

Isabel ran to Margaret, gathering the child into her arms. Margaret fought Isabel's hold, craning to see Josiah. As the last of the dog's howls echoed in death, the fire reached out again.

"No!" Margaret cried.

Isabel tried to regain her hold, but the flighty girl slipped from her hands. Margaret jumped before the string of fire, blocking her face. But the fire didn't want her. It wanted its demon. The flames curled around her, dipping behind her back for the knight.

A black force, as dark and formless as a shadow, was pulled from Josiah's bleeding body. The demon screeched—a terrible sound that sent chills over their flesh. The fire then consumed the shadow, destroying him with his dog in the bubbling and melting canvas of their portrait.

Margaret fell to her knees next to Josiah. Blood streamed from gaping wounds in his neck, his arm, and his chest. There was a hole where his heart should be. They watched as the hole filled in, his heart forming within the wound. It began to beat. Shaking, Margaret shouted, "Isabel!"

Isabel came forward, looking down at the trembling man. He'd risked himself to save Margaret. Somehow, he was given back his heart, but the wound above the heart didn't lessen. Josiah's spirit was dying. Of that, Isabel was certain.

"Isabel," Margaret pleaded. Tears streamed down her face. She cradled Josiah's head in her hands. "Help him."

Isabel shook her head helplessly. Tears poured over her cheeks, matching the child's. She dropped to her knees next to them. Seeing a wound in his side, she tore her gown and pressed her hands to it. Josiah grunted. His eyes briefly sought Isabel. He nodded in approval. She'd done what he asked. She'd saved Margaret and sacrificed him. His approval, however, didn't lessen their sorrow.

"Why is he bleeding like this?" Margaret cried in panic. Her small hands pushed against his breast to stay the blood.

Isabel felt his heart beating beneath her palms, but there was too much blood. The wounds were too deep.

"Isabel, he shouldn't be bleeding like this," Margaret insisted. "We are dead. We do not bleed like this! What is happening?"

"He's dying," Isabel whispered. "He never got the chance before."

Josiah's eyes opened. Isabel stiffened. They were the color of a storm-riddled sky. Their bluish-gray depths shone as he gazed up at Margaret. The black color had left his eyes just as the evil had left his body. He lifted his hand to cup Margaret's cheek, but the effort was too great, and his fingers fell again to his side.

"Lady Margaret." A slight smile formed on his lips. His lids drifted closed.

"No," she cried, shaking her head. "Josiah, no. Stay with me."

Isabel froze at the intense heartache that passed between the two. She couldn't doubt the look, the harboring of hopeless love. She thought of Dougal. He was gone. She'd lost him.

Margaret leaned down. She pressed her mouth to Josiah. The knight's eyes shot open in surprise at the unexpected contact. Margaret's tears poured over him. The sorrow of her pain coursed through him. As she pulled her trembling mouth away, he smiled up at her—a kind, reassuring smile. Then, within the blinking of an eye, he disappeared, dissolving into the earth.

Margaret fell atop the leaves that had just cradled his body. Her small hands dug into the dirt, grasping fistfuls of forest litter in her torment. Isabel stiffly pulled Margaret to her feet. The girl wailed as Isabel lifted her. Taking her by the shoulders, Isabel tried to lead the girl out of the forest.

"Where is my father?" Margaret cried. "Where did Josiah go?"

"I don't know," Isabel whispered.

Margaret tore out of her arms, running away into the mist. Isabel tried to follow, but her body was too frail, her mind too tired. Instead, her body dissolved into the night air, and she was carried away with its will.

37

The bright rays of the summer sun warmed the gardens. The fragrant scents of flowers, trees and grass rode on the gentle winds. The white cotton of the clouds floated against the delicate blue of the heavens. Rothfield Park was peaceful. The land was quiet with the appearance of a new morning.

Isabel didn't find Margaret though she'd looked. She didn't find anyone. She was alone. Tearfully, she had clawed her way through the forest. She tore furiously at tree limbs as she darted past. With blind precision, she found herself in the garden settled on the stone bench, and there she sat, having no will to go on. With Dougal gone, she had nothing.

Mist still came with the dusk, but its thickness was tempered, and it clung mostly to the trees.

Isabel wasn't frightened of it. She knew it could be controlled. The mist wasn't good or evil, just a thing to be used and commanded by either.

Alone on the bench, she watched the passing of time, the stirrings of mornings, and the restlessness of nights. Time had no meaning for her. Days were undifferentiated from years. She kept vigil, only fading when her spirit grew too weary to continue. And after a rest, she would again appear in her spot, waiting for someone to come to her.

Except to fade, not once did she leave her post. One day the quietly beckoning call of Jane made her turn her head. Jane was married to the colonel in the garden in front of family and friends. Isabel watched, happy for her sister. She wished she were alive so she could join in the celebration.

The family's guests didn't notice the onlooker, didn't sense her presence. Only once did Jane turn, catching Isabel's gaze briefly in the sunlight. The bride smiled, proud and happy, but her ghostly sister had vanished like the sun slipping behind a cloud.

Isabel saw her parents, looking a bit older but none the worse for wear. She saw Edward and Harriet, neither speaking to the other. Edward even sat beside Isabel on the bench, never knowing she was there. Isabel watched his face in silence, and before she knew it, he was gone.

The day faded like all the others. Snow came, sending only the slightest of chills through her. Isabel still didn't move. Then, on a particularly chilly day, she saw the colonel pushing through the massive banks of snow. Tugging his coat over his shoulders, he came to the bench. His eyes squinted at the empty space. Quietly, he said, "Your sister wishes for you to come in out of the cold. It's Christmas, and you should be with your family."

Isabel blinked in surprise, watching the white puffs of air coming from his cold lips. The colonel stroked his mustache lightly.

"I assume you're here, sister," he murmured. "I can't see you now, but I have seen you in the moonlight at this post. I don't know why you wait, but you're welcome as long as you like. The bench is yours. No one will bother you here."

With that, the colonel turned, stomping his way back into the house.

"I wait," Isabel whispered, "because there is little else that I can do. I don't wish to live without my sweet Dougal. And if he is around, he will come for me here. For this is the place we first met."

Detecting the call of a bird, she moved her gaze to the sky. Wistfully, she sighed. It was again spring.

Isabel adjusted on the bench, stretching her

hands above her head. A rabbit hopped nearby, sniffing at a peeking flower. Her legs felt like lead. Standing for the first time since her vigil began, she yawned. Then, hearing the soft thud of footfall on the path, she turned around. Her heart sped as her eyes hungrily sought the distance. She waited breathlessly, but as the intruder came into view, her smile wavered. It was Reverend Stillwell.

"Miss Drake!"

"Reverend?" Her legs trembling, she fell to the ground and began to weep.

"There now." The vicar gathered her up into his arms. Slowly he lifted her back onto the bench. "What is it?"

"I thought you were Dougal," she said, wiping her eyes. "I was waiting for him."

"Oh, child," the vicar said. He patted her shoulder lightly before drawing away. Isabel studied his kindly face, his pleasant eyes. "I shouldn't have stayed away so long."

"How long has it been?" she asked wearily.

The vicar's eyes widened in surprise. "You don't know? What have you been doing?"

"I have been right here." Suddenly, she heard the singing of a child. Margaret skipped up the path. Isabel's heart again sped. "Margaret?"

"Yes, Margaret is staying with me," the vicar answered.

"With you?" Isabel asked. "Then—?"

Margaret stopped to pick a flower near the rabbit. The creature hopped over to smell her outreached hand. The vicar waited patiently.

"Then you have not seen him?" Isabel whispered.

"No. No one has seen him. I believe he has made his peace. His spirit has moved on." Reverend Stillwell saw the frown marring her brow. "Be happy for him, Miss Drake. It's a good place he has gone to."

Isabel nodded with difficulty.

"Have you been here all year?" the vicar asked.

Isabel sighed. "I prayed he would come. But now there is no hope for it. It's useless. I can't live. I can't move on. I can't have the man I love."

"You still wish to live?"

"Yes," she answered. "If I'm not thinking of Dougal, I'm thinking of how much I miss being alive."

Looking at the vicar, she asked, "How is Margaret?"

"She cries a lot. She misses her father and Sir Josiah. It's not my place to say, but I believe that sometimes the child's affections for the knight are beyond a child's affections for a guardian. I have been told what happened, what you did." The vicar rubbed the back of his neck thoughtfully. "I would have come to you sooner about it, but I have been busy helping the lost souls, whom you freed, to find their way."

"Lost souls?" Isabel gasped in surprise.

"You don't know?"

"No, I came straight here that morning and have not left."

"What you did that night." He shook his head in awe. "Your gallantry and Sir Josiah's sacrifice released all of the demon's captured souls. Their spirits marched through the countryside in a long procession. You should have seen it. There were many in need of my counsel."

"I had no idea," she whispered.

"It's why…" the vicar began quietly.

Isabel turned to him.

His eyes lowered as he began again, "It's why I have been sent to make you a great offer."

"Offer?" She thought of Dougal. Unable to hide her hope, she said, "Dougal?"

"No," said the vicar. "I can't bring him back."

"Then, what?" she said in disappointment.

"I have been sent to offer you the gift of life," the vicar said.

"Life?" Isabel questioned.

"Yes, if you want it," he answered. "It's what you want, is it not? To live?"

She watched Margaret in the distance. The

girl's face was wistful and sad, not the happy countenance of a true child. Isabel thought of everything that the child never had a chance to experience—of everything she, herself, had missed. And here was her opportunity to get it all back.

"Yes," she agreed. She thought mournfully of Dougal. "I do want to live. I want it more than almost anything."

"So you've made your decision then? You'll take this gift of life?" the vicar asked.

Isabel watched Margaret pick another flower. Her heart pounded. This was her chance. Either way, Dougal was lost to her.

"Yes," she whispered. "I will take the gift."

38

"I am so glad you have returned to us," Jane gushed happily. She looked over at her sister lying on her bed to make sure she was real. "I nearly fainted yesterday, seeing you in the foyer for the first time in so long. I have missed you so much."

"I missed you, too." Isabel crawled off the bed, moving slowly over to the window. Pressing her forehead against the glass, she looked out over the estate. An acute sadness surrounded her, one that she couldn't hide.

"I daresay that since first seeing your spirit, I have started seeing them all the time. I saw a maidservant this morning in the dining room. Though I don't think she saw me. She was cleaning something that wasn't there." Jane paused to examine her needlepoint before selecting a pink thread. "I swear people must think I'm crazy, always talking to walls and such."

"That would be Charlotte," Isabel answered. "She's harmless. She likes to keep busy."

"Oh." Jane giggled. "It's a good thing Mother is gone. I assume she will never visit. At my wedding, she refused to come into the house. She's convinced some painting jumped out of her hands and ran away."

Isabel giggled. Jane raised a suspicious eyebrow. Before her sister could ask about it, Isabel said, "I can't believe I'm to be an aunt. I daresay the colonel is almost choking with pride."

"As well he should," Jane answered, patting her still flat stomach. Lifting her needlepoint, she scrutinized the rose pattern. "I'm so glad you'll be here to help me with it."

"Do you know he came to talk to me?" Isabel asked.

"Who?" Jane lowered her sewing to her lap.

"The colonel," Isabel replied, "last winter when I was on the bench. I think it was right before Christmas. He asked me to come inside. He said I would always be welcomed here."

"He did?" Jane smiled. "He never told me."

"He couldn't see me," Isabel continued. "I think part of him even doubted I was there."

"He knew. We both knew you were there."

Isabel turned, forcing a sad smile before glancing back out over the distance.

"Isabel?" Standing, Jane crossed to the window and stood beside Isabel. "Why were you on the bench so long? Why did you not come inside?"

"I was waiting." Isabel closed her eyes to the pain. She could recall every detail of Dougal as if no time had passed. She thought of him—of his green-gray eyes that haunted her, his dark hair, the small birthmark on his cheek. She ached to smell his scent, to taste his mouth, to feel his skin.

Jane didn't understand. "It must be a spirit thing. I suppose time passes differently for you now that you're alive again."

"How so?" Isabel mumbled absently.

"Well, there is this man in the library who seems to be waiting for something too." Jane looked up, startled when Isabel gasped.

Isabel's hands violently shook as she stared at her sister's door.

"I…" Isabel began, but she was unable to finish her sentence. Her heart fluttered wildly. Without a backward glance, she ran from her sister's room.

Isabel raced through the home, tearing around the front hall. Her feet slid on the slick floor. Then, pausing by the library, she gasped for breath. Her fingers shook as she reached out to touch the door.

Closing her eyes, she pushed it open. The door creaked. She stepped inside, unable to look. Weakly, she whispered, "Dougal?"

"Isabel?"

A smile spread over her features. Her heart fluttered. With a cry, she turned to the sound. It was Dougal. He stood by her father's desk. Her entire body shaking, she stared at him, too afraid to move.

"Dougal," she said breathlessly. "Can it be true? You're here?"

Dougal crossed the floor and pulled her into his embrace. He pressed his lips to hers. Isabel moaned against his mouth. Pulling back, she looked up to make sure he was real. Her hands ran over his face and neck.

"I love you," she whispered in a rush, knowing it was the most important thing she ever needed to say.

"Oh, Isabel," he answered, pulling her back to his beating heart. "I love you, too."

Isabel clutched him to her. "Never leave me again. I couldn't bear it."

"What happened?"

"I thought you had moved on," she whispered. Tears of happiness filled her eyes.

"Moved on?" he chuckled, the idea being the

most absurd thing he'd ever heard. Then, seeing her tears, he questioned, "Why are you shaking?"

Isabel gazed into his eyes. "You don't remember?"

"Remember? You banished me away from you but moments ago," he answered. He lifted a fistful of Forget Me Nots. "I went to the field to pick your favorite flowers and came here for when you would call me back. Please don't be upset. I love you. I knew you would come back. And so you have. Now we can face the dangers in the mist together."

The flowers in his hand were perfect, unwilted by the passing of time. Just like their clothes and the rooms, their environments appeared just as the spirits wanted them to be.

"I am not afraid of the mist. The mist is not evil. It's only what we allow it to be. We control the mist," Isabel said. "The demon Josiah used it to feed into our fears."

"Josiah?" Dougal questioned in mounting alarm. "He's the demon?"

"Was," Isabel said. "Dougal, a year has passed. The demon is gone. We're safe."

"But..." He glanced at the flowers. "I only just picked these."

"I promise to tell you the entire story another time," she answered. "Right now, I just want to hold you."

"Margaret?" he asked in fear.

Isabel froze.

"What is it?" he shot. "Has something happened to her?"

"Yes," Isabel said carefully.

"What? You must tell me."

"She's alive," Isabel whispered.

"Then let us find her."

"We can't just yet," Isabel said. "I don't know where she is."

"Why? We just need to call out to her. Our spirits will find each other."

"When I said she was alive, I meant alive-alive." Isabel's eyes shone lovingly. She refused to move from Dougal's embrace, and he was content to let her stay there. "As in *of the living*?"

"But, how?" he said in disbelief.

"It's a long story," Isabel said. Then she told him of what had happened since their last parting. Finally, finishing with the choice that Reverend Stillwell had given her, she said, "I was offered the gift of life, so I took it. And I gave it to Margaret. She's alive, Dougal, and so beautiful. You won't recognize her."

"Father?"

Isabel and Dougal turned to the door. The young woman who returned their eager stares smiled prettily. Her blonde hair was swept up into a coiffure, the plaits bound together with green ribbons and flowers. Her matching green eyes glittered brilliantly from a slender beautiful face.

"Margaret?" Dougal gasped in awe at an adult version of his little girl.

"I knew that you were finally here." When Margaret came forward, Isabel stepped aside to let her father hug her. "I could feel you talking about me," Margaret said.

"But, how?" he murmured, touching his daughter's face. Her slender features suited the old wisdom in her eyes better than the body of a child.

"It seems I had a few stipulations added to the gift," Isabel said. "I told the vicar that Margaret should gain a more appropriate age for her wisdom and that she should have the happiness her heart deserved."

Margaret's cheeks reddened. Then, nodding eagerly at her father, she said, "Isabel gave up her own chance at life for me. And Lady Jane has agreed to let me stay as her ward. She and the colonel have been very kind to me. They say they will throw me a ball to bring me out into society properly."

Dougal looked over his daughter's head at Isabel. He mouthed, "Thank you."

"I wanted to live," she admitted, "but it would have been no life without you. You are my life.

Without you, there is nothing. Part of me still hoped that one day I would find you. And I have."

"And you'll never lose me," he promised, "nor me, you."

"Ugh," teased Margaret, wrinkling her nose. Isabel giggled. Smiling slyly, Margaret inquired, as she had long ago, "So *are* you going to be my mother?"

"Yes," Dougal answered for her. Then loudly, he said, "Reverend Stillwell, you're needed."

Almost instantly, the vicar materialized. Scratching his head, he glanced around at the three. "How?"

"Time has a funny way of moving for us spirits," Isabel laughed.

"That it does." Dougal leaned down to kiss Isabel. Isabel moaned, forgetting others were watching.

"You need to marry them," Margaret whispered to the vicar. Then she wryly added, "Quickly."

Reverend Stillwell beamed. Clearing his throat, he then said, "Hold on there. Do you both choose each other?"

"Yes," Dougal assured him, breaking only slightly from the kiss.

"Yes," Isabel echoed in between kisses. She never wanted to let him go.

"Then you're married," the vicar stated.

"What?" Isabel laughed, looking doubtfully at the man. "That can't be right."

"Ah, we are dead." The vicar shrugged. "What else do we need? Not like anyone else is going to come to the ceremony."

Margaret rushed forward, giving them both quick hugs and her congratulations. Then, pulling back, she asked, "So will you come to my ball?"

"I don't see why not," Dougal said. "What delightful pranks we can play on your guests."

"Oh, Father! You won't ruin it for Jane, will you?" Margaret beseeched. Her eyes belied the fact that it wasn't Jane who she was worried about.

"No, dear, he won't ruin it for Jane," Isabel assured her, shooting a mock glare of warning at her husband. Dougal laughed.

"Now, if you'll excuse us, we have a honeymoon to attend." Dougal grabbed his wife and faded with her into the air. The vicar's face became bright red. Margaret gave the transparent man a mock hug, lifting her arms wide and round and then pretending to kiss his vanishing cheek.

Isabel's lips meanwhile met Dougal's. And under the power of his will, he brought them to a bedchamber. The dust disappeared from the bed as they arrived next to it. Isabel glanced around.

Raising an eyebrow at the unfamiliar room, she smiled in question. "Is this your room?"

He nodded. "Yes."

"You're going to have to show me how you did that." She pulled him close.

"I shall explain later. But for now, kiss me," he said.

And there were no more words between them. Nothing else mattered—not the past nor the future, for together, they would have eternity.

39

EPILOGUE

Dougal lifted his hand to Isabel, escorting her through the entryway into the front hall of Rothfield Park. Bowing politely at the colonel and his wife, Dougal smiled while the current lord of the manor uncomfortably tried to acknowledge him and not seem out of sorts to his living guests.

Isabel, seeing her husband's ploy, hit him on the arm.

"Behave," she scolded. "You promised Margaret."

"No one saw me," he answered innocently.

"That is exactly my point. You'll send the poor colonel to an early grave, and then I shall not be able to protect you from him."

Dougal chuckled. He glanced around the front hall decorated with vases teeming with wildflowers, sweeping ribbons, and giant bows. He hugged his wife closer to his side.

"You realize," he offered as he glanced suggestively over her body, "that no one can see us. We could dance naked if we want."

"Oh, really?" Isabel warned, feigning ire. Then, unable to resist his handsome face, she grinned. "Jane, Margaret, and the colonel can see us."

"I keep forgetting," he whispered in penitence, but Isabel didn't believe it for a second.

"Do hush," Isabel ordered. "Where is our daughter? I can't wait to see her in her new dress."

"Patience." He looked over the crowd. His own anxiousness showed as he searched for Margaret.

Isabel smiled secretively up at him. The afterlife was good to them. She'd never been happier or more in love.

The first strains of a waltz began. The sweet melody fell over the hall as partners joined together. Isabel, catching her daughter's flushed face among the crowd, stiffened.

"Is that," she began, narrowing her eyes in suspicion.

Dougal followed her gaze. Margaret stood out from the crowd in a gown of shimmering white. Gemstones sparkled at her throat in gleaming perfection, but the stones paled next to her beauty as she gazed into the eyes of her dance partner.

"Josiah?" Isabel finished. "But how?"

Dougal, seeing the happiness on his daughter's face, only smiled. He'd spoken with the former knight earlier in the day about his intentions toward his daughter. Josiah had been most polite.

Dougal said, "I think it has something to do with the dark worshiper's betrayal. They broke the demonic pact he made by killing him and his family. And do not discount his sacrifice that night in the forest. Not to mention your stipulation that Margaret deserved happiness."

"How would you know that?"

"Do not question it," Dougal said with a loving pull on her arm. "You'll never understand my ways."

"Quite so, husband," Isabel whispered, tears of blissfulness sparkling in her eyes as she watched the girl. Her heart bubbled over with joy.

Dougal swept his arm before his waist, bowing low to his wife. Then, straightening, he offered her his arms to dance.

"My lady," he murmured, "I believe the honor is mine."

"Eternally." Isabel curtsied.

As they waltzed about the room, they were unmindful of the other guests. The two ghosts were unseen or felt by anyone but each other. Eventually, Dougal swept her away from the other dancers, past the front door, down the steps into the dimming evening.

Dougal and Isabel lingered at the estate through the passing years. And every so often, someone would swear they had seen their spirits beneath the stars of an endless night. They were said to be dancing in a tuneless breeze through a mysterious fog that gathered and swept around the trees and flowers of Rothfield Park.

THE END

We hope you enjoyed Forget Me Not by Michelle M. Pillow. To learn more about Michelle and her books, visit MichellePillow.com.

NEWSLETTER

To stay informed about when a new book in the series installments is released, sign up for updates:

Sign up for Michelle's Newsletter

michellepillow.com/author-updates

ABOUT MICHELLE M. PILLOW

New York Times & *USA TODAY*
Bestselling Author

Michelle loves to travel and try new things, whether it's a paranormal investigation of an old Vaudeville Theatre or climbing Mayan temples in Belize. She believes life is an adventure fueled by copious amounts of coffee.

Newly relocated to the American South, Michelle is involved in various film and documentary projects with her talented director husband. She is mom to a fantastic artist. And she's managed by a dog and cat who make sure she's meeting her deadlines.

For the most part she can be found wearing pajama pants and working in her office. There may or may not be dancing. It's all part of the creative process.

Come say hello! Michelle loves talking with readers on social media!

www.MichellePillow.com

- facebook.com/AuthorMichellePillow
- twitter.com/michellepillow
- instagram.com/michellempillow
- bookbub.com/authors/michelle-m-pillow
- goodreads.com/Michelle_Pillow
- amazon.com/author/michellepillow
- youtube.com/michellepillow
- pinterest.com/michellepillow

PLEASE LEAVE A REVIEW

Please take a moment to share your thoughts by reviewing this book.
Thank you for reading!

Be sure to check out Michelle's other titles at www.michellepillow.com

COMPLIMENTARY EXCERPTS
TRY BEFORE YOU BUY!

LOVE POTIONS
WARLOCKS MACGREGOR® SERIES

by Michelle M. Pillow
Contemporary Paranormal Scottish Warlocks

A little magickal mischief never hurt anyone...

Erik MacGregor, from a clan of ancient Scottish warlocks, isn't looking for love. After centuries, it's not even a consideration...until he moves in next door to Lydia Barratt. It's clear that the shy beauty wants nothing to do with him, but he's drawn to her nonetheless and determined to win her over.

Lydia Barratt just wants to be left alone to grow flowers and make lotions in her old Victorian house. The last thing she needs is a demanding Scottish man meddling in her private life. Just because he's gorgeous and totally rocks a kilt doesn't mean she's going to fall for his seductive manner.

But Erik won't give up and just as Lydia let's her guard down, his sister decides to get involved. Her little love potion prank goes terribly wrong, making Lydia the target of his sudden embarrassingly obsessive behavior. They'll have to find a way to pull Erik out of the spell fast when it becomes clear that Lydia has more than a lovesick warlock to worry about. Evil lurks within the shadows and it plans to use Lydia, alive or dead, to take out Erik and his clan for good.

❧

Love Potions Excerpt

"Ly-di-ah! I sit beneath your window, laaaass, singing 'cause I loooove your a—"

"For the love of St. Francis of Assisi, someone call a vet. There is an injured animal screaming in pain outside," Charlotte interrupted the flow of music in ill-humor.

Lydia lifted her forehead from the kitchen table. Her windows and doors were all locked, and yet Erik's endlessly verbose singing penetrated the barrier of glass and wood with ease.

Charlotte held her head and blinked heavily.

Her red-rimmed eyes were filled with the all too poignant look of a hangover. She took a seat at the table and laid her head down. Her moan sounded something like, "I'm never moving again."

"You need fluids," Lydia prescribed, getting up to pour unsweetened herbal tea from the pitcher in the fridge. She'd mixed it especially for her friend. It was Gramma Annabelle's hangover recipe of willow bark, peppermint, carrot, and ginger. The old lady always had a fresh supply of it in the house while she was alive. Apparently, being a natural witch also meant in partaking in natural liquors. Annabelle had kept a steady supply of moonshine stashed in the basement. If the concert didn't stop soon she might try to find an old bottle.

"Ly-di-ah!"

"Omigod. Kill me," Charlotte moaned. "No. Kill him. Then kill me."

"Ly-di-ah!"

Erik had been singing for over an hour. At first, he'd tried to come inside. She'd not invited him and the barrier spell sent him sprawling back into the yard. He didn't seem to mind as he found a seat on some landscaping timbers and began his serenade. The last time she'd asked him to be quiet, he'd gotten louder and overly enthusiastic. In fact, she'd been too scared to pull back the curtains for a clearer look, but she was pretty sure he'd been dancing on her lawn, shaking his kilt.

"Omigod," Charlotte muttered, pushing up and angrily going to a window. Then grimacing, she said, "Is he wearing a tux jacket with his kilt?"

"Don't let him see you," Lydia cried out in a panic. It was too late. The song began with renewed force.

"He's..." Charlotte frowned. "I think it's dancing."

Since the damage was done, Lydia joined Charlotte at the window. Erik grinned. He lifted his arms to the side and kicked his legs, bouncing around the yard like a kid on too much sugar. "Maybe it's a traditional Scottish dance?"

Both women tilted their heads in unison as his kilt kicked up to show his perfectly formed ass.

"He's not wearing..." Charlotte began.

"I know. He doesn't," Lydia answered. Damn, the man had a fine body. Too bad Malina's trick had turned him insane.

To learn more about Michelle's books visit:
www.MichellePillow.com

MAIDEN AND THE MONSTER
MEDIEVAL HISTORICAL ROMANCE BY MICHELLE M. PILLOW

Winner of the 2006 Romantic Times Reviewers' Choice Award

Vladamir of Kessen, Duke of Lakeshire Castle, is feared as a demon in the land of Wessex. The Kings have granted him a title of nobility in exchange for his part as a political prisoner. Discontent, he bides his time in his new home until war will once again rip through the land. But boredom soon turns to devious pleasure as the daughter of his most hated enemy is left for dead at his castle gate. Now the monster bides his time plotting revenge.

Lady Eden of Hawks' Nest doesn't know what to think of the man who saved her life, but she can't wrench her thoughts away. His words are those of a tyrant, true to his vicious reputation, but his touch is that of a man, stirring passion and lust when there should only be fear. It would seem the infamous monster is not as monstrous as he appears.

To learn more about Michelle's books visit:
www.MichellePillow.com

MICHELLE'S BESTSELLING SERIES
SHAPE-SHIFTER ROMANCES

Dragon Lords Series
Barbarian Prince
Perfect Prince
Dark Prince
Warrior Prince
His Highness The Duke
The Stubborn Lord
The Reluctant Lord
The Impatient Lord
The Dragon's Queen

❧

Lords of the Var® Series
The Savage King
The Playful Prince

MICHELLE'S BESTSELLING SERIES

The Bound Prince
The Rogue Prince
The Pirate Prince

❃

Captured by a Dragon-Shifter Series
Determined Prince
Rebellious Prince
Stranded with the Cajun
Hunted by the Dragon
Mischievous Prince
Headstrong Prince

❃

Space Lords Series
His Frost Maiden
His Fire Maiden
His Metal Maiden
His Earth Maiden
His Woodland Maiden

❃

Learn more at www.MichellePillow.com

Made in the USA
Monee, IL
11 January 2021

57209052R00233